ICEBOUND

A NOVEL BY
Dean Koontz

Published by Random House Large Print
in association with Ballantine Books
New York 1995

Originally published in different form under the title
Prison of Ice by J. P. Lippincott in 1976.

Library of Congress Cataloging-in-Publication Data

Koontz, Dean R. (Dean Ray), 1945–
    Icebound : a novel / by Dean Koontz.—1st large
    print ed.
        p.   cm.
    ISBN 0-679-75942-5 (PB)
    1. Large type books.   I. Title.
PS3561.055127   1995   94-23988
813′.54—dc20   CIP

Manufactured in the United States of America

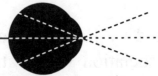

This Large Print Book carries the
Seal of Approval of N.A.V.H.

This corrected version
is still for
that special
and singular lady
Winona Garbrick.
I'm sure you're up there.
Watching. Red pencil in hand.

BEFORE . . .

From *The New York Times*:

[1]
POLAR ICE PUREST WATER
IN THE WORLD

MOSCOW, Feb. 10—According to Russian scientists, the water constituting the Arctic icecap has a far lower bacteria count than any water we now drink or with which we irrigate crops, a discovery that might make this vast frozen reservoir a valuable resource of the future. Because tapping the polar icecap might be cheaper than any current or foreseeable desalinization process, especially since the water would not have to be purified, some Russian researchers speculate that millions of acres of farmland might be irrigated with melted icebergs in the next decade.

[2]
SCIENTISTS BELIEVE ICEBERGS
COULD PROVIDE FRESH WATER

BOSTON, Sept. 5—Speaking before the annual convention of the American Society of Environmental Engineers, Dr. Harold Carpenter said today that chronic shortages of water in

California, Europe, and other regions could be alleviated by a controlled melting of icebergs towed south from the Arctic Circle. Dr. Carpenter's wife and research partner, Dr. Rita Carpenter, said the concerned nations should consider pooling the capital for the necessary research and development—an investment that would, she said, "be repaid a hundredfold within 10 years."

According to the Carpenters, co-recipients of last year's National Science Foundation Prize, the basic concept is simple. A large iceberg would be "blown loose" from the edge of the icefield and allowed to drift south in natural currents. Later, enormous steel towing cables would be affixed to the berg. A trawler would then tow the ice to a conversion facility at the shore near thirsty farmland. "Because the North Atlantic and North Pacific are cold oceans, perhaps less than 15 percent of the ice would melt before it could be converted to water at the shore and piped to drought-stricken farms," Dr. Harold Carpenter said.

The Carpenters both cautioned that no one could be certain the idea was workable. "There are still a great many problems to overcome," Dr. Rita Carpenter said. "Extensive research on the polar icecap . . ."

[3]
DROUGHT AFFECTS
CALIFORNIA CROPS

SACRAMENTO, Calif., Sept. 20—State
Department of Agriculture officials estimate that
California's water shortages may have been
responsible for as much as a $50 million loss in
second-season crops as diverse as oranges, lemons,
cantaloupes, lettuce. . . .

[4]
SUFFICIENT RELIEF SUPPLIES
UNAVAILABLE FOR THOUSANDS
STARVING IN DROUGHTS

UNITED NATIONS, Oct. 18—The director of the
United Nations Disaster Relief Office announced
that poor harvests in the United States, Canada, and
Europe have made it impossible for drought-
stricken Africans and Asians to purchase grain and
produce from the usually food-rich Western
nations. Already, more than 200,000 people have
died in . . .

[5]
SPECIAL U.N. FUND TO SEND
SCIENTISTS TO POLAR ICECAP

UNITED NATIONS, Jan. 6—Eleven members of the United Nations today contributed to a unique fund that will pay for a series of scientific experiments on the Arctic icecap. The primary intent of the project will be to study the feasibility of towing huge icebergs south, where they can be tapped for the irrigation of crops.

"It might sound like science fiction," said one British official, "but since the 1960's, most environmental specialists have come to see the very real potential." If such a scheme should prove workable, the major food-producing nations might never suffer bad harvests again. Although the icebergs could not be towed into the warm seas of southern Asia and Africa, the entire world would profit by the insured good harvests of the few countries that the project would directly benefit . . .

[6]
TEAM OF U.N. SCIENTISTS
ESTABLISHES RESEARCH STATION
ON ARCTIC ICEFIELD

THULE, Greenland, Sept. 28—This morning, scientists under the direction of Drs. Harold and Rita Carpenter, co-recipients of this year's Rothschild Prize in earth science, landed on the Arctic icecap between Greenland and Spitsbergen, Norway. They began construction of a research station two miles from the edge of the icefield where they will conduct United Nations–funded studies for at least nine months. . . .

[7]
ARCTIC EXPEDITION TO BLOW LOOSE
PIECE OF POLAR ICECAP TOMORROW

THULE, Greenland, Jan. 14—At midnight tomorrow, scientists at the United Nations–funded Edgeway Station will detonate a series of explosive devices to separate a half-mile-square iceberg from the edge of the winter icecap, just 350 miles off the northeast coast of Greenland. Two United Nations trawlers equipped with electronic tracking gear, are waiting 230 miles to the south, where they will monitor the progress of the "bugged" iceberg.

In an experiment designed to determine if Atlantic currents change substantially in northern regions during the severe Arctic winter . . .

One

❄

SNARE

NOON
DETONATION IN TWELVE HOURS

With a crystal-shattering shriek, the bit of the power drill bored deep into the Arctic ice. Gray-white slush churned out of the hole, sluiced across the crusted snow, and refroze in seconds. The flared auger was out of sight, and most of the long steel shank also had disappeared into the four-inch-diameter shaft.

Watching the drill, Harry Carpenter had a curious premonition of imminent disaster. A faint flicker of alarm. Like a bird shadow fluttering across a bright landscape. Even inside his heavily insulated clothing, he shivered.

As a scientist, Harry respected the tools of logic, method, and reason, but he had learned never to discount a hunch—especially on the ice, where strange things could happen. He was unable to identify the source of his sudden uneasiness, though occasional dark forebodings were to be expected on a job involving high explosives. The chance of one of the charges detonating prematurely, killing them all, was slim to nil. Nevertheless . . .

Peter Johnson, the electronics engineer who doubled as the team's demolitions expert, switched off the drill and stepped back from it. In his white

Gore-Tex/Thermolite storm suit, fur-lined parka, and fur-lined hood, Pete resembled a polar bear—except for his dark brown face.

Claude Jobert shut down the portable generator that supplied power to the drill. The resultant hush had an eerie quality of expectancy so intense that Harry glanced behind himself and then up into the sky, half convinced that something was rushing or falling toward him.

If Death kissed anyone today, it was more likely to rise up from below than to descend upon them. As the bleak afternoon began, the three men were preparing to lower the last hundred-pound explosive charge deep into the ice. It was the sixtieth demolitions package that they had handled since the previous morning, and they were all uneasily conscious of standing upon enough high-yield plastic explosives to destroy them in an apocalyptic flash.

No fertile imagination was required to picture themselves dying in these hostile climes: The ice-cap was a perfect graveyard, utterly lifeless, and it encouraged thoughts of mortality. Ghostly bluish-white plains led off in all directions, somber and moody during that long season of nearly constant darkness, brief twilight, and perpetual overcast. At the moment, visibility was fair because the day had drawn down to that time when a vague, cloud-filtered crescent of sunlight painted the horizon. However, the sun had little to illuminate in the stark landscape. The only points of elevation were the jagged pressure ridges and hundreds of slabs of ice—some only as large as a man, others bigger than houses—that had popped from the field and stood on end like gigantic tombstones.

Pete Johnson, joining Harry and Claude at a pair of snowmobiles that had been specially rebuilt for the rigors of the pole, told them, "The shaft's twenty-eight yards deep. One more extension for the bit, and the job's done."

"Thank God!" Claude Jobert shivered as if his thermal suit provided no protection whatsoever. In spite of the transparent film of petroleum jelly that protected the exposed portions of his face from frostbite, he was pale and drawn. "We'll make it back to base camp tonight. Think of that! I haven't been warm one minute since we left."

Ordinarily, Claude didn't complain. He was a jovial, energetic little man. At a glance, he seemed fragile, but that was not the case. At five seven and a hundred thirty pounds, he was lean, wiry, hard. He had a mane of white hair now tucked under his hood, a face weathered and made leathery by a lifetime in extreme climates, and bright blue eyes as clear as those of a child. Harry had never seen hatred or anger in those eyes. Until yesterday, he had never seen self-pity in them, either, not even three years ago, when Claude lost his wife, Colette, in a sudden, senseless act of violence; he had been consumed by grief but had never wallowed in self-pity.

Since they had left the comfort of Edgeway Station, however, Claude had been neither jovial nor energetic, and he had complained frequently about the cold. At fifty-nine, he was the oldest member of the expedition, eighteen years older than Harry Carpenter, which was the outer limit for anyone working in those brutal latitudes.

Although he was a fine arctic geologist specializing in the dynamics of ice formation and movement, the current expedition would be his last trip to either pole. Henceforth, his research would be done in laboratories and at computers, far from the severe conditions of the icecap.

Harry wondered if Jobert was bothered less by the bitter cold than by the knowledge that the work he loved had grown too demanding for him. One day Harry would have to face the same truth, and he wasn't sure that he would be able to exit with grace. The great chaste spaces of the Arctic and Antarctic enthralled him: the power of the extreme weather, the mystery that cloaked the white geometric landscapes and pooled in the purple shadows of every seemingly unplumbable crevasse, the spectacle on clear nights when the aurora borealis splashed the sky with shimmering streamers of light in jewellike colors, and the vast fields of stars when the curtains of the aurora drew back to reveal them.

In some ways he was still the kid who had grown up on a quiet farm in Indiana, without brothers or sisters or playmates: the lonely boy who'd felt stifled by the life into which he'd been born, who'd daydreamed of traveling to far places and seeing all the exotic marvels of the world, who'd wanted never to be tied down to one plot of earth, and who'd yearned for adventure. He was a grown man now, and he knew that adventure was hard *work.* Yet, from time to time, the boy within him was abruptly overcome by wonder, stopped whatever he was doing, slowly turned in a circle to look at the dazzlingly white world around him, and thought: *Holy jumping catfish, I'm really here, all the way from Indiana to the end of the earth, the top of the world!*

Pete Johnson said, "It's snowing."

Even as Pete spoke, Harry saw the lazily spiraling flakes descending in a silent ballet. The day was windless, though the calm might not endure much longer.

Claude Jobert frowned. "We weren't due for this storm until this evening."

The trip out from Edgeway Station—which lay four air miles to the northeast of their temporary camp, six miles by snowmobile past ridges and deep chasms—had not been difficult. Nevertheless, a bad storm might make the return journey impossible. Visibility could quickly deteriorate to zero, and they could easily get lost because of compass distortion. And if their snowmobiles ran out of fuel, they would freeze to death, for even their thermal suits would be insufficient protection against prolonged exposure to the more murderous cold that would ride in on the back of a blizzard.

Deep snows were not as common on the Greenland cap as might have been expected, in part because of the extreme lows to which the air temperature could sink. At some point in virtually every blizzard, the snowflakes metamorphosed into spicules of ice, but even then visibility was poor.

Studying the sky, Harry said, "Maybe it's a local squall."

"Yes, that's just what Online Weather said last week about *that* storm," Claude reminded him. "We were to have only local squalls on the periphery of the main event. Then we had so much snow and ice it would've kept Père Noël home on Christmas Eve."

"So we'd better finish this job quickly."

"Yesterday would be good."

As if to confirm the need for haste, a wind sprang up from the west, as crisp and odorless as a wind could be only if it was coming off hundreds of miles of barren ice. The snowflakes shrank and began to descend at an angle, no longer spiraling prettily like flakes in a crystal bibelot.

Pete freed the drill from the shank of the buried

bit and lifted it out of its supportive frame, handling it as if it weighed a tenth of its actual eighty-five pounds.

A decade ago he had been a football star at Penn State, turning down offers from several NFL teams. He hadn't wanted to play out the role that society dictated for every six-foot-four-inch, two-hundred-pound black football hero. Instead, he had won scholarships, earned two degrees, and taken a well-paid position with a computer-industry think tank.

Now he was vital to Harry's expedition. He maintained the electronic data-gathering equipment at Edgeway, and having designed the explosive devices, he was the only one who could deal with them in full confidence if something went wrong. Furthermore, his tremendous strength was an asset out there on the inhospitable top of the world.

As Pete swung the drill out of the way, Harry and Claude lifted a three-foot bit extension from one of the cargo trailers that were coupled to the snowmobiles. They screwed it onto the threaded shank, which was still buried in the ice.

Claude started the generator again.

Pete slammed the drill in place, turned the keyless chuck to clamp the jaws tight around the shank, and finished boring the twenty-nine-yard-deep shaft, at the bottom of which they would plant a tubular charge of explosives.

While the machine roared, Harry gazed at the heavens. Within the past few minutes, the weather had deteriorated alarmingly. Most of the ashen light had faded from behind the oppressive overcast. So much snow was falling that the sky no longer was mottled with grays and black; nothing whatsoever of the actual cloud cover could be seen through the crystalline torrents. Above them was only a deep, whirling whiteness. Already shrinking and becoming grainlike, the flakes lightly pricked his greased face. The wind escalated to perhaps twenty miles an hour, and its song was a mournful drone.

Harry still sensed oncoming disaster. The feeling was formless, vague, but unshakable.

As a boy on the farm, he had never realized that adventure was hard work, although he *had* understood that it was dangerous. To a kid, danger had been part of the appeal. In the process of growing up, however, as he'd lost both parents to illness and learned the violent ways of the world, he had ceased to be able to see anything romantic about death. Nevertheless, he admitted to a certain perverse nostalgia for the innocence that had once made it possible to find a pleasurable thrill in the taking of mortal risks.

Claude Jobert leaned close and shouted above the noise from the wind and the grinding auger: "Don't worry, Harry. We'll be back at Edgeway soon. Good brandy, a game of chess, Benny Goodman on the CD player, all the comforts."

Harry Carpenter nodded. He continued to study the sky.

12:20

In the telecommunications shack at Edgeway Station, Gunvald Larsson stood at the single small window, chewing nervously on the stem of his unlit pipe and peering out at the rapidly escalating storm. Relentless tides of snow churned through the camp, like ghost waves from an ancient sea that had evaporated millennia ago. Half an hour earlier, he'd scraped the ice off the outside of the triple-pane window, but already feathery new patterns of crystals were regrowing along the perimeter of the glass. In an hour, another blinding cataract would have formed.

From Gunvald's slightly elevated viewpoint, Edgeway Station looked so isolated—and contrasted so boldly with the environment in which it stood—that it might have been humanity's only outpost on an alien planet. It was the only splash of color on the white, silver, and alabaster fields.

The six canary-yellow Nissen huts had been air-lifted onto the icecap in prefabricated sections at tremendous effort and expense. Each one-story structure measured twenty by fifteen feet. The walls—layers of sheet metal and lightweight foam insulation—were riveted to hooped girders, and the floor of each hut was countersunk into the ice. As unattractive as slum buildings and hardly less cramped than packing crates, the huts were none-theless dependable and secure against the wind.

A hundred yards north of the camp, a smaller structure stood by itself. It housed the fuel tanks that fed the generators. Because the tanks held diesel fuel, which could burn but couldn't explode, the danger of fire was minimal. Nevertheless, the thought of being trapped in a flash fire fanned by an arctic gale was so terrifying—especially when there was no water, just useless ice, with which to fight it—that excessive precautions had to be taken for everyone's peace of mind.

Gunvald Larsson's peace of mind had been shattered hours ago, but he was not worried about fire. Earthquakes were what troubled him now. Specifically, suboceanic earthquakes.

The son of a Swedish father and a Danish mother, he had been on the Swedish ski teams at two winter Olympics, had earned one silver medal, and was proud of his heritage; he cultivated the image of an imperturbable Scandinavian and usually possessed an inner calm that matched his cool exterior. His wife said that, like precision calipers, his quick blue eyes continuously measured the world. When he wasn't working outdoors, he usually wore slacks and colorful ski sweaters; at the moment, in fact, he was dressed as though lolling in a mountain lodge after a pleasant day on the slopes rather than sitting in an isolated hut on the winter icecap, waiting for calamity to strike.

During the past several hours, however, he had lost a large measure of his characteristic composure. Chewing on the pipestem, he turned away from the frost-fringed windowpane and scowled at the computers and the data-gathering equipment that lined three walls of the telecommunications shack.

Early the previous afternoon, when Harry and the others had gone south toward the edge of the ice, Gunvald had stayed behind to monitor incoming calls on the radio and to keep a watch over the station. This was not the first time that all but one of the expedition members had left Edgeway to conduct an experiment in the field, but on previous occasions, someone other than Gunvald had remained behind. After weeks of living in a tiny community with eight too-close neighbors, he had been eager for his session of solitude.

By four o'clock the previous day, however, when Edgeway's seismographs registered the first quake, Gunvald had begun to wish that the other members of the team had not ventured so near to the edge of the ice, where the polar cap met the sea. At 4:14, the jolt was confirmed by radio reports from Reykjavik, Iceland, and from Hammerfest, Norway. Severe slippage had occurred in the seabed sixty miles northeast of Raufarhöfn, Iceland. The shock was on the same chain of interlinked faults that had triggered destructive volcanic eruptions on Iceland more than three decades ago. This time there had been no damage on any land bordering the Greenland Sea, although the tremor had registered a solid 6.5 on the Richter scale.

Gunvald's concern arose from the suspicion that the quake had been neither an isolated incident nor the main event. He had good reason to believe that it was a foreshock, precursor to an event of far greater magnitude.

From the outset the team had intended to study, among other things, ocean-bed temblors in the Greenland Sea to learn more about local sub-oceanic fault lines. They were working in a geologically active part of the earth that could never be trusted until it was better known. If dozens of ships were to be towing colossal icebergs in those waters, they would need to know how often the sea was disturbed by major submarine quakes and by resultant high waves. A tsunami—a titanic wave radiating from the epicenter of a powerful quake—could endanger even a fairly large ship, although less in the open sea than if the vessel was near a shoreline.

He should have been pleased with the opportunity to observe, at such close quarters, the characteristics and patterns of major temblors on the Greenland Sea fault network. But he wasn't pleased at all.

Using a microwave uplink to orbiting communications satellites, Gunvald was able to go on-line and access any computers tied into the worldwide Infonet. Though he was geographically isolated, he had at his disposal virtually all the research databases and software that would have been available in any city.

Yesterday, he had tapped those impressive resources to analyze the seismographic data on the recent quake. What he discovered had made him uneasy.

The enormous energy of the temblor had been released less by lateral seabed movement than by violent upward thrust. That was precisely the type of ground movement that would put the greatest amount of strain on the interlinked faults lying to the east of the one on which the first event had transpired.

Edgeway Station itself was in no imminent danger. If major seabed slippage occurred nearby, a tsunami might roll beneath the icecap and precipitate some changes: Primarily, new chasms and pressure ridges would form. If the quake were related to submarine volcanic activity, in which millions of cubic tons of molten lava gushed out of the ocean floor, perhaps even temporary holes of warm water would open in the icecap. But most of the polar terrain would be unchanged, and the likelihood was slim that the base camp would be either damaged or destroyed.

The other expedition members, however, couldn't be as certain of their safety as Gunvald was of his own. In addition to creating pressure ridges and chasms, a hot tsunami was likely to snap off sections of the ice at the edge of the winter field. Harry and the others might find the cap falling out from under them while the sea rushed up dark, cold, and deadly.

At nine o'clock last night, five hours after the first tremor, the second quake—5.8 on the Richter scale—had hit the fault chain. The seabed had shifted violently one hundred five miles north-northeast of Raufarhöfn. The epicenter had been thirty-five miles nearer Edgeway than that of the initial shaker.

Gunvald took no comfort from the fact that the second quake had been less powerful than the first. The diminution in force was not absolute proof that the more recent temblor had been an aftershock to the first. Both might have been foreshocks, with the main event still to come.

During the Cold War, the United States had planted a series of extremely sensitive sonic monitors on the floor of the Greenland Sea, as well as in many other strategic areas of the world's oceans, to detect the nearly silent passage of nuclear-armed enemy submarines. Subsequent to the collapse of the Soviet Union, some of those sophisticated devices had begun doing double duty, both monitoring submarines and providing data for scientific purposes. Since the second quake, most of the deep-ocean listening stations in the Greenland Sea had been transmitting a faint but almost continuous low-frequency grumble: the ominous sound of growing elastic stress in the crust of the earth.

A slow-motion domino reaction might have begun. And the dominoes might be falling toward Edgeway Station.

During the past sixteen hours, Gunvald had spent less time smoking his pipe than chewing nervously on the stem of it.

. . .

At nine-thirty the previous night, when the radio confirmed the location and force of the second shock, Gunvald had put through a call to the temporary camp six miles to the southwest. He told Harry about the quakes and explained the risks that they were taking by remaining on the perimeter of the polar ice.

"We've got a job to do," Harry had said. "Forty-six packages are in place, armed, and ticking. Getting them out of the ice again before they all detonate would be harder than getting a politician's hand out of your pocket. And if we don't place the other fourteen tomorrow, without all sixty synchronized charges, we likely won't break off the size berg we need. In effect, we'll be aborting the mission, which is out of the question."

"I think we should consider it."

"No, no. The project's too damned expensive to chuck it all just because there *might* be a seismic risk. Money's tight. We might not get another chance if we screw up this one."

"I suppose you're right," Gunvald acknowledged, "but I don't like it."

The open frequency crackled with static as Harry said, "Can't say I'm doing cartwheels, either. Do you have any projection about how long it might take major slippage to pass through an entire fault chain like this one?"

"You know that's anybody's guess, Harry. Days, maybe weeks, even months."

"You see? We have more than enough time. Hell, it can even take longer."

"Or it can happen much faster. In hours."

"Not this time. The second tremor was less violent than the first, wasn't it?" Harry asked.

"And you know perfectly well that doesn't mean the reaction will just play itself out. The third might be smaller or larger than the first two."

"At any rate," Harry said, "the ice is seven hundred feet thick where we are. It won't just splinter apart like the first coat on a winter pond."

"Nevertheless, I strongly suggest you wrap things up quickly tomorrow."

"No need to worry about that. Living out here in these damned inflatable igloos makes any lousy shack at Edgeway seem like a suite at the Ritz-Carlton."

After that conversation, Gunvald Larsson had gone to bed. He hadn't slept well. In his nightmares, the world crumbled apart, dropped away from him in enormous chunks, and he fell into a cold, bottomless void.

At seven-thirty in the morning, while Gunvald had been shaving, with the bad dreams still fresh in his mind, the seismograph had recorded a third tremor: Richter 5.2.

His breakfast had consisted of a single cup of black coffee. No appetite.

At eleven o'clock the fourth quake had struck only two hundred miles due south: 4.4 on the Richter scale.

He had not been cheered to see that each event was less powerful than the one that preceded it. Perhaps the earth was conserving its energy for a single gigantic blow.

The fifth tremor had hit at 11:50. The epicenter was approximately one hundred ten miles due south. Much closer than any previous tremor, essentially on their doorstep. Richter 4.2.

He'd called the temporary camp, and Rita Carpenter had assured him that the expedition would leave the edge of the icecap by two o'clock.

"The weather will be a problem," Gunvald worried.

"It's snowing here, but we thought it was a local squall."

"I'm afraid not. The storm is shifting course and picking up speed. We'll have heavy snow this afternoon."

"We'll surely be back at Edgeway by four o'clock," she'd said. "Maybe sooner."

At twelve minutes past noon another slippage had occurred in the subsea crust, one hundred miles south: 4.5 on the Richter scale.

. . .

Now, at twelve-thirty, when Harry and the others were probably planting the final package of explosives, Gunvald Larsson was biting so hard on his pipe that, with only the slightest additional pressure, he could have snapped the stem in two.

12:30

Almost six miles from Edgeway Station, the temporary camp stood on a flat section of ice in the lee of a pressure ridge, sheltered from the pressing wind.

Three inflatable, quilted, rubberized nylon igloos were arranged in a semicircle approximately five yards from that fifty-foot-high ridge of ice. Two snowmobiles were parked in front of the structures. Each igloo was twelve feet in diameter and eight feet high at the center point. They were firmly anchored with long-shanked, threaded pitons and had cushiony floors of lightweight, foil-clad insulation blankets. Small space heaters powered by diesel fuel kept the interior air at fifty degrees Fahrenheit. The accommodations weren't either spacious or cozy, but they were temporary, to be used only while the team planted the sixty packages of explosives.

A hundred yards to the south, on a plateau that was five or six feet above the camp, a six-foot steel pipe rose from the ice. Fixed to it were a thermometer, a barometer, and an anemometer.

With one gloved hand, Rita Carpenter brushed snow from the goggles that protected her eyes and then from the faces of the three instruments on the pole. Forced to use a flashlight in the steadily deepening gloom, she read the temperature, the atmospheric pressure, and the wind velocity. She didn't like what she saw. The storm had not been expected to reach them until at least six o'clock that night, but it was bearing down hard and was liable to be on them in full force before they had finished their work and completed the return journey to Edgeway Station.

Awkwardly negotiating the forty-five-degree slope between the plateau and the lower plain, Rita started back toward the temporary camp. She could move *only* awkwardly because she was wearing full survival gear: knitted thermal underwear, two pairs of socks, felt boots, fleece-lined outer boots, thin woolen trousers and shirt, quilted thermal nylon suit, a fur-lined coat, a knitted mask that covered her face from chin to goggles, a fur-lined hood that laced under her chin, and gloves. In this cruel weather, body heat had to be maintained at the cost of easy mobility; awkwardness, clumsiness, and discomfort were the burdens of survival.

Though Rita was warm enough, the bitter-cold wind and the barren landscape chilled her emotionally. By choice, both she and Harry had spent a large portion of their professional lives in the Arctic and Antarctic; however, she did not share Harry's love of the vast open spaces, the monochromatic vistas, the immense curve of sky, and the primal storms. In fact, she'd driven herself to return repeatedly to those polar regions primarily because she was afraid of them.

Since the winter when she was six years old, Rita had stubbornly refused to surrender to *any* fear, ever again, no matter how justified surrender might be. . . .

Now, as she approached the igloo on the west end of camp, with the wind hammering her back, she suddenly suffered a phobic reaction so intense that it nearly brought her to her knees. Cryophobia: the fear of ice and frost. Frigophobia: the fear of cold. Chionophobia: the fear of snow. Rita knew those terms because she suffered from mild forms of all three phobias. Frequent confrontation with the sources of her anxieties, like inoculations against influenza, had ensured that she usually suffered only minor discomfort, uneasiness, seldom flat-out terror. Sometimes, however, she was overwhelmed by memories against which no number of inoculations was sufficient protection. Like now.

The tumultuous white sky seemed to descend at the speed of a falling rock, to press relentlessly upon her as though the air and the clouds and the sheeting snow had magically metamorphosed into a massive slab of marble that would crush her into the unyielding, frozen plain. Her heart pounded hard and fast, then much harder and faster than before, then faster still, until its frantic cadence drummed, drummed, drummed so loudly in her ears that it drowned out the quarrelsome moaning of the wind.

Outside the igloo entrance, she halted and held her ground, refusing to run from that which terrified her. She required herself to endure the isolation of that bleak and gloom-shrouded realm, as someone who had an irrational fear of dogs might force himself to pet one until the panic passed.

That isolation, in fact, was the aspect of the Arctic that most troubled Rita. In her mind, since she was six years old, winter had been inextricably associated with the fearful solitude of the dying, with the gray and distorted faces of corpses, with the frost-glazed stares of dead and sightless eyes, with graveyards and graves and suffocating despair.

She was trembling so violently that the beam of her flashlight jittered across the snow at her feet.

Turning away from the inflatable shelter, she faced not into the wind but crosswise to it, studying the narrow plain that lay between the plateau and the pressure ridge. Eternal winter. Without warmth, solace, or hope.

It was a land to be respected, yes, all right. But it was not a beast, possessed no awareness, had no conscious intention to do her harm.

She breathed deeply, rhythmically, through her knitted mask.

To help quell her irrational fear of the icecap, she told herself that she had a greater problem waiting in the igloo beside her. Franz Fischer.

She had met Fischer eleven years ago, shortly after she earned her doctorate and took her first research position with a division of International Telephone and Telegraph. Franz, who had also worked for ITT, was attractive and not without charm when he chose to reveal it, and they'd been together for nearly two years. It hadn't been an altogether calm, relaxed, and loving relationship. But at least she had never been bored by it. They'd separated nine years ago, as the publication of her first book approached, when it became clear that Franz would never be entirely comfortable with a woman who was his professional and intellectual equal. He expected to dominate, and she would not be dominated. She had walked out on him, met Harry, gotten married a year later, and never looked back.

Because he had come into Rita's life after Franz, Harry felt, in his unfailingly sweet and reasonable way, that their history was none of his concern. He was secure in his marriage and sure of himself. Even knowing of that relationship, therefore, he had recruited Franz to be the chief meteorologist at Edgeway Station, because the German was the best man for the job.

In this one instance, unreasonable jealousy would have served Harry—and all of them—better than rationality. Second best would have been preferable.

Nine years after their separation, Franz still insisted on playing the lover scorned, complete with stiff upper lip and soulful eyes. He was neither cold nor rude; to the contrary, he strove to create the impression that at night he nursed a badly broken heart in the lonely privacy of his sleeping bag. He never mentioned the past, showed any improper interest in Rita, or conducted himself in less than a gentlemanly fashion. In the confines of a polar outpost, however, the care with which he displayed his wounded pride was as disruptive, in its way, as shouted insults would have been.

The wind groaned, the snow churned around her, and the ice stretched out of sight as it had since time immemorial—but gradually her racing heartbeat subsided to a normal rate. She stopped shaking. The terror passed.

She'd won again.

When at last Rita entered the igloo, Franz was on his knees, packing instruments into a carton. He had taken off his outer boots, coat, and gloves. He dared not work up a sweat, because it would chill his skin, even inside his thermal suit, and leach precious heat from him when he went outdoors. He glanced up at her, nodded, and continued packing.

He possessed a certain animal magnetism, and Rita could see why she had been drawn to him when she was younger. Thick blond hair, deep-set dark eyes, Nordic features. He was only five nine, just an inch taller than she, but at forty-five he was as muscular and as trim as a boy.

"Wind is up to twenty-four miles," she said, pushing back her hood and removing her goggles. "Air temp's down to ten degrees Fahrenheit and falling."

"With the wind-chill factor, it'll be minus twenty or worse by the time we break camp." He didn't look up. He seemed to be talking to himself.

"We'll make it back all right."

"In zero visibility?"

"It won't get that bad so fast."

"You don't know polar weather like I do, no matter how much of it you've seen. Take another look outside, Rita. This front's pushing in a lot faster than predicted. We could find ourselves in a total whiteout."

"Honestly, Franz, your gloomy Teutonic nature—"

A thunderlike sound rolled beneath them, and a tremor passed through the icecap. The rumble was augmented by a high-pitched, nearly inaudible squeal as dozens of ice strata moved against one another.

Rita stumbled but kept her balance, as though lurching down the aisle of a moving train.

The rumble quickly faded away.

Blessed stillness returned.

Franz finally met her eyes. He cleared his throat. "Larsson's much-heralded big quake?"

"No. Too small. Major movement on this fault chain would be much larger than that, much bigger all down the line. That little shake would hardly have registered on the Richter scale."

"A preliminary tremor?"

"Maybe," she said.

"When can we expect the main event?"

She shrugged. "Maybe never. Maybe tonight. Maybe a minute from now."

Grimacing, he continued packing instruments into the waterproof carton. "And you were talking about *my* gloomy nature . . ."

12:45

Pinned by cones of light from two snowmobiles, Roger Breskin and George Lin finished anchoring the radio transmitter to the ice with four two-foot-long belaying pins, and then ran a systems check on the equipment. Their long shadows were as strange and distorted as those of savages hunched over an idol, and the eerie song of the wind might have been the voice of the violent god to whom they prayed.

Even the murky glow of the winter twilight had now been frozen out of the sky. Without the snow-mobile headlamps, visibility would drop to ten yards.

The wind had been brisk and refreshing that morning, but as it gathered speed, it had become an increasingly deadly enemy. A strong gale in those latitudes could press a chill through layer upon layer of thermal clothing. Already the fine snow was being driven so hard that it appeared to be sheeting past them on a course parallel to the ice-cap, as if falling horizontally out of the west rather than out of the sky, destined never to touch ground. Every few minutes they were forced to scrape their goggles and break the crust of snow off the knitted masks that covered the lower half of their faces.

Standing behind the amber headlights, Brian Dougherty averted his face from the wind. Flexing his fingers and toes to ward off the cold, he wondered why he had come to this godforsaken termi-nus. He didn't belong here. *No one* belonged here. He had never before seen a place so barren; even great deserts were not as lifeless as the icecap. Every aspect of the landscape was a blunt reminder that all of life was nothing but a prelude to inevita-ble and eternal death, and sometimes the Arctic so sensitized him that in the faces of the other members of the expedition he could see the skulls beneath the skin.

Of course that was precisely why he had come to the icecap: adventure, danger, the possibility of death. He knew at least that much about himself, though he had never dwelt on it and though he had only a shadowy notion of *why* he was obsessed with taking extreme risks.

He had compelling reasons for staying alive, after all. He was young. He was not wildly handsome, but he wasn't the Hunchback of Notre Dame, either, and he was in love with life. Not least of all, his family was enormously wealthy, and in fourteen months, when he turned twenty-five, he would gain control of a thirty-million-dollar trust fund. He didn't have a clue in hell as to what he'd *do* with all that money, if anything, but it surely was a comfort to know that it would be his.

Furthermore, the family's fame and the sympathy accorded to the whole Dougherty clan would open any doors that couldn't be battered down with money. Brian's uncle, once President of the United States, had been assassinated by a sniper. And his father, a United States Senator from California, had been shot and crippled during a primary campaign nine years ago. The tragedies of the Doughertys were the stuff of endless magazine covers from *People* to *Good Housekeeping* to *Playboy* to *Vanity Fair*, a national obsession that sometimes seemed destined to evolve into a formidable political mythology in which the Doughertys were not merely ordinary men or women but demigods and demigoddesses, embodiments of virtue, goodwill, and sacrifice.

In time, Brian could have a political career of his own if he wished. But he was still too young to face the responsibilities of his family name and tradition. In fact, he was fleeing from those responsibilities, from the thought of ever meeting them. Four years ago, he'd dropped out of Harvard after only eighteen months of law studies. Since then he had traveled the world, "bumming" on American Express and Carte Blanche. His escapist adventures had put him on the front pages of newspapers on every continent. He had confronted a bull in one of Madrid's rings. He'd broken an arm on an African photographic safari when a rhinoceros attacked the jeep in which he was riding, and while shooting the rapids on the Colorado River, he had capsized and nearly drowned. Now he was passing the long, merciless winter on the polar ice.

His name and the quality of several magazine articles that he had written were not sufficient credentials to obtain a position as the official chronicler of the expedition. But the Dougherty Family Foundation had made an $850,000 grant to the Edgeway project, which had virtually guaranteed that Brian would be accepted as a member of the team.

For the most part, he had been made to feel welcome. The only antagonism had come from George Lin, and even that had amounted to little more than a brief loss of temper. The Chinese scientist had apologized for his outburst. Brian was genuinely interested in their project, and his sincerity won friends.

He supposed his interest arose from the fact that he was unable to imagine himself making an equal commitment to any lifelong work that was even half as arduous as theirs. Although a political career was part of his legacy, Brian loathed that vile game: Politics was an illusion of service that cloaked the corruption of power. It was lies, deceptions, self interest, and self-aggrandizement: suitable work only for the mad and the venal and the naïve. Politics was a jeweled mask under which hid the true disfigured face of the Phantom. Even as a young boy, he'd seen too much of the inside of Washington, enough to dissuade him from ever seeking a destiny in that corrupt city. Unfortunately, politics had infected him with a cynicism that made him question the value of *any* attainment or achievement, either inside or outside the political arena.

He *did* take pleasure in the act of writing, and he intended to produce three or four articles about life in the far, far north. Already, in fact, he had enough material for a book, which he felt increasingly compelled to write.

Such an ambitious undertaking daunted him. A book—whether or not he had the talent and maturity to write well at such length—was a major commitment, which was precisely what he had been avoiding for years.

His family thought that he had been attracted to the Edgeway Project because of its humanitarian potential, that he was getting serious about his future. He hadn't wanted to disillusion them, but they were wrong. Initially he'd been drawn to the expedition merely because it was another adventure, more exciting than those upon which he'd embarked before but no more meaningful.

And it still *was* only an adventure, he assured himself, as he watched Lin and Breskin checking out the transmitter. It was a way to avoid, for a while longer, thinking about the past and the future. But then . . . why this compulsion to write a book? He couldn't convince himself that he had anything to say that would be worth anyone's reading time.

The other two men got to their feet and wiped snow from their goggles.

Brian approached them, shouting over the wind, "Are you done?"

"At last!" Breskin said.

The two-foot-square transmitter would be sheathed in snow and ice within hours, but that wouldn't affect its signal. It was designed to operate in arctic conditions, with a multiple-battery power supply inside layers of insulation originally developed for NASA. It would put out a strong signal—two seconds in duration, ten times every minute—for eight to twelve days.

When that segment of ice was blasted loose from the winter field with almost surgical precision, the transmitter would drift with it into those channels known as Iceberg Alley and from there into the North Atlantic. Two trawlers, part of the United Nations Geophysical Year Fleet, were standing at the ready two hundred thirty miles to the south to monitor the continual radio signal. With the aid of geosynchronous polar satellites, they would fix the position of the berg by triangulation and home in on it until it could be identified visually by the waterproof, self-expanding red dye that had been spread across wide areas of its surface.

The purpose of the experiment was to gain a basic understanding of how the winter sea currents affected drift ice. Before any plans could be made to tow ice south to drought-stricken coastal areas, scientists must learn how the sea would work against the ships and how it might be made to work for them.

It wasn't practical to send trawlers to the very edge of the polar cap to grapple with the giant berg. The Arctic Ocean and the Greenland Sea were choked with ice floes and difficult to navigate at that time of year. Depending on what the project experiments revealed, however, they might find that it was not necessary for the tow ships to connect with the ice even immediately south of Iceberg Alley. Instead, the bergs might be allowed to ride the natural currents for a hundred or two hundred miles before effort was expended to haul them farther south and coastward.

"Could I get a few pictures?" Brian asked.

"No time for that," George Lin said shortly. He brushed his hands together, briskly knocking thin plates of ice from his heavy gloves.

"Take just a minute."

"Got to get back to Edgeway," Lin said. "Storm could cut us off. By morning we'd be part of the landscape, frozen solid."

"We can spare a minute," Roger Breskin said. He wasn't half shouting as they were, but his bass voice carried over the wind, which had escalated from an unearthly groan to a soft ululant howl.

Brian smiled thankfully.

"You crazy?" Lin asked. "See this snow? If we delay—"

"George, you've already wasted a minute carping." Breskin's tone was not accusatory, merely that of a scientist stating an observable fact.

Although Roger Breskin had emigrated to Canada from the United States only eight years ago, he was every bit as quiet and calm as the stereotypical Canadian. Self-contained, reclusive, he did not easily make friends *or* enemies.

Behind his goggles, Lin's eyes narrowed. Grudgingly he said, "Take your pictures. I guess Roger wants to see himself in all the fancy magazines. But hurry."

Brian had no choice but to be quick. Weather conditions allowed no time for setting up shots and focusing to perfection.

"This okay?" Roger Breskin asked, standing to the right of the transmitter.

"Great."

Roger dominated the frame in the viewfinder. He was five eleven, one hundred ninety pounds, shorter and lighter than Pete Johnson but no less muscular than the former football star. He had been a weight lifter for twenty of his thirty-six years. His biceps were enormous, webbed with veins that resembled steel tubes. In arctic gear, he was an impressively bearish figure who seemed to belong in these vast frozen wastes as none of the others did.

Standing to the left of the transmitter, George Lin was as unlike Breskin as a hummingbird is unlike an eagle. He was shorter and slimmer than Roger, but the differences were not merely physical. While Roger stood as silent and still as a pinnacle of ice, Lin swayed from side to side as if he might explode with nervous energy. He had none of the patience that was reputed to be a trait of the Asian mind. Unlike Breskin, he didn't belong in these frozen wastes, and he knew it.

George Lin had been born Lin Shen-yang, in Canton, mainland China, in 1946, shortly before

Mao Tse-tung's revolution had ousted the Kuomin-tang government and established a totalitarian state. His family had not managed to flee to Taiwan until George was seven. In those early years, something monstrous had happened to him in Canton that had forever traumatized and shaped him. Occasionally he alluded to it, but he refused ever to speak of it directly, either because he was not capable of deal-ing with the horror of those memories—or because Brian's skills as a journalist were insufficient to extract the story.

"Just hurry," Lin urged. His breath billowed in skeins of crystalline yarn that unraveled in the wind.

Brian focused and pressed the shutter release.

The electronic flash was reflected by the snow-scape, and figures of light leaped and danced with figures of shadow. Then the deep darkness swarmed back to crouch at the edges of the headlamps.

Brian said, "One more for—"

The icecap rose abruptly, precipitously, like the motorized floor in a carnival fun house. It tilted left, right, then dropped out from under him.

He fell, slammed so hard into the ice that even the heavy padding of his insulated clothing did not adequately cushion him, and the painful impact knocked his bones against one another as if they were *I Ching* sticks clattering in a metal cup. The ice heaved up again, shuddered and bucked, as though striving mightily to fling him off the top of the earth and out into space.

One of the idling snowmobiles crashed onto its side, inches from his head, and sharp shards of ice exploded in his face, glittery needles, stinging his skin, barely sparing his eyes. The skis on the machine rattled softly and quivered as if they were insectile appendages, and the engine choked off.

Dizzy, shocked, heart stuttering, Brian cautiously raised his head and saw that the transmitter was still firmly anchored. Breskin and Lin were sprawled in the snow, having been pitched about as though they were dolls, as he himself had been. Brian started to get up—but he fell again as the wasteland leaped more violently than it had the first time.

Gunvald's suboceanic earthquake had come at last.

Brian tried to brace himself within a shallow depression in the ice, wedging between the natural contours to avoid being thrown into the snowmobiles or the transmitter. Evidently a massive tsunami was passing directly under them, hundreds of millions of cubic yards of water rising with all the vengeful fury and force of an angry god awakening.

Inevitably, additional waves of still great but diminishing power would follow before the icecap stabilized.

The overturned snowmobile revolved on its side.

The headlights swept across Brian twice, harrying shadows like wind-whipped leaves that had blown in from warmer latitudes, and then stopped as they illuminated the other men.

Behind Roger Breskin and George Lin, the ice suddenly cracked open with a deafening *boom!* and gaped like a ragged, demonic mouth. Their world was coming apart.

Brian shouted a warning.

Roger grasped one of the large steel anchor pins that fixed the transmitter in place, and he held on with both hands.

The ice heaved a third time. The white field tilted toward the new, yawning crevasse.

Although he tried desperately to brace himself, Brian slid out of the depression in which he had sought shelter, as though there were no inhibiting friction whatsoever between him and the ice. He shot toward the chasm, grabbed the transmitter as he sailed past it, crashed hard against Roger Breskin, and held on with fierce determination.

Roger shouted something about George Lin, but the wailing of the wind and the rumble of fracturing ice masked the meaning of his words.

Squinting through snow-filmed goggles, unwilling to risk his precarious hold to wipe them clean, Brian looked over his shoulder.

Screaming, George Lin slid toward the brink of the new crevasse. He flailed at the slick ice. As the last surge of the tsunami passed beneath them and as the winter cap settled down, Lin fell out of sight into the chasm.

Franz had suggested that Rita finish packing the gear and that he handle the heavy work of loading it into the cargo trailers. He was so unconsciously condescending toward "the weaker sex" that Rita rejected his suggestion. She pulled up her hood, slipped the goggles over her eyes once more, and lifted one of the filled cartons before he could argue with her.

Outside, as she loaded the waterproof box into one of the low-slung cargo trailers, the first tremor jolted the ice. She was pitched forward onto the cartons. A blunt cardboard corner gouged her cheek. She rolled off the trailer and fell into the snow that had drifted around the machine during the past hour.

Dazed and frightened, she scrambled to her feet as the primary crest of the tsunami arrived. The snowmobile engines were running, warming up for the ride back to Edgeway, and their headlamps pierced the falling snow, providing enough light for her to see the first broad crack appear in the nearly vertical wall of the fifty-foot-high pressure ridge that had sheltered—and now threatened—the temporary camp. A second crack split off the first, then a third, a fourth, ten, a hundred, like the intricate web of fissures in an automobile windshield that has been hit by a stone. The entire facade was going to collapse.

She shouted to Fischer, who was still in the igloo at the west end of the camp. "Run! Franz! *Get out!*"

Then she took her own advice, not daring to look back.

The sixtieth package of explosives was no different from the fifty-nine that had been placed in the ice before it: two and a half inches in diameter, sixty inches long, with smooth, rounded ends. A sophisticated timing device and detonator occupied the bottom of the cylinder and was synchronized to the timers in the other fifty-nine packages. Most of the tube was filled with plastic explosives. The upper end of the cylinder terminated in a steel loop, and a gated carabiner connected a tempered-steel chain to the loop.

Harry Carpenter wound the chain off the drum of a small hand winch, lowering the package— thirty pounds of casing and one hundred pounds of plastic explosives—into the narrow hole, working carefully because the charge was equivalent to three thousand pounds of TNT. He let down seventy-eight feet of chain before he felt the cylinder touch bottom in the eighty-seven-foot shaft. He connected another carabiner to the free end of the chain, pulled the links snug against the shaft wall, and secured the carabiner to a peg that was embedded in the ice beside the hole.

Pete Johnson was hunkered beside Harry. He looked over his shoulder at the Frenchman and called out above the keening wind: "Ready here, Claude."

A barrel, which they had filled with snow, stood on electric heating coils in one of the cargo trailers. It brimmed with boiling water. Steam roiled off the surface of the water, froze instantly into clouds of glittering crystals, and was dispersed into the whirling snow, so it seemed as if an endless procession of ghosts was arising from a magical cauldron and fleeing to the far reaches of the earth.

Claude Jobert fixed a metal-ring hose to a valve on the barrel. He opened the valve and handed the nozzle to Carpenter.

Loosening the petcock, Harry let hot water pour out of the hose into the deep shaft. In three minutes the hole was sealed: The bomb was suspended in new ice.

If he left the shaft open, the explosion would vent upward to no purpose. The charge had been shaped to blow downward and expend its energy to all sides, and the hole must be tightly sealed to achieve the desired effect. At midnight, when that charge detonated with all the others, the new ice in the shaft might pop out like a cork from a bottle, but the greater force of the blast would not be dissipated.

Pete Johnson rapped his gloved knuckles against the newly formed plug. "Now we can get back to Edge—"

The icecap jolted up, lurched forward, tilted sharply in front of them, squealed like a great monster, and then groaned before collapsing back into its original plane.

Harry was thrown on his face. His goggles jammed hard against his cheeks and eyebrows. Tears streamed as pain swelled across his cheekbones. He felt warm blood trickling from his nostrils, and the taste of blood was in his mouth.

Pete and Claude had fallen and were holding each other. Harry caught a brief glimpse of them, grotesquely locked in each other's embrace as though they were a pair of wrestlers.

The ice shook again.

Harry rolled against one of the snowmobiles. The machine was bouncing up and down. He clung to it with both hands and hoped that it would not roll over on him.

His first thought had been that the plastic explosives had blown up in his face and that he was dead or dying. But as the ice swelled once more, he realized that tidal waves must be surging beneath the polar cap, no doubt spawned by a seabed quake.

As the third wave struck, the white world around Harry cracked and canted, as if a prehistoric creature were rising from a long sleep beneath him, and he found himself suspended at the top of an ice ramp. Only inertia kept him high in the air, at the top of the incline. At any moment he might slide to the bottom along with the snowmobile, and perhaps be crushed beneath the machine.

In the distance, the sound of shattering, grinding ice pierced the night and the wind: the ominous protests of a brittle world cracking asunder. The roar grew nearer by the second, and Harry steeled himself for the worst.

Then, as suddenly as the terror had begun—no more than a minute ago—it ended. The ice plain dropped, became a level floor, and was still.

Having sprinted far enough to be safely out of any icefall from the looming pressure ridge, Rita stopped running and spun around to look back at the temporary camp. She was alone. Franz had not emerged from the igloo.

A truck-size piece of the ridge wall cracked off and fell with eerie grace, smashing into the unin-habited igloo at the east end of the crescent-shaped encampment. The inflatable dome popped as if it were a child's balloon.

"Franz!"

A much larger section of the ridge collapsed. Sheets, spires, boulders, slabs of ice crashed into the camp, fragmenting into cold shrapnel, flatten-ing the center igloo, overturning a snowmobile, ripping open the igloo at the west end of the camp, from which Franz had still not escaped, casting up thousands of splinters of ice that glinted like showers of sparks.

She was six years old again, screaming until her throat seized up—and suddenly she wasn't sure if she had called out for Franz or for her mother, for her father.

Whether she had called a warning to him or not, Franz crawled out of the ruined nylon dome even as the deluge was tumbling around him, and he scrambled toward her. Mortar shells of ice exploded to the left and right of him, but he had the grace of a broken-field runner and the speed born of terror. He raced beyond the avalanche to safety.

As the ridge stabilized and ice stopped falling, Rita was shaken by a vivid vision of Harry crushed beneath a shining white monolith elsewhere in the cruel black-and-white polar night. She staggered, not because of the movement of the icefield, but because the thought of losing Harry rocked her. She ceased trying to keep her balance, sat on the ice, and began to shake uncontrollably.

Only the snowflakes moved, cascading out of the darkness in the west and into the darkness in the east. The sole sound was the dour-voiced wind singing a dirge.

Harry held on to the snowmobile and pulled himself erect. His heart thudded so hard that it seemed to knock against his ribs. He tried to work up some saliva to lubricate his parched throat. Fear had dried him out as thoroughly as a blast of Sahara heat could have done. When he regained his breath, he wiped his goggles and looked around.

Pete Johnson helped Claude to his feet. The Frenchman was rubber-legged but evidently uninjured. Pete didn't even have weak knees; perhaps he was every bit as indestructible as he appeared to be.

Both snowmobiles were upright and undamaged. The headlights blazed into the vast polar night but revealed little in the seething sea of windblown snow.

High on adrenaline, Harry briefly felt like a boy again, flushed with excitement, pumped up by the danger, exhilarated by the very fact of having survived.

Then he thought of Rita, and his blood ran colder than it would have if he'd been naked in the merciless polar wind. The temporary camp had been established in the lee of a large pressure ridge, shadowed by a high wall of ice. Ordinarily, that was the best place for it. But with all the shaking that they had just been through, the ridge might have broken apart. . . .

The lost boy faded into the past, where he belonged, became just a memory among other memories of Indiana fields and tattered issues of *National Geographic* and summer nights spent staring at the stars and at far horizons.

Get moving, he thought, awash in a fear far greater than that which he had felt for himself only moments ago. Get packed, get moving, get to her.

He hurried to the other men. "Anyone hurt?"

"Just a little rattled," Claude said. He was a man who not only refused to surrender to adversity but was actually buoyed by it. With a brighter smile than he'd managed all day, he said, "Quite a ride!"

Pete glanced at Harry. "What about you?"

"Fine."

"You're bleeding."

When Harry touched his upper lip, bright chips of frozen blood like fragments of rubies adhered to his glove. "Nosebleed. It's already stopped."

"Always a sure cure for nosebleed," Pete said.

"What's that?"

"Ice on the back of the neck."

"You should be abandoned here for that one."

"Let's get packed and moving."

"They may be in serious trouble at camp," Harry said, and he felt his stomach turn over again when he considered the possibility that he might have lost Rita.

"My thought exactly."

The wind pummeled them as they worked. The falling snow was fine and thick. The blizzard was racing in on them with surprising speed, and in unspoken recognition of the growing danger, they moved with a quiet urgency.

As Harry was strapping down the last of the instruments in the second snowmobile's cargo trailer, Pete called to him. He wiped his goggles and went to the other machine.

Even in the uncertain light, Harry could see the worry in Pete's eyes. "What is it?"

"During that shaking, I guess ... did the snow-mobiles do a lot of moving around?"

"Hell, yes, they bounced up and down as if the ice was a damn trampoline."

"Just up and down?"

"What's wrong?"

"Not sideways at all?"

"What?"

"Well, I mean, is it possible they slid around, sort of swiveled around?"

Harry turned his back on the wind and leaned closer to Pete. "I was holding tight to one of them. It didn't turn. But what's that have to do with anything?"

"Bear with me. What direction were the snow-mobiles facing before the tsunami?"

"East."

"You're sure?"

"Absolutely."

"Me too. I remember east."

"Toward the temporary camp."

Their breath collected in the sheltered space

between them, and Pete waved a hand through the crystals to disperse them. He bit his lower lip. "Then am I losing my mind or what?"

"Why?"

"Well, for one thing . . ." He tapped the Plexiglas face of the snowmobile's compass, which was fixed to the hood in front of the windshield.

Harry read the compass. According to the needle, the snowmobile was facing due south, a ninety-degree change from where it had stood before the ice was shaken by the seismic waves.

"That's not all," Johnson said. "When we parked here, I know damned well the wind was hitting this snowmobile from behind and maybe even slightly to my left. I remember how it was hammering the back of the sled."

"I remember too."

"Now it's blowing across the flank, from my right side when I'm behind the handlebars. That's a damned big difference. But blizzard winds are steady. They don't change ninety degrees in a few minutes. They just don't, Harry. They just don't ever."

"But if the wind didn't change and the snowmobiles didn't move, that means the ice we're on . . ."

His voice trailed away.

They were both silent.

Neither of them wanted to put his fear into words.

At last Pete finished the thought: ". . . so the

ice must have revolved one full quarter of the compass."

"But how's that possible?"

"I have one good idea."

Harry nodded reluctantly. "Yeah, so do I."

"Only one explanation makes sense."

"We better have a look at the compass on my machine."

"We're in deep shit, Harry."

"It's not a field of daisies," Harry agreed.

They hurried to the second vehicle, and the fresh snow crunched and squeaked under their boots.

Pete tapped the Plexiglas face of the compass. "This one's facing south too."

Harry brushed at his goggles but said nothing. Their situation was so dire that he didn't want to have to put it into words, as if the worst wouldn't actually have happened until they spoke of it.

Pete surveyed the inhospitable wasteland that surrounded them. "If the damn wind picks up and the temperature keeps dropping . . . and it *will* keep dropping . . . then how long could we survive out here?"

"With our current supplies, not even one day."

"The nearest help . . ."

"Would be those UNGY trawlers."

"But they're two hundred miles away."

"Two hundred and thirty."

"And they're not going to head north into a

major storm, not with so many ice floes to negotiate."

Neither of them spoke. The banshee shriek of the wind filled their silence. Furies of hard-driven snow stung the exposed portions of Harry's face, even though his skin was protected by a layer of Vaseline.

Finally, Pete said, "So now what?"

Harry shook his head. "Only one thing's certain. We won't be driving back to Edgeway Station this afternoon."

Claude Jobert joined them in time to hear that last exchange. Even though the lower part of his face was covered by a snow mask and though his eyes were only half visible behind his goggles, his alarm was unmistakable. He put one hand on Harry's arm. "What's wrong?"

Harry glanced at Pete.

To Claude, Pete said, "Those waves . . . they broke up the edge of the icefield."

The Frenchman tightened his grip on Harry's arm.

Clearly not wanting to believe his own words, Pete said, "We're adrift on an iceberg."

"That can't be," Claude said.

"Outrageous, but it's true," Harry said. "We're moving farther away from Edgeway Station with every passing minute . . . and deeper into this storm."

Claude was a reluctant convert to the truth. He

looked from Harry to Pete, then around at the forbidding landscape, as if he expected to see something that would refute what they had told him. "You can't be sure."

"All but certain," Pete disagreed.

Claude said, "But under us . . ."

"Yes."

". . . those bombs . . ."

"Exactly," Harry said. "Those bombs."

Two

✳

SHIP

1:00
DETONATION IN ELEVEN HOURS

One of the snowmobiles was on its side. The safety cutout had switched off the engine when the machine overturned, so there had been no fire. The other snowmobile was canted against a low hummock of ice. The four headlamps parted the curtains of snow, illuminating nothing, pointing away from the precipice over which George Lin had disappeared.

Although Brian Dougherty was convinced that any search for the Chinese was a waste of time, he scrambled to the edge of the new crevasse and sprawled facedown on the ice at the jagged brink. Roger Breskin joined him, and they lay side by side, peering into a terrible darkness.

Queasiness coiled and slithered in Brian's gut. He tried to dig the metal toes of his boots into the iron-hard ice, and he clutched at the flat surface. If another tsunami set the world adance, he might be tipped or flung into the abyss.

Roger directed his flashlight outward, toward the distant wall of the crevasse. Except for falling snow, nothing was revealed within the reach of the yellow beam. The light dwindled away into perfect blackness.

"Isn't a crevasse," Brian said. "It's a damned canyon!"

"Not that either."

The beam moved slowly back and forth: Nothing lay out there. Nothing whatsoever. Less than astronauts could see when they peered from a porthole into deep space.

Brian was baffled. "I don't understand."

"We've broken off from the main icefield," Roger explained with characteristic yet nonetheless remarkable equanimity.

Brian needed a moment to absorb that news and grasp the full horror of it. "Broken off . . . You mean we're adrift?"

"A ship of ice."

The wind gusted so violently that for half a minute Brian could not have been heard above it even if he'd shouted at the top of his voice. The snowflakes were as busy and furious as thousands of angry bees, stinging the exposed portions of his face, and he pulled up his snow mask to cover his mouth and nose.

When the gust died out at last, Brian leaned toward Roger Breskin. "What about the others?"

"Could be on this berg too. But let's hope they're still on safe ice."

"Dear God."

Roger directed the flashlight away from the darkness where they had expected to find the far wall of a crevasse. The tight beam speared down and out into the humbling void.

They wouldn't be able to see the face of the cliff

that dropped away just in front of them unless they eased forward and hung partly over the precipice. Neither of them was eager to expose himself to that extreme risk.

The pale light angled to the left and right, then touched upon the choppy, black, unfrozen sea that raged eighty or ninety feet below them. Flat tables of ice, irregular chunks of ice, gnarled rafts of ice, and delicate ever-changing laces of ice bobbled and swirled in the deep troughs of frigid dark water, crashed together on the crests of the waves; touched by the light, they glittered as if they were diamonds spread on black velvet.

Mesmerized by the chaos that the flashlight revealed, swallowing hard, Brian said, "George fell into the sea. He's gone."

"Maybe not."

Brian didn't see how there could be a hopeful alternative. His queasiness had slid into full-blown nausea.

Pushing with his elbows against the ice, Roger inched forward until he was able to peer over the brink and straight down the face of the precipice.

In spite of his nausea—and though he was still concerned that another tsunami might sweep under them and cast him into George Lin's grave—Brian moved up beside Roger.

The flashlight beam found the place where their ice island met the sea. The cliff did not plunge cleanly into the water. At its base, it was shattered into three ragged shelves, each six or eight yards wide and six to eight feet below the one above it. The shelves were as fissured and sharp-edged and jumbled as the base of any rocky bluff on dry land. Because another six hundred feet or more of the berg lay below sea level, the towering storm waves could not pass entirely under it; they crashed across the three shelves and broke against the glistening palisades, exploding into fat gouts of foam and icy spray.

Caught by that maelstrom, Lin would have been dashed to pieces. It might have been a more merciful death if he had plunged suddenly into those hideously cold waters and suffered a fatal heart attack before the waves had a chance to hammer and grind him against the jagged ice.

The light moved slowly backward and upward, revealing more of the cliff. From the three shelves at the bottom, for a distance of fifty feet, the ice sloped up at approximately a sixty-degree angle— not sheer by any measure, but much too steep to be negotiated by anyone other than a well-equipped and experienced mountain climber. Just twenty feet below them, another shelf crossed the face of the berg. This one was only a few feet wide. It angled back into the cliff. Above that shelf, the ice was sheer all the way to the brink where they lay.

After he had paused to scrape the crusted snow from his goggles, Roger Breskin used the flashlight to explore that shallow shelf below them.

Eight feet to the right of them, twenty feet down, previously cloaked in darkness, George Lin lay where he had fallen onto the narrow ledge. He was on his left side, his back against the cliff, facing out toward the open sea. His left arm was wedged under him, and his right arm was across his chest. He had assumed the foetal position, with his knees drawn up as far as his bulky arctic clothing would allow and his head tucked down.

Roger cupped his free hand to his mouth and shouted: "George! You hear me? George!"

Lin didn't move or respond.

"You think he's alive?" Brian asked.

"Must be. Didn't fall far. Clothes are quilted, insulated—absorbed some impact."

Brian cupped both hands around his mouth and shouted at Lin.

The only answer came from the steadily increasing wind, and it was easy to believe that its shriek was full of gleeful malevolence, that this wind was somehow alive and daring them to remain at the brink just a moment longer.

"Have to go down and get him," Roger said.

Brian studied the slick, vertical wall of ice that dropped twenty feet to the ledge. "How?"

"We've got rope, tools."

"Not climbing gear."

"Improvise."

"Improvise?" Brian said with astonishment. "You ever done any climbing?"

"No."

"This is nuts."

"No choice."

"Got to be another way."

"Like what?'

Brian was silent.

"Let's look at the tools," Roger said.

"We could die trying to rescue him."

"Can't just walk away."

Brian stared down at the crumpled figure on the ledge. In a Spanish bullring, on the African veldt, on the Colorado River, skin-diving in a shark run off Bimini . . . In far-flung places and in so many imaginative ways, he had tempted death without much fear. He wondered why he was hesitating now. Virtually every risk he'd ever taken had been pointless, a childish game. This time he had a good reason for risking everything: A human life was at stake. Was that the problem? Was it that he didn't want to be a hero? Too damned many heroes in the Dougherty family, power-thirsty politicians who had become heroes for the history books.

"Let's get working," Brian said at last. "George'll freeze if he lies there much longer."

1:05

Harry Carpenter leaned into the handlebars and squinted through the curve of Plexiglas at the white landscape. Hard sprays of snow and spicules of sleet slanted through the headlights. The windshield wiper thumped monotonously, crusted with ice but still doing its job reasonably well. Visibility had decreased to ten or twelve yards.

Although the machine was responsive and could be stopped in a short distance, Harry kept it throttled back. He worried that unwittingly he might drive off a cliff, because he had no way of knowing where the iceberg ended.

The only vehicles in use by the Edgeway expedition were custom-stretched snowmobiles with rotary-combustion engines and specially engineered twenty-one-wheel, three-track bogie suspensions. Each machine could carry two adults in bulky thermal clothing on a thirty-six-inch padded bench. The driver and passenger rode in tandem, one behind the other.

Of course the machines had been adapted further for operations in the rugged polar winter, in which conditions were dramatically more severe than those encountered by snowmobile enthusiasts back in the States. Aside from the dual starter system and the pair of special heavy-duty arctic batteries, the major modification on each vehicle was the addition of a cabin that extended from the hood to the end of the stretched passenger bench. That enclosure was fabricated of riveted aluminum sheets and thick Plexiglas. An efficient little heater had been mounted over the engine, and two small fans conducted the warm air to the driver and passenger.

Perhaps the heater was a luxury, but the enclosed cabin was an absolute necessity. Without it, the continuous pounding of the wind would have chilled any driver to the bone and might have killed him on a trip longer than four or five miles.

A few of the sleds had been further modified in unique ways. Harry's was one of those, for he was transporting the power drill. Most tools were carried in the shallow storage compartment that was hidden under the hinged top of the passenger bench, or in a small open-bed trailer towed behind. But the drill was too large for the storage compartment and too important to the expedition to be exposed to the shocks that rattled the bed of a cargo trailer; therefore, the last half of the bench was fitted with locking braces, and the drill was now dogged down tightly behind Harry, occupying the space where a passenger ordinarily would have been.

With those few modifications, the sled was well suited for work on the Greenland ice. At thirty miles per hour, it could be stopped within eighty feet. The twenty-inch-wide track provided excellent stability on moderately rough terrain. And although it weighed six hundred pounds in its adapted form, it had a top speed of forty-five miles per hour.

At the moment, that was considerably more power than Harry could use. He was holding the snowmobile to a crawl. If the brink of the iceberg abruptly loomed out of the storm, he'd have at most thirty or thirty-five feet in which to comprehend the danger and stop the machine. If he were going at all fast, he would not be able to stop in time. Hitting the brakes at the penultimate moment, he would pitch out into the night, down into the sea. Haunted by that mental image, he kept the engine throttled back to just five miles per hour.

Though caution and prudence were necessary, he had to make the best possible time. Every minute spent in transit increased the likelihood that they would become disoriented and hopelessly lost.

They had struck out due south from the sixtieth blasting shaft, maintaining that heading as well as they could, on the assumption that what had been east prior to the tsunami was now south. In the first fifteen or twenty minutes after the tidal wave, the iceberg would probably have drifted around on the compass as much as it was going to, finding its natural bow and stern; logically, it should now be sailing straight on course. If their assumption was wrong and if the berg was still turning, the temporary camp would no longer lay due south, either, and they would pass the igloos at a considerable distance, stumbling upon them only by accident, if at all.

Harry wished he could find the way back by visual references, but the night and the storm cloaked all landmarks. Besides, on the icecap, one monotonous landscape looked pretty much like another, and even in broad daylight it was possible to get lost without a functioning compass.

He glanced at the side-mounted mirror beyond the ice-speckled Plexiglas. The headlamps of the second sled—carrying Pete and Claude—sparkled in the frigorific darkness behind him.

Although distracted for only a second, he quickly returned to his scrutiny of the ice ahead, half expecting to see a yawning gulf just beyond the black tips of the snowmobile skis. The calcimined land still rolled away unbroken into the long night.

He also expected to see a glimmer of light from the temporary camp. Rita and Franz would realize that without a marker the camp would be difficult if not impossible to find in such weather. They would switch on the snowmobile lights and focus on the ridge of ice behind the camp: The glow, reflected and intensified, would be an unmistakable beacon.

But he was unable to see even a vague, shimmering luminescence ahead. The darkness worried him, for he took it to mean that the camp was gone, buried under tons of ice.

Although he was ordinarily optimistic, Harry sometimes was overcome by a morbid fear of losing his wife. Deep down, he didn't believe that he really deserved her. She had brought more joy into his life than he had ever expected to know. She was precious to him, and fate had a way of taking from a man that which he held closest to his heart.

Of all the adventures that had enlivened Harry's life since he'd left that Indiana farm, his relationship with Rita was by far the most exciting and rewarding. She was more exotic, more mysterious, more capable of surprising and charming and delighting him, than all the wonders of the world combined.

He told himself that the lack of signal lights ahead was most likely a positive sign. The odds were good that the igloos still stood on the solid winter field and not on the berg. And if the temporary camp was still back there on the icecap, then Rita would be secure at Edgeway Station within a couple of hours.

But no matter whether Rita was on the berg or the cap, the pressure ridge that loomed behind the camp might have collapsed, crushing her.

Hunching farther over the handlebars, he squinted through the falling snow: nothing.

If he found Rita alive, even if she was trapped with him, he would thank God every minute of the rest of his life—which might total precious few. How could they get off this ship of ice? How would they survive the night? A quick end might be preferable to the special misery of a slow death by freezing.

Just thirty feet ahead, in the headlights, a narrow black line appeared on the snow-swept plain: a crack in the ice, barely visible from his perspective.

He hit the brakes hard. The machine slid around thirty degrees on its axis, skis clattering loudly. He turned the handlebars into the slide until he felt the track gripping again, and then he steered back to the right.

Still moving, gliding like a hockey puck, Jesus, twenty feet from the looming pit and *still* sliding . . .

The dimensions of the black line grew clearer. Ice was visible beyond it. So it must be a crevasse. Not the ultimate brink with only night on the far side and only the cold sea at the base of it. Just a crevasse.

. . . sliding, sliding . . .

On the way out from camp, the ice had been flawless. Apparently the subsea activity had also opened this chasm.

. . . fifteen feet . . .

The skis rattled. Something knocked against the undercarriage. The snow cover was thin. Ice offered poor traction. Snow billowed from the skis, from the churning polyurethane track, like clouds of smoke.

. . . ten feet . . .

The sled stopped smoothly, rocking imperceptibly on its bogie suspension, so near the crevasse that Harry was not able to see the edge of the ice over the sloped front of the machine. The tips of the skis must have been protruding into empty air beyond the brink. A few more inches, and he would have been balanced like a teeter-totter, rocking between death and survival.

He slipped the machine into reverse and backed up two or three feet, until he could see the precipice.

He wondered if he were clinically mad for wanting to work in this deadly wasteland.

Shivering, but not because of the cold, he pulled his goggles from his forehead, fitted them over his eyes, opened the cabin door, and got out. The wind had the force of a blow from a sledgehammer, but he didn't mind it. The chill that passed through him was proof that he was alive.

The headlights revealed that the crevasse was only about four yards wide at the center and narrowed drastically toward both ends. It was no more than fifteen yards long, not large but certainly big enough to have swallowed him. Gazing down into the blackness under the headlights, he suspected that the depth of the chasm could be measured in hundreds of feet.

He shuddered and turned his back to it. Under his many layers of clothing, he felt a bead of sweat, the pure distillate of fear, trickle down the hollow of his back.

Twenty feet behind his sled, the second snowmobile was stopped with its engine running, lights blazing. Pete Johnson squeezed out through the cabin door.

Harry waved and started toward him.

The ice rumbled.

Surprised, Harry halted.

The ice moved.

For an instant he thought that another seismic wave was passing beneath them. But they were adrift now and wouldn't be affected by a tsunami in the same way as they had been when on the fixed icecap. The berg would only wallow like a ship in rough seas and ride out the turbulence without damage; it wouldn't groan, crack, heave, and tremble.

The disturbance was entirely local—in fact, it was directly under his feet. Suddenly the ice opened in front of him, a zigzagging crack about an inch wide, wider, wider, now as wide as his hand, then even wider. He was standing with his back to the brink, and the badly fractured wall of the newly formed crevasse was disintegrating beneath him.

He staggered, flung himself forward, jumped across the jagged fissure, aware that it was widening under him even as he was in mid-leap. He fell on the far side and rolled away from that treacherous patch of ice.

Behind him, the wall of the crevasse calved off thick slabs that crashed into the depths, and thunder rose from below. The plain shivered.

Harry pushed up onto his knees, not sure if he was safe yet. Hell, no. The edge of the chasm continued to disintegrate into the pit, the crevasse widened toward him, and he scrambled frantically away from it.

Gasping, he glanced back in time to see his snowmobile, its rotary engine humming, as it slid into the chasm. It slammed against the far wall of the crevasse and was pinned there for an instant by a truck-size slab of ice. The fuel in the main and auxiliary tanks exploded. Flames gushed high into the wind but quickly subsided as the burning wreckage sought the depths. Around and under him, red-orange phantoms shimmered briefly in the milky ice; then the fire puffed out, and darkness took command.

1:07

Cryophobia. The fear of ice.

Their circumstances made it far harder than usual for Rita Carpenter to repress that persistent, debilitating terror.

Portions of the pressure ridge had partially collapsed while other sections had been radically recontoured by the tsunami. Now a shallow cave—approximately forty feet deep and thirty feet wide—pocked those white ramparts. The ceiling was as high as twenty feet in some places and as low as ten in others: one half smooth and slanted, the other half composed of countless boulders and partitions of ice jammed together in a tight, mutually supportive, white-on-white mosaic that had a malevolent beauty and reminded Rita of the surreal stage sets in *The Cabinet of Dr. Caligari*, a very old movie.

She hesitated in the entrance to that cold haven, reluctant to follow Franz Fischer across the threshold, plagued by the irrational feeling that she would be moving not merely forward a few feet but simultaneously backward in time to that winter day when she was six, to the rumble and the roar and the living death of the white tomb. . . .

Clenching her teeth, struggling to repress a sense of almost paralyzing dread, she went inside. The storm raged behind her, but she found comparative quiet within those white walls, as well as relief from the biting wind and snow.

With her flashlight, Rita studied the ceiling and the walls, searching for indications that the structure was in imminent danger of collapsing. The cave appeared to be stable enough at the moment, although another powerful tsunami, passing under the ice, might bring down the ceiling.

"Risky," she said, unable to prevent her voice from breaking nervously.

Franz agreed. "But we don't have any choice."

All three inflatable shelters had been destroyed beyond repair. To remain outside in the increasingly fierce wind for an extended period of time would be courting hypothermia, in spite of their insulated storm suits. Their desperate need for shelter outweighed the danger of the cave.

They went outside again and carried the short-wave radio—which appeared to have survived the destruction of the camp—into the ice cave and set it on the floor against the rear wall. Franz ran wires in from the backup battery of the undamaged snowmobile, and they hooked up the transceiver. Rita switched it on, and the selection band glowed sea green. The crackle of static and an eerie whistling shivered along the walls of ice.

"It works," she said, relieved.

Adjusting his hood to make it tighter at the throat, Franz said, "I'll see what else I can salvage." Leaving the flashlight with her, he went out into the storm, shoulders hunched and head tucked down in anticipation of the wind.

Franz had no sooner stepped outside than an urgent transmission came through from Gunvald at Edgeway Station.

Rita crouched at the radio and quickly acknowledged the call.

"What a relief to hear your voice," Gunvald said. "Is everyone all right?"

"The camp was destroyed, but Franz and I are okay. We've taken shelter in an ice cave."

"Harry and the others?"

"We don't know what's happened to them," she said, and her chest tightened with anxiety as she spoke. "They're out on work details. We'll give

them fifteen minutes to show up before we go looking." She hesitated and cleared her throat. "The
thing is . . . we're adrift."

For a moment, Gunvald was too stunned to
speak. Then: "Are you certain?"

"A change in wind direction alerted us. Then the
compasses."

"Give me a moment," Larsson said with audible
distress. "Let me think."

In spite of the storm and the strong magnetic dis-
turbances that accompanied bad weather in those
latitudes, Larsson's voice was clear and easy to follow. But then he was only four air miles away. As
the storm accelerated, and as the iceberg drifted farther south, they were certain to have severe communications problems. Both understood that they
would soon lose contact, but neither mentioned it.

Larsson said, "What's the size of this iceberg of
yours? Do you have any idea?"

"None at all. We haven't had an opportunity to
reconnoiter. Right now, we're just searching for
whatever's salvageable in the wreckage of the
camp."

"If the iceberg isn't very large . . ." Gunvald's
voice faded into static.

"I can't read you."

Shatters of static.

"Gunvald, are you still there?"

His voice returned: ". . . if the berg isn't large . . .
Harry and the others might not be adrift with you."

Rita closed her eyes. "I hope that's true."

"Whether they are or aren't, the situation is far from hopeless. The weather's still good enough for me to get a message by satellite relay to the United States Air Force base at Thule. Once I've alerted them, they can contact those UNGY trawlers standing south of you."

"But what then? No sensible captain would bring a trawler north into a bad winter storm. He'd lose his ship and his crew trying to save us."

"They've got the most modern rescue aircraft at Thule, some damn rugged helicopters capable of maneuvering in almost any conditions."

"There isn't a plane yet invented that can fly safely in this kind of storm—let alone set down on an iceberg in gale-force winds."

The radio produced only crackling static and warbling electronic squeals, but she sensed that Gunvald was still there.

Yes, she thought. It leaves me speechless too.

She glanced up at the angled slabs that had jammed together to form the ceiling. Snow and shavings of ice sifted down through a few of the cracks.

Finally the Swede said, "Okay, you're right about the aircraft. But we can't give up hope of rescue."

"Agreed."

"Because . . . well . . . listen, Rita, this storm could last three or four days."

"Or longer," she acknowledged.

"You haven't got enough food for that."

"Hardly any. But food isn't so terribly impor-tant," Rita said. "We can last longer than four days without food."

They both knew that starvation was not the dan-ger. Nothing mattered as much as the bone-freezing, unrelenting cold.

Gunvald said, "Take turns getting warm in the snowmobiles. Do you have a good supply of fuel?"

"Enough to get back to Edgeway—if that were possible. Not a hell of a lot more than that. Enough to run the engines for a few hours, not a few days."

"Well, then . . ."

Silence. Static.

He came back after several seconds. ". . . put through that call to Thule all the same. They have to know about this. They might see an answer that we've overlooked, have a less emotional perspective."

She said, "Edgeway came through unscathed?"

"Fine here."

"And you?"

"Not a bruise."

"Glad to hear it."

"I'll live. And so will you, Rita."

"I'll try," she said. "I'll sure as hell try."

1:10

Brian Dougherty siphoned gasoline from the tank of the upright snowmobile and poured it onto a two-foot section of ice at the brink of the cliff.

Roger Breskin twisted open a chemical match and tossed it into the gasoline. Flames erupted, flapped like bright tattered flags in the wind, but burned out within seconds.

Kneeling where the fire had been, Brian examined the edge of the precipice. The ice had been jagged; now it was smooth and slick. A climber's rope would slide over it without fraying.

"Good enough?" Roger asked.

Brian nodded.

Roger stooped and snatched up the free end of a thirty-five-foot rope that he had tied to the frame of the snowmobile and had also anchored to a long, threaded piton identical to those used to secure the radio transmitter. He quickly looped it around Brian's chest and shoulders, fashioning a harness of sorts. He tied three sturdy knots at the center of the younger man's chest and said, "It'll hold. It's nylon, thousand-pound test. Just remember to grip the rope above your head with both hands so you'll keep at least some of the pressure off your shoulders."

Because he did not trust himself to speak without a nervous stammer, Brian nodded.

Roger returned to the snowmobile, which was

facing toward the precipice and which he had disconnected from its cargo trailer. He climbed into
the cabin and closed the door. He held the brakes
and revved the engine.

Trembling, Brian stretched out on his stomach,
flat on the ice. He took a deep breath through his
knitted ski mask, hesitated only briefly, and pushed
himself feet-first over the edge of the cliff.
Although he didn't drop far, his stomach lurched,
and a thrill of terror like an electrical current siz-
zled through him. The rope pulled tight, checking
his descent when the crown of his head was only
inches below the top of the iceberg.

As yet, too little of the line hung past the brink
to enable him to reach overhead and get a firm grip
on it. He was forced to take the strain entirely with
his shoulders. Immediately a dull ache arose in his
joints, across his back, and up the nape of his neck.
The ache would rapidly escalate into a sharp pain.

"Come on, come on, Roger," he muttered. "Be
quick."

Brian was facing the ice wall. He brushed and
bumped against it as the punishing wind pummeled
him.

He dared to turn his head to the side and peer
down, expecting to be able to see nothing but a
yawning black gulf. Away from the glare of the
snowmobile lights, however, his eyes adjusted
swiftly to the gloom, and the vague natural phosphorescence of the ice allowed him to make out the

sheer palisade against which he hung, as well as the broken shelves of jagged blocks at the bottom. Sixty or seventy feet below, the whitecaps on the churning sea exhibited a ghostly luminescence of their own as they rose in serried ranks from out of the night and crashed with spumous fury against the iceberg.

• • •

Roger Breskin throttled the snowmobile down so far that it almost stalled.

He considered the problem one last time: Dougherty was six feet tall, and the ledge was twenty feet below; therefore, he had to lower Dougherty about twenty feet in order to put him on the ledge *and* allow him six feet of line to ensure him sufficient mobility to deal with George Lin. They had marked off twenty feet of the line with a swatch of bright red cloth, so when that marker disappeared over the brink, Dougherty would be in position. But the rope had to be let down as slowly as possible, or the kid might be knocked unconscious against the side of the iceberg.

Furthermore, the snowmobile was only forty feet from the precipice; if the machine slid forward too fast, Roger might not be able to stop in time to save himself, let alone Dougherty and Lin. He was worried that the sled's lowest speed would prove dangerously fast for this job, and he hesitated now that he was ready to begin.

• • •

A violent gust of wind hammered Brian from behind and to the right, pressing him against the face of the cliff but also pushing him leftward, so he hung at a slight angle. When the wind relented after a moment, declining to about thirty miles an hour, he rocked back to the right, then began to swing gently like a pendulum, in a two- or three-foot arc.

He squinted up at the point where the rope met the edge of the cliff. Even though he had carefully smoothed the ice with burning gasoline, any friction whatsoever was bound to wear on the nylon line.

He closed his eyes and slumped in the harness, waiting to be lowered onto the ledge. His mouth was as dry as that of any desert wanderer, and his heart was beating so fast and hard that it seemed capable of cracking his ribs.

Because Roger was highly experienced with the snowmobile, it had seemed logical and reasonable that Brian should be the one to go down to retrieve George Lin. Now he wished that he himself had been the snowmobile expert. What the hell was taking so long?

His impatience evaporated when he suddenly dropped as if the rope had been cut. He landed on the ledge with such force that pain shot up his legs to the top of his spine. His knees crumpled as though they were sodden cardboard. He fell against the face of the cliff, bounced off, and toppled off the narrow ledge, out into the wind-shattered night.

He was too terrified to scream.

· · ·

The snowmobile lurched and rushed forward too fast.

Roger hit the brakes immediately after he released them. The red cloth vanished over the brink, but the machine was still moving. Because the ice had been swept free of snow and polished by the incessant wind, it provided little traction. As smoothly as a shuffleboard puck gliding along polished pine, the snowmobile slid another ten feet, headlights spearing out into an eternal blackness, before it finally stopped less than ten feet from the edge of the cliff.

· · ·

The harness jerked tight across Brian's chest and under his arms. Compared to the throbbing pain in his legs and the ache in his back, however, the new agony was endurable.

He was surprised that he was still conscious— and alive.

Unclipping his flashlight from the tool belt that encircled his waist, he cut open the perfect blackness around him with a blade of light, and torrents of snowflakes gushed over him.

Trying not to think about the icy sea below, he peered up at the ledge that he had overshot. It was four feet above his head. A yard to his left, the gloved fingers of George Lin's inert right hand trailed over the shelf.

Brian was swinging in a small arc again. His

lifeline was scraping back and forth along the ledge, which had *not* been melted by burning gasoline. It gleamed sharply. Splinters and shavings of ice sprinkled down on him as the rope carved a shallow notch in that abrasive edge.

A flashlight beam stabbed down from above.

Brian raised his eyes and saw Roger Breskin peering at him from the top of the cliff.

Lying on the ice, his head over the precipice and his right arm extended with a flashlight, Roger cupped his free hand to his mouth and shouted something. The wind tore his words into a meaningless confetti of sound.

Brian raised one hand and waved weakly.

Roger shouted louder than before: "You all right?" His voice sounded as if it came from the far end of a five-mile-long railroad tunnel.

Brian nodded as best he could: Yes, I'm all right. There was no way to convey, with only a nod, the degree of his fear and the worry that was caused by the lingering pain in his legs.

Breskin shouted, but only a few of his words reached Brian: "Going . . . snowmobile . . . reverse . . . draw you . . . up."

Again, Brian nodded.

". . . slowly . . . a chance . . . too fast again . . . battered . . . the ice."

Roger disappeared, obviously hurrying back to the snowmobile.

Leaving his flashlight on, Brian clipped it to his

tool belt, with the beam shining down on his right foot. He reached overhead and gripped the taut line with both hands, hoisting himself slightly to take a measure of the strain off his upper arms, which were on the verge of dislocating from his shoulder sockets.

The snowmobile drew up some of the line. The movement was smooth compared to the style of his descent, and he was not thrown against the cliff.

From the knees down, his legs were still below the ledge. He swung them up and over, planted both feet on the narrow shelf of ice, crouching there. He let go of the rope and stood up.

His ankles ached, his knees felt as if they were made of jelly, and pain laced his thighs. But his legs held him.

He took a large piton—a five-inch shaft tapered to a sharp point, topped by a one-inch-diameter eye loop—from a zippered pocket of his coat. He freed a small hammer from his tool belt and pounded the pin into a tight crack in the face of the cliff.

Again, Roger's flashlight shone down from the top.

When the anchoring pin was secure, Brian unhooked an eight-foot-long coil of nylon rope from his belt. Before descending, he had knotted one end of it to a carabiner; now he linked the carabiner to the piton and screwed shut its safety gate.

He tied the other end of the line around his waist. The resultant tether would bring him up short of death if he slipped and fell off the ledge, yet he was free enough to attend to George Lin. Thus belayed, he untied the knots that held the harness together across his chest and under his arms. When he was free from the main line, he coiled it and hung it around his neck.

To avoid some of the wind's vicious force, he got on his hands and knees and crawled to Lin. Roger Breskin's light followed him. He took his own flashlight from his belt and placed it on the ledge, against the cliff face, with the beam shining on the unconscious man.

Unconscious—or dead?

Before he could know the answer to that question, he had to get a look at Lin's face. Turning the man onto his back was not an easy chore, because Brian had to be careful that the scientist did not roll off into the abyss. By the time Lin was on his back, he'd regained consciousness. His amber skin—at least those few square inches of his face that were exposed—was shockingly pale. Against the slit in his mask, his mouth worked without making an audible sound. Behind his frost-spotted goggles, his eyes were open; they expressed some confusion but didn't appear to be the eyes of a man in severe pain or delirium.

"How do you feel?" Brian shouted above the shrill wind.

Lin stared at him uncomprehendingly and tried to sit up.

Brian pressed him down. "Be careful! You don't want to fall."

Lin turned his head and stared at the darkness from which the snow streamed ever faster. When he looked at Brian again, his pallor had deepened.

"Are you badly hurt?" Brian asked. Because of the thermal clothing Lin wore, Brian couldn't determine if the man had any broken bones.

"Some chest pain," Lin said barely loudly enough to be heard above the storm.

"Heart?"

"No. When I went over the edge . . . the ice was still rocking . . . from the wave . . . the cliff face was slanted. I *slid* down . . . and landed here hard on my side. That's all I remember."

"Broken ribs?"

Lin took a deep breath and winced. "No. Probably not. Only bruised, I think. Damn sore. But nothing's fractured."

Brian removed the coil of rope from around his neck. "I'll have to make a harness under your arms, across your chest. Can you tolerate that?"

"Do I have a choice?"

"No."

"So I'll tolerate it."

"You'll have to sit up."

Groaning, Lin eased cautiously into a sitting

position, with his back toward the cliff and his legs dangling in the void.

Brian quickly fashioned a harness, tied a tight double knot over Lin's breastbone, and got to his feet. He reached down and helped the injured man to stand. They turned in place to put the sea and the murderous wind at their backs. Dry, almost granular snow snapped against the wall of ice, bounced from it, and spun against their faces.

"Ready?" Roger called from twenty feet above.

"Yeah. But take it easy!"

Lin clapped his hands rapidly, loudly. Platelets of ice fell from his gloves. He flexed his fingers. "Feel numb . . . all over. I can move my fingers . . . but hardly feel them."

"You'll be okay."

"Can't feel . . . toes at all. Sleepy. Not good."

He was right about that. When the body became so cold that it encouraged sleep to maintain precious heat, death could not be far away.

"As soon as you're topside, get into the sled," Brian said. "Fifteen minutes, you'll be as warm as toast."

"You got me just in time. Why?"

"Why what?"

"You risked your life."

"Not really."

"Yes, you did."

"Well, wouldn't you have done the same?"

The taut line was pulled upward, taking George

Lin with it. The ascent was smooth. At the top of the precipice, however, Lin got stuck, with his shoulders past the brink and the rest of him dangling in the wind. He was too weak to pull himself to safety.

Roger Breskin's years of training as a weight lifter served him well. He left the snowmobile and easily manhandled George Lin the last few feet onto the top of the iceberg. He untied the harness from the man's shoulders and threw the main line down to Brian.

"Check with you . . . soon as . . . George settled!" he shouted. Even though his voice was wind-tattered, the anxiety in it was evident.

Only an hour ago, Brian couldn't have conceived that Roger—rock solid as he was, with his bull's neck and his massive biceps and his powerful hands and his air of total self-reliance—might ever be afraid of anything whatsoever. Now that the other man's fear was evident, Brian was less ashamed of the terror that knotted his own guts. If a tough sonofabitch like Roger was susceptible to fear, then even one of the stoical Doughertys might be permitted that emotion a few times in his life.

He picked up the main line and harnessed himself to it. Then he untied the safety tether at his waist, loosened the other end from the piton, coiled it, and hooked it to his tool belt. He plucked the flashlight from the ledge and also fastened it to the belt. He would have salvaged the piton, too, if he'd had the means and the strength to pry it out of the ice. Their supplies, the fuel, and the tools were priceless. They dared waste or discard nothing. No one could predict what scrap, now insignificant, might eventually be essential to their survival.

He was thinking in terms of *their* survival rather than his own, for he knew that he was the least likely member of the expedition to come through the forthcoming ordeal with his life. Although he had taken four weeks of training at the U.S. Army Arctic Institute, he was not as familiar with the ice-cap or as well conditioned to it as were the others. Furthermore, he stood six one and weighed a hundred seventy pounds. Emily, his oldest sister, had called him String Bean since he was sixteen. But he was broad at the shoulders, and his lean arms were muscular: a string bean, then, but not a weakling. A weakling could never have ridden the Colorado River rapids, run with the shark hunters off Bimini, climbed mountains in Washington State. And as long as he had a warm igloo or a heated room at Edgeway Station to which he could return after a long day of exposure to the debilitating cold, he could hold up pretty well. But this was different. The igloos might no longer exist; and even if they did exist, there might not be sufficient fuel in the snowmobile tanks or life in the batteries to keep them warm for longer than another day. Survival, in this case, demanded a special strength and stamina that came only with experience. He was all but certain that he did not have the fortitude to pull through.

What he would most regret about dying was his mother's grief. She was the best of the Doughertys, above the muck of politics, and she had experienced too much grief already. God knew, Brian had caused her more than a little of it with his—

A flashlight beam found him in the darkness.

"Are you ready to go?" Roger Breskin shouted.

"Whenever you are."

Roger returned to the snowmobile.

No sooner had Brian braced himself than the rope was drawn up, putting a new and more terrible strain on his aching shoulders. Battered by the wind, half dazed by pain, unable to stop thinking about the immense watery grave that lapped far below him, he slid along the face of the cliff as smoothly as George Lin had done five minutes ago. When he came to the brink, he was able to push and kick over the top without Roger's help.

He got up and took a few uncertain steps toward the snowmobile's headlamps. His ankles and thighs were sore, but the pain would diminish with exercise. He had come through virtually unscathed. "Incredible," he said. He began to untie the knots that held the harness together. "Incredible."

"What are you talking about?" Roger asked as he joined him.

"Didn't expect to make it."

"You didn't trust me?"

"It wasn't that. I thought the rope would snap or the cliff crack apart or something."

"You're going to die eventually," Roger said, his deep voice almost theatrical in its effect. "But this wasn't your place. It wasn't the right time."

Brian was as amazed to hear Roger Breskin waxing philosophical as he had been to learn that the man knew fear.

"If you're not hurt, we'd better get moving."

Working his throbbing shoulders, Brian said, "What now?"

Roger wiped his goggles. "Put the second snowmobile right side up and see if it still works."

"And then?"

"Find the temporary camp. Join up with the others."

"What if the camp isn't on this iceberg with us?"

Roger didn't hear the question. He had already turned away and started toward the toppled snowmobile.

The cabin of the remaining snowmobile would seat only two men; therefore, Harry elected to ride behind in the open cargo trailer. Claude was willing to surrender his place, and Pete Johnson insisted on giving up his seat behind the handlebars, as though riding in the trailer were desirable, when in fact the exposure might prove deadly. Harry cut them short and pulled rank in order to obtain that worst of all positions for himself.

The trailer contained the eighteen-inch-square hot plate and the steel barrel in which they'd melted snow to obtain water to fill the blasting holes. They tipped the barrel off the trailer and rolled it out of their way; the wind caught it and swept it off into the night, and in seconds the hollow clatter of its bounding progress faded into the cacophonous symphony of the storm. The hot plate was small, and because it might come in handy later, Claude found a place for it inside the cabin.

Three or four inches of snow had accumulated in the trailer bed, drifting against the two-foot-high walls. Harry brushed it out with his hands.

The wind gusted behind them, wailing like Apaches in a Western movie, rushed under the trailer and made it bounce lightly up and down on the ice.

"I still think you should drive," Pete argued when the gale subsided slightly.

Harry was nearly finished cleaning the snow out of the trailer. "I drove my own buggy straight into an ice chasm—and you'd trust me with yours?"

Pete shook his head. "Man, do you know what's wrong with you?"

"I'm cold and scared."

"Not that."

"Well, I *have* neglected clipping my toenails for weeks. But I don't see how you could know."

"I mean what's wrong inside your head."

"This isn't an ideal time for psychoanalysis, Pete. Jeez, you Californians are obsessed with therapy." Harry brushed the last of the snow out of the trailer. "I suppose you think I want to sleep with my mother—"

"Harry—"

"—or murder my father."

"Harry—"

"Well, if that's what you think, then I don't see how we can just go on being friends."

"You've got a hero complex," Pete said.

"For insisting I ride in the trailer?"

"Yeah. We should draw straws."

"This isn't a democracy."

"It's only fair."

"Let me get this straight—you're *demanding* to ride in the back of the bus?"

Pete shook his head, tried to look serious, but couldn't repress his smile. "Honky fool."

"And proud of it."

Harry turned his back squarely to the wind and pulled on the drawstring at his chin, loosening his hood. He reached inside the neck of his coat and got hold of the thick woolen snow mask that had been folded against his throat. He tugged it over his mouth and nose; now not even a fraction of his face was exposed. What the mask did not cover, the hood and the goggles concealed. He drew the hood tight once more and knotted the drawstring. Through the mask, he said, "Pete, you're too damned big to ride in the cargo trailer."

"You're not exactly a dwarf yourself."

"But I'm small enough to curl up on my side and get down out of the worst of the wind. You'd have to sit up. It's the only way you'd fit. And sitting up, you'd freeze to death."

"Okay, okay. You're determined to play hero. Just remember—no medals are given at the end of this campaign."

"Who needs medals?" Harry climbed into the cargo trailer and sat in the middle. "I'm after sainthood."

Johnson leaned toward him. "You think you can get into heaven with a wife who knows more dirty jokes than all the men in the Edgeway group combined?"

"Isn't it obvious, Pete?"

"What?"

"God has a sense of humor."

Pete scanned the storm-whipped icecap and said, "Yeah. A real *dark* sense of humor." He returned to the cabin door, glanced back, and with considerable affection again said, "Honky fool." Then he got behind the handlebars and closed the door.

Harry took a last look at that portion of the icefield revealed by the backwash of the snowmobile's headlamps. He did not often think in metaphors, but something about the top-of-the-world gloom, some quality of the landscape, required metaphors. Perhaps the nearly incomprehensible hostility of the cruel land could only be properly grasped in metaphorical terms that made it less alien, less frightening. The icefield was a crouching dragon of monstrous dimensions. The smooth, deep darkness was the dragon's gaping mouth. The awful wind was its scream of rage. And the snow, whistling by so thickly now that he had trouble seeing even twenty feet, was the beast's spittle or perhaps foam dripping from its jaws. If it chose to do so, it could gobble them up and leave no trace.

The snowmobile began to move.

Turning away from the dragon, Harry lay on his left side. He drew his knees toward his chest, kept his head tucked down, and folded his hands under his chin. That was all the protection he could give himself.

Conditions in the trailer were even worse than he had expected—and he had expected them to be nothing short of intolerable. The suspension system was primitive at best, and every irregularity of the icecap was instantly transmitted through the skis and wheels to the cargo bed. He bounced and slid from one side of the narrow space to the other. Even his heavy clothing could not fully cushion him from the cruelest shocks, and the ribs on his right side soon reverberated with soft pain. The wind roared at him from every direction; blasts of frigid air searched busily and relentlessly for a chink in his arctic armor.

Aware that dwelling on his condition would only make it seem much worse, he guided his thoughts into other channels. He closed his eyes and conjured a vivid picture of Rita. But in order not to think of her as she might be—cold, frightened, miserable, injured, or even dead—he cast his mind back in time, back to the day they had first met. The second Friday of May. Nearly nine years ago. In Paris . . .

. . .

He had been attending a four-day conference of scientists who had participated in the previous United Nations Geophysical Year. From all over the world, three hundred men and women of different disciplines had met in Paris for seminars, lectures, and intense discussions paid for by a special UNGY fund.

At three o'clock Friday afternoon, Harry addressed a handful of geophysicists and meteorologists who were interested in his Arctic studies. He spoke for half an hour in a small room off the hotel mezzanine. When he had made his final point, he put away his notes and suggested they switch to a question-and-answer format.

During the second half of the meeting, he was surprised and enchanted by a young and beautiful woman who asked more intelligent, incisive questions than any of the twenty eminent gray heads in the room. She looked as though she might be half Irish and half Italian. Her amber-olive skin seemed to radiate heat. Wide mouth, ripe lips: very Italian. But the Irish was in her mouth too, for she had a curious, lopsided smile that gave her an elfin quality. Her eyes were Irish green, clear—but almond shaped. Long, lustrous auburn hair. In a group that opted for tweeds, sensible spring suits, and plain dresses, she was a standout in tan corduroy jeans and a dark-blue sweater that accentuated her exciting figure. But it was her mind—quick, inquisitive, well informed, well trained—that most engaged Harry. Later he realized that he'd more than likely snubbed others in the audience by spending so much time with her.

When the meeting broke up, he reached her before she left the room. "I wanted to thank you for making this a more interesting session than it might otherwise have been, but I don't even know your name."

She smiled crookedly. "Rita Marzano."

"Marzano. I thought you looked half Italian, half Irish."

"Half English, actually." Her smile developed into a full, lopsided grin. "My father was Italian, but I was raised in London."

"Marzano . . . that's familiar. Yes, of course, you've written a book, haven't you? The title . . ."

"Changing Tomorrow."

Changing Tomorrow was popularized science, a study of mankind's future projected from current discoveries in genetics, biochemistry, and physics.

It had been published in the United States and was on some best-seller lists.

"Have you read it?" she asked.

"No," he admitted.

"My British publisher shipped four hundred copies to the convention. They're on sale in the news corner off the lobby." She glanced at her watch. "I'm scheduled for an autograph session now. If you'd like a signed copy, I won't make you wait in line."

That night he was unable to put the book down until he turned the last page at three o'clock in the morning. He was fascinated by her methods—her way of ordering facts, her unconventional but logical approaches to problems—because they were startlingly like his own thought processes. He felt almost as though he had been reading his own book.

He slept through the Saturday morning lectures and spent most of the afternoon looking for Rita. He couldn't find her. When he wasn't looking for her, he was thinking about her. As he showered and dressed for the evening's gala affair, he realized he couldn't recall a word spoken in the one lecture to which he had gone.

For the first time in his life, Harry Carpenter had begun to wonder what life was like for a settled man sharing a future with one woman. He was what many women would call "a good catch": five-eleven, a hundred sixty pounds, pleasant-looking if not handsome, with gray eyes and aristocratic features. But he had never wanted to be anyone's catch. He'd always wanted a woman who was his equal, who neither clung nor dominated, a woman with whom he could share his work and hopes and ideas, from whom he could get feedback that interested him. He thought perhaps he had found her.

But he didn't know what to do about it. At thirty-three, with eight years of university education behind him, he had spent far too many hours in academic pursuits and too few learning the rituals of courtship.

The program for the evening included a film study of the major UNGY projects, a banquet, and a floor show, followed by dancing to a twelve-piece band. Ordinarily, he would have gone only to the film, if that. But there was a good chance that he'd see Rita Marzano at one of the social functions.

She was last in line at the hotel's exhibition hall, where the film was to be shown. She seemed to be alone, and she smiled crookedly when she saw him.

With a candor that he could not control and a blush that he hoped she didn't notice, he said, "I've been looking for you all day."

"I got bored and went shopping. Do you like my new dress?"

The dress couldn't enhance her beauty, but it complemented all that nature had given her. It was floor-length, long-sleeved, green with beige buttons. Her eyes picked up the shade of the dress while her auburn hair seemed brighter by contrast. The neckline revealed a décolletage uncommon at the dry conferences of scientists, and the clinging, silky fabric vaguely outlined her nipples. With little effort she could have entranced him as quickly as a flute entrances a cobra.

"I like it," he said, trying not to stare.

"Why were you looking for me all day?"

"Well, of course, the book. I'd like to talk about it if you have a free minute."

"Minute?"

"Or an hour."

"Or an evening?"

Damn if he wasn't blushing again. He felt like an Indiana farm boy. "Well . . ."

She looked along the exhibition-hall line, turned to Harry again, and grinned. "If we skip out on this, we'll have all evening to talk."

"Aren't you interested in the film?"

"No. Besides, dinner will be awful. The floor show will be too conventional. And the dance band will be out of tune."

"Dinner together?"

"That would be lovely."

"Drinks first at Deux Magots?"

"Marvelous."

"Lapérouse for dinner?"

She frowned. "That's pretty expensive. You

needn't take me first class. I'm as happy with beer as with champagne."

"This is a special occasion. For me if not for you."

Dinner was perfect. Paris offered no more romantic atmosphere than that in the upstairs room at Lapérouse. The low ceiling and the murals on the crack-webbed walls made the restaurant warm and cozy. From their table they had a view of the night-clad city, and below them lay the light-stained, oily river like a storybook giant's discarded black silk scarf. They ate flawless *oie rôtie aux pruneaux,* and for dessert there were tiny tender strawberries in a perfect zabaglione. Throughout the meal, they unraveled an endless skein of conversation, immediately as comfortable as friends who had been dining together for a decade. Halfway through the roast goose, Harry realized that they had not yet discussed her book but had rambled on about art, literature, music, cooking, and much more, without once finding themselves at a loss for words. When he finished his cognac, he was reluctant to let the night end so soon.

She shared that reluctance. "We've been Frenchmen for dinner. Now let's be tourists."

"What do you have in mind?"

The Crazy Horse Saloon was an all-out assault on the senses. The customers were Americans, Germans, Swedes, Italians, Japanese, Arabs, British, Greeks, even a few Frenchmen, and their conversations intertwined to produce a noisy babble frequently punctuated with laughter. The air was thick with cigarette smoke, perfume, and whiskey. When the band played, it generated enough sound to shatter crystal. The few times Harry wanted to speak to Rita, he was forced to scream, although they were just two feet apart, on opposite sides of a minuscule cocktail table.

The stage show made him forget the noise and smoke. The girls were gorgeous. Long legs. Full, high-set breasts. Tiny waists. Galvanizing faces. More variety than the eye could take in. More beauty than the mind could easily comprehend or the heart appreciate. Dozens of girls, most bare-breasted. All manner of costumes, most skimpy: leather straps, chains, furs, boots, jeweled dog collars, feathers, silk scarves. Their eyes were heavily mascaraed, and some wore sequined designs on their faces and bodies.

Rita said, "After an hour, this gets to be a bore. Shall we go?" Outside, she said, "We haven't talked about my book, and that's really what you wanted to do. Tell you what. We'll walk to the Hôtel George V, have some champagne, and talk."

He was somewhat confused. She seemed to be sending conflicting signals. Hadn't they gone to the Crazy Horse to be turned on? Hadn't she expected him to make a pass afterward? And now she was ready to talk books?

As they crossed the lobby of the George V and

boarded the elevator, he said, "Do they have a rooftop restaurant here?"

"I don't know. We're going to my room."

His confusion deepened. "You're not staying at the convention hotel? I know it's dull, but this is terribly expensive."

"I've made a tidy sum from *Changing Tomorrow*. I'm splurging, for once. I have a small suite overlooking the gardens."

In her room a bottle of champagne stood beside her bed in a silver bucket full of crushed ice.

She pointed to the bottle. "Moët. Open it, please?"

He took it out of the bucket—and saw her wince.

"The sound of the ice," she said.

"What about it?"

She hesitated. "Puts my teeth on edge. Like fingernails screeching against a blackboard."

By then he was so attuned to her that he knew she wasn't telling him the truth, that she had winced because the rattle of the ice had reminded her of something unpleasant. For a moment her eyes were faraway, deep in a memory that furrowed her brow.

"The ice is hardly melted," he said. "When did you order this?"

Shedding the troubling memory, she focused on him and grinned again. "When I went to the ladies' room at Lapérouse."

Incredulous, he said *"You're* seducing *me!"*

"It's very late in the twentieth century, you know."

Mocking himself, he said, "Yes, well, actually, I've noticed women sometimes wear pants these days."

"Are you offended?"

"By women in pants?"

"By me trying to get you out of yours."

"Good heavens, no."

"If I've been too bold ..."

"Not at all."

"Actually, I've never done anything like this before. I mean, going to bed on a first date."

"Neither have I."

"Or on a second or a third, for that matter."

"Neither have I."

"But it feels right, doesn't it?"

He eased the bottle into the ice and pulled her into his arms. Her lips were the texture of a dream, and her body against his felt like destiny.

They skipped the rest of the convention and stayed in bed. They had their meals sent up. They talked, made love, and slept as if they were drugged.

• • •

Someone was shouting his name.

Stiff with cold, crusted with snow, Harry raised himself from the bed of the cargo trailer and from the delicious memories. He looked over his shoulder.

Claude Jobert was staring at him through the rear window of the snowmobile cabin. "Harry!

Hey, Harry!" He was barely audible above the wind and the engine noise. "Lights! Ahead! Look!"

At first he didn't understand what Claude meant. He was stiff, chilled, and still half in that Paris hotel room. Then he lifted his gaze and saw that they were driving directly toward a hazy yellow light that sparkled in the snowflakes and shimmered languidly across the ice. He pushed up on his hands and knees, ready to jump from the trailer the instant that it stopped.

Pete Johnson drove the snowmobile along the familiar ice plateau and down into the basin where the igloos had been. The domes were deflated, crushed by enormous slabs of ice. But one snowmobile was running, headlights ablaze, and two people in arctic gear stood beside it, waving.

One of them was Rita.

Harry launched himself out of the trailer while the snowmobile was still in motion. He fell into the snow, rolled, stumbled onto his feet, and ran to her.

"Harry!"

He grabbed her, nearly lifted her above his head, then put her down and lowered his snow mask and tried to speak and couldn't speak and hugged her instead.

Eventually, voice quivering, she said, "Are you hurt?"

"Nosebleed."

"That's all?"

"And it's stopped. You?"

"Just frightened."

He knew that she struggled always against her fear of snow, ice, and cold, and he never ceased to admire her unwavering determination to confront her phobias and to work in the very climate that most tested her. "You've good reason this time," he said. "Listen, you know what we'll do if we get off this damned berg?"

She shook her head and shoved up her misted goggles, so he could see her lovely green eyes. They were wide with curiosity and delight.

"We'll go to Paris," he told her.

Grinning, she said, "To the Crazy Horse Saloon."

"George V."

"A room overlooking the gardens."

"Moët."

He pulled up his own goggles, and she kissed him.

Clapping one hand on Harry's shoulder, Pete Johnson said, "Have some consideration for those whose wives don't like frostbite. And didn't you hear what I said? I said, 'The gang's all here.' " He pointed to a pair of snowmobiles racing toward them through the snow.

"Roger, Brian, and George," Rita said with obvious relief.

"Must be," Johnson said. "Not likely to run across a bunch of strangers out here."

"The gang's all here," Harry agreed. "But where in the name of God does it go next?"

1:32

On the fourteenth day of a hundred-day electronic-espionage mission, the Russian nuclear submarine *Ilya Pogodin* reached its first monitoring station on schedule. The captain, Nikita Gorov, ordered the maneuvering room to hold the boat steady in the moderate southeasterly currents northwest of Jan Mayen Island, forty miles from the coast of Greenland and one hundred feet beneath the stormy surface of the North Atlantic.

The *Ilya Pogodin* had been named after an official Hero of the Soviet People, in the days before the corrupt bureaucracy had failed and the totalitarian state had crumbled under the weight of its own inefficiency and venality. The boat's name had not been changed: in part because the navy was tradition bound; in part because the new quasi-democracy was fragile, and care still had to be taken not to offend the bitter and potentially murderous old-guard Party members who had been driven from power but who might one day come storming back to reopen the extermination camps and the institutions of "reeducation"; and in part because Russia was now so fearfully poor, so totally bankrupted by Marxism and by legions of pocket-lining politicians, that the country could spare no funds for the repainting of boat names or for the alteration of records to reflect those changes.

Gorov was unable to obtain even adequate maintenance for his vessel. In these trying days after the fall of empire, he was too worried about the integrity of the pressure hull, the nuclear power plant, and the engines to spare any concern for the fact that the *Ilya Pogodin* was named after a despicable thief and murderer who had been nothing more noble than a dutiful defender of the late, unlamented regime.

Although the *Pogodin* was an aging fleet submarine that had never carried nuclear missiles, only some nuclear-tipped torpedoes, it was nonetheless a substantial boat, measuring three hundred sixty feet from bow to stern, with a forty-two-foot beam and a draft of thirty-two feet six inches. It displaced over eight thousand tons when fully submerged.

The southeasterly currents had a negligible influence on the boat. It would never drift more than one hundred yards from where Gorov had ordered it held steady.

Peter Timoshenko, the young communications officer, was in the control center at Gorov's side. Around them, the windows and gauges of the electronic equipment pulsed and glowed and blinked in the half-light: red, amber, green, blue. Even the ceiling was lined with scopes, graphs, display screens, and control panels. When the maneuvering room acknowledged Gorov's order to hold the boat steady, and when the engine room and reactor room had been made aware of it, Timoshenko said, "Request permission to run up the aerial, Captain."

"That's what we're here for."

• • •

Timoshenko stepped into the main companionway and walked thirty feet to the communications shack, a surprisingly small space packed full of radio equipment capable of receiving and sending encrypted messages in ultrahigh frequency (UHF), high frequency (HF), very low frequency (VLF), and extremely low frequency (ELF). He sat at the primary console and studied the display screens and scopes on his own extensive array of transceivers and computers. He smiled and began to hum as he worked.

In the company of most men, Peter Timoshenko felt awkward, but he was always comfortable with the companionship of machines. He had been at ease in the control room, but this place, with its even heavier concentration of electronics, was his true home.

"Are we ready?" another technician asked.

"Yes." Timoshenko flicked a yellow switch.

Topside, on the outer hull of the *Ilya Pogodin*, a small helium balloon was ejected from a pressurized tube on the sail. It rose rapidly through the dark sea, expanding as it went, trailing the multicommunications wire behind it. When the balloon broke the surface, the technicians in the *Pogodin* were able to monitor every message sent to, from, and within the eastern coast of Greenland via virtually every communications medium except note-passing and underground telephone lines. Because it was the same dull gray-blue as the winter sea, the balloon—and the short, complicated antenna attached to it—couldn't have been seen from the deck of a ship even ten yards away.

On land and in civilian society, Timoshenko was frequently self-conscious. He was tall, lanky, raw-boned, awkward, and often clumsy. In restaurants and nightclubs, on city streets, he suspected that people were watching him and were quietly amused by his lack of grace. In the *Pogodin*, however, secure in his deep domain, he felt blessedly invisible, as though the sea were not a part of the world above the surface but a parallel dimension to it, and as though he were a spirit slipping through those cold depths, able to hear the inhabitants in the world above without being heard, to see without being seen, safe from their stares, not an object of amusement any longer. A ghost.

• • •

After giving Timoshenko a while to deploy the aerial and scan a wide spectrum of frequencies, Captain Gorov stepped into the doorway of the communications shack. He nodded at the assistant technician. To Timoshenko, he said, "Anything?"

The communications officer was smiling and holding a single earphone to his left ear. "Full input."

"Of interest?"

"Not much as yet. There's a group of American Marines winter-testing some equipment near the coast."

Although they were living in the long shadow of the Cold War's passage, in a world where old enemies were supposed to have become neutral toward one another or were even said to have become fine friends, the greater part of the former Soviet intelligence apparatus remained intact, both at home and abroad. The Russian Navy continued to conduct extensive information-gathering along the coastlines of every major Western nation, as well as at most points of strategic military importance in the Third World. Change, after all, was the only constant. If enemies could become friends virtually overnight, they could become *enemies* again with equivalent alacrity.

"Keep me informed," Gorov said. Then he went to the officer's mess and ate lunch.

1:40

Crouched at the shortwave radio, in contact with Edgeway Station, Harry said, "Have you gotten through to Thule?"

Although Gunvald Larsson's voice was filtered through a sieve of static, it was intelligible. "I've been in continuous contact with them and with

Norwegian officials at a meteorological station on Spitsbergen for the past twenty-five minutes."

"Can either of them reach us?"

"The Norwegians are pretty much locked in by ice. The Americans have several Kaman Huskies at Thule. That's their standard rescue helicopter. The Huskies have auxiliary fuel tanks and long-range capability. But conditions at ground level aren't really good enough to allow them to lift off. Terrific winds. And by the time they got to you—if they *could* get to you—the weather would have deteriorated so much they probably wouldn't be able to put down on your iceberg."

"There doesn't just happen to be an icebreaker or a battleship in our neighborhood?"

"The Americans say not."

"So much for miracles."

"Do you think you can ride it out?"

Harry said, "We haven't taken an inventory of our remaining supplies, but I'm sure we don't have enough fuel to keep us warm any longer than another twenty-four hours."

A loud burst of static echoed like submachine-gun fire in the ice cave.

Gunvald hesitated. Then: "According to the latest forecasts, this is bigger than any other major weather pattern we've had all winter. We're in for a week of bitter storms. One atop the other. Not even a brief respite between them."

A week. Harry closed his eyes against the sight

of the ice wall beyond the radio, for in that prismatic surface, he saw their fate too clearly. Even in thermal clothing, even sheltered from the wind, they could not survive for a week with no heat. They were virtually without food; hunger would weaken their resistance to the subzero temperatures.

"Harry, did you read me?"

He opened his eyes. "I read you. It doesn't look good, does it? Then again, we're drifting south, out of the bad weather."

"I've been studying the charts here. Do you have any idea how many miles per day that berg of yours will travel?"

"At a guess . . . thirty, maybe forty."

"That's approximately the same figure I've arrived at with the charts. And do you know how much of that represents real southward movement?"

Harry thought about it. "Twenty miles per day?"

"At best. Perhaps as little as ten."

"Ten. You're sure? Strike that. Stupid of me. Of course, you're sure. Just how large *is* this storm pattern?"

"Harry, it ranges one hundred and twenty miles south of your last known position. You'd need eight or ten days or even longer to get out of the blizzard to a place where those helicopters could reach you."

"What about the UNGY trawlers?"

"The Americans have relayed the news to them. Both ships are making for you at their best possible speed. But according to Thule, seas are extremely rough even beyond the storm area. And those trawlers are two hundred and thirty miles away. Under the current conditions, their best speed won't amount to much."

They had to know precisely where they stood, no matter how tenuous their position might be. Harry said, "Can a ship that size push a hundred miles or more into a storm as bad as this one without being torn to pieces?"

"I think those two captains are courageous—but not suicidal," Gunvald said flatly.

Harry agreed with that assessment.

"They'll be forced to turn back," Gunvald said.

Harry sighed. "Yeah. They won't have any choice. Okay, Gunvald, I'll call you again in fifteen minutes. We've got to have a conference here. There's a chance we'll think of something."

"I'll be waiting."

Harry put the microphone on top of the radio. He stood and regarded the others. "You heard."

Everyone in the ice cave was staring either at Harry or at the now silent radio. Pete, Roger, and Franz stood near the entrance; their goggles were in place, and they were ready to go outside and pick through the ruins of the temporary camp. Brian Dougherty had been studying a chart of the Greenland Sea and the North Atlantic; but listening to Gunvald, he had realized that pinpointing the location of the trawlers was useless, and he had folded the chart. Before Harry had called Edgeway Station, George Lin had been pacing from one end of the cave to the other, exercising his bruised muscles to prevent stiffness. Now he stood motionless, not even blinking, as if frozen alive. Rita and Claude knelt on the floor of the cave, where they'd been taking an inventory of the contents of a carton of foodstuffs that had been severely damaged by the collapsing pressure ridge. To Harry, for a moment, they seemed to be not real people but lifeless mannequins in a strange tableau—perhaps because, without some great stroke of luck, they were already as good as dead.

Rita said what they were all thinking but what no one else cared to mention: "Even if the trawlers can reach us, they won't be here until tomorrow at the earliest. They can't possibly make it in time to take us aboard before midnight. And at midnight all sixty bombs go off."

"We don't know the size or the shape of the iceberg," Fischer said. "Most of the charges may be in the ice shafts that are still part of the main winter field."

Pete Johnson disagreed. "Claude, Harry, and I were at the end of the bomb line when the first tsunami passed under us. I think we followed a fairly direct course back to camp, the same route we took going out. So we must have driven right by or across all sixty charges. And I'd bet my right arm this berg isn't anywhere near large enough to withstand all those concussions."

After a short silence Brian cleared his throat. "You mean the iceberg's going to be blown into a thousand pieces?"

No one responded.

"So we're all going to be killed? Or dumped into the sea?"

"Same thing," Roger Breskin said matter-of-factly. His bass voice rebounded hollowly from the ice walls. "The sea's *freezing*. You wouldn't last five minutes in it."

"Isn't there anything we can do to save ourselves?" Brian asked as his gaze traveled from one member of the team to another. "Surely there's *something* we could do."

Throughout the conversation, George Lin had been as motionless and quiet as a statue, but suddenly he turned and took three quick steps toward Dougherty. "Are you scared, boy? You *should* be scared. Your almighty family can't bail you out of this one!"

Startled, Brian backed away from the angry man.

Lin's hands were fisted at his sides. "How do you like being helpless?" He was shouting. "How do you like it? Your big, rich, politically powerful family doesn't mean a goddamned thing out here. Now you know what it's like for the rest of us, for all us little people. Now you have to scramble to save yourself. Just exactly like the rest of us."

"That's enough," Harry said.

Lin turned on him. His face had been transformed by hatred. "His family sits back with all its money and privileges, isolated from reality but so damned sure of its moral superiority, yammering about how the rest of us should live, about how we should sacrifice for this or that noble cause. It was people like them who started the trouble in China, brought in Mao, lost us our homeland, tens of millions of people butchered. You let them get a foot in the door, and the communists come right after them. The barbarians and the cossacks, the killers and the human animals storm right in after them. The—"

"Brian didn't put us on this berg," Harry said sharply. "And neither did his family. For God's sake, George, he saved your life less than an hour ago."

When Lin realized that he'd been ranting, the flush of anger drained from his cheeks. He seemed confused, then embarrassed. He shook his head as if to clear it. "I . . . I'm sorry."

"Don't tell me," Harry said. "Tell Brian."

Lin turned to Dougherty but didn't look him in the face. "I'm sorry. I really am."

"It's all right," Brian assured him.

"I don't . . . I don't know what came over me. You did save my life. Harry's right."

"Forget it, George."

After a brief hesitation, Lin nodded and went to

the far end of the cave. He walked back and forth, exercising his aching muscles, staring at the ice over which he trod.

Harry wondered what experiences in the little man's past had prepared him to regard Brian Dougherty as an antagonist, which he had done since the day they'd met.

"Is there anything at all we can do to save ourselves?" Brian asked again, graciously dismissing the incident with Lin.

"Maybe," Harry said. "First we've got to get some of those bombs out of the ice and defuse them."

Fischer was amazed. "Impossible!"

"Most likely."

"How could they ever be retrieved?" Fischer asked scornfully.

Claude rose to his feet beside the carton of half-ruined food. "It isn't impossible. We've got an auxiliary drill, ice axes, and the power saw. If we had a lot of time and patience, we might be able to angle down toward each bomb, more or less dig steps in the ice. But, Harry, we needed a day and a half just to bury them. Digging them out will be hugely more difficult. We would need at least a week to retrieve them, maybe two."

"We only have ten hours," Fischer reminded them unnecessarily.

Leaving the niche in the wall by the cave entrance and stepping to the middle of the room,

Pete Johnson said, "Wait a minute. You folks didn't listen to the man. Harry said we had to defuse *some* of the bombs, not all of them. And he didn't say we'd have to dig them out, the way Claude's proposing." He looked at Harry. "You want to explain yourself?"

"The nearest package of explosives is three hundred yards from our position. Nine hundred feet. If we can retrieve and disarm it, then we'll be nine hundred and forty-five feet from the *next* nearest bomb. Each charge is forty-five feet from the one in front of it. So, if we take up ten of them, we'll be over a quarter of a mile from the nearest explosion. The other fifty will detonate at midnight—but none of them will be directly under us. Our end of the iceberg might well survive the shock. With luck, it might be large enough to sustain us."

"Might," Fischer said sourly.

"It's our best chance."

"Not a good one," the German noted.

"I didn't say it was."

"If we can't *dig* up the explosives, which you apparently agree is out of the question, then how do we get to them?"

"With the auxiliary drill. Reopen the shafts."

Fischer frowned. "Perhaps not so wise. What if we drill into a bomb casing?"

"It won't explode," Harry assured him.

Johnson said, "The plastic charge responds only

to a certain voltage of electric current. Neither shock nor heat will do the job, Franz."

"Besides," Harry said, "the bits for the ice drill aren't hard enough to cut through a steel casing."

"And when we've opened the shaft?" the German asked with obvious skepticism. "Just reel in the bomb by its chain, as if it's a fish on a line?"

"Something like that."

"No good. You'll chew the chain to pieces when you reopen the shaft with the drill."

"Not if we use the smaller bits. The original shaft is four inches in diameter. But the bomb is only two and a half inches in diameter. If we use a three-inch bit, we might be able to slip past the chain. After all, it's pulled flat against the side of the original shaft."

Franz Fischer wasn't satisfied. "Even if you can open the hole without shredding the chain, it'll still be welded to the ice, and so will the bomb casing."

"We'll snap the upper end of the chain to a snowmobile and try to pop it and the cylinder out of the shaft."

"Won't work," Fischer said dismissively.

Harry nodded. "Maybe you're right."

"There must be another way."

"Such as?"

Brian said, "We can't just lie down and wait for the end, Franz. That doesn't make a whole hell of a lot of sense." He turned to Harry. "But if your plan works, if we can get the bombs out of the ice, will it be possible to uncover ten of them in ten hours?"

"We won't know till we try," Harry said, resolutely refusing either to play into Fischer's stubborn pessimism or to raise false hopes.

Pete Johnson said, "If we can't get ten, maybe eight. If not eight, surely six. Every one we get buys us more security."

"Even so," Fischer said, his accent thickening as he became more defensive of his negativism, "what will we have gained? We'll still be adrift on an iceberg, for God's sake. We'll still have enough fuel to keep us warm only until tomorrow afternoon. We'll still freeze to death."

Getting to her feet, Rita said, "Franz, goddammit, stop playing devil's advocate, or whatever it is you're doing. You're a good man. You can help us survive. Or for the lack of your help, we may all die. Nobody is expendable here. Nobody is dead weight. We need you on our side, pulling with us."

"My sentiments exactly," Harry said. He pulled his hood over his head and laced it tightly beneath his chin. "And if we can buy some time by retrieving a few of the bombs, even just three or four— well, there's always the chance we'll be rescued sooner than seems possible right now."

"How?" Roger asked.

"One of those trawlers—"

Glancing at Rita, but with no less contention in

his voice, as though he and Harry were somehow engaged in a competition to win her backing, Fischer said, "You and Gunvald already agreed that the trawlers can't possibly reach us."

Harry shook his head emphatically. "Our fate here isn't written in stone. We're intelligent people. We can make our own fate if we put our minds to it. If one of those captains is damned good and *damned-all* bullheaded, and if he has a really top-flight crew, and if he's a bit lucky, he might get through."

"Too many ifs," Roger Breskin said.

Fischer was grim. "If he's Horatio Hornblower, if he's the fucking grandfather of all the sailors who ever lived, if he's not a mere man but a supernatural force of the sea, then I guess we'll have a chance."

"Well, if he *is* Horatio Hornblower," Harry said impatiently, "if he does show up here tomorrow, all flags flying and sailing like the clappers, I want to be around to say hello."

They were silent.

Harry said, "What about the rest of you?"

No one disagreed with him.

"All right, we'll need every man on the bomb-recovery project," Harry said, fitting the tinted goggles over his eyes. "Rita, will you stay here and watch over the radio, put through that call to Gunvald?"

"Sure."

Claude said, "Someone should finish searching the camp before the snow drifts over the ruins."

"I'll handle that too," Rita said.

Harry went to the mouth of the cave. "Let's get moving. I can hear those sixty clocks ticking. I don't want to be too near them when the alarms go off."

Three

❄

PRISON

2:30
DETONATION IN NINE HOURS
THIRTY MINUTES

Within a minute or two of lying down, Nikita Gorov knew that he was not going to be able to get any rest. From out of the past, one small ghost materialized to haunt him and ensure that he would not find the peace of sleep. When he closed his eyes, he could see little Nikolai, his Nikki, running toward him through a soft yellow haze. The child's arms were open wide, and he was giggling. But the distance between them could not be closed, regardless of how long or fast Nikki ran or how desperately Gorov reached out for him: They were separated by only ten or twelve feet, but each inch was an infinity. The captain wanted nothing half as much as to touch his son, but the unbreachable veil between life and death separated them.

With a soft, involuntary sigh of despair, Gorov opened his eyes and looked at the silver-framed photograph on the corner desk: Nikolai and himself standing in front of a piano-accordion player on a Moscow River cruise ship. At times, when the past lay especially heavy on him, Gorov was monstrously depressed by the photograph. But he could not remove it. He could not put it in a drawer or throw it away any more than he could chop off his right hand merely because Nikolai had often held it.

Suddenly charged with nervous energy, he got up from his bunk. He wanted to pace, but his quarters were too small. In three steps he had walked the length of the narrow aisle between the bed and the closet. He couldn't allow the crew to see how distraught he was. Otherwise, he might have paced the main companionway.

Finally he sat at the desk. He took the photograph in both hands, as if by confronting it—and his agonizing loss—he could soothe the pain in his heart and calm himself.

He spoke softly to the golden-haired boy in the picture. "I am not responsible for your death, Nikki."

Gorov knew that was true. He believed it as well, which was more important than merely knowing it. Yet oceans of guilt washed through him in endless, corrosive tides.

"I know you never blamed me, Nikki. But I wish I could hear you tell me so."

• • •

In mid-June, seven months ago, the *Ilya Pogodin* had been sixty days into an ultrasecret, ninety-day electronic-surveillance mission on the Mediterranean route. The boat had been submerged nine miles off the Egyptian coast, directly north of the city of Alexandria. The multicommunications aerial was up, and thousands of bytes of data, important and otherwise, were filing into the computer banks every minute.

At two o'clock in the morning, the fifteenth of June, a message came in from the Naval Intelligence Office at Sevastopol, relayed from the Naval Ministry in Moscow. It required a confirmation from the *Ilya Pogodin,* thereby shattering the radio silence that was an absolute necessity during a clandestine mission.

When the code specialist had finished translating the encrypted text, Gorov was wakened by the night communications officer. He sat in his bunk and read from the pale-yellow paper.

The message began with latitude and longitude coordinates, followed by orders to rendezvous in twenty-two hours with the *Petr Vavilov,* a Vostok-class research ship that was currently in the same part of the Mediterranean to which the *Pogodin* was assigned. That much of it pleasantly piqued Gorov's curiosity: A midnight meeting in the middle of the sea was a more traditional and intriguing piece of cloak-and-dagger work than that to which he was accustomed in an age of electronic spying. But the rest of it brought him straight to his feet, trembling.

YOUR SON IN SERIOUS CONDITION KREMLIN
HOSPITAL STOP YOUR PRESENCE REQUIRED
MOSCOW SOONEST STOP ALL TRANSPORTATION
HAS BEEN ARRANGED STOP FIRST OFFICER

ZHUKOV TO ASSUME COMMAND YOUR SHIP STOP
CONFIRM RECEIPT
CONFIRM RECEIPT

At midnight Gorov passed control of his submarine to Zhukov and transferred to the *Petr Vavilov*.
From the main deck of the research ship, a helicopter took him to Damascus, Syria, where he boarded
a Russian diplomatic jet for a scheduled flight to
Moscow. He arrived at Sheremetyevo Airport at
three o'clock on the afternoon of the sixteenth.

Boris Okudzhava, a functionary from the Naval
Ministry, met him at the terminal. Okudzhava had
eyes as dirty gray as laundry water. A cherry-sized
wart disfigured the left side of his nose. "A car is
waiting, Comrade Gorov."

"What's wrong with Nikki? What's wrong with
my son?"

"I'm no doctor, Comrade Gorov."

"You must know something."

"I think we'd better not waste time here. I'll
explain in the car, comrade."

"It's not 'comrade' anymore," Gorov said as
they hurried away from the debarkation gate.

"Sorry. Just long habit."

"Is it?"

Although the social and economic policies of the
communists had been thoroughly discredited,
although their thievery and mass murders had been
exposed, more than a few former true believers

yearned for the reestablishment of the old order. They still enjoyed considerable influence in many quarters, including the nuclear-weapons industry, where production of warheads and missiles continued unabated. For many of them, repudiation of hard-line Marxist ideology was merely a self-serving recognition of the shift of power to more democratic forces, not a genuine change of heart or mind. They labored with apparent diligence for the new Russia while waiting hopefully for a chance to resurrect the Supreme Soviet.

As they left the busy terminal and stepped outside into the mild late-spring afternoon, Okudzhava said, "The next revolution should be for more freedom, not less. If anything, we haven't gone far enough. Too many of the old *nomenklatura* remain in power, calling themselves champions of democracy, praising capitalism while undermining it at every turn."

Gorov dropped the matter. Boris Okudzhava was not a good actor. The excessive ardency with which he spoke revealed the truth: The grotesque wart alongside his nose flushed bright red, as though it were a telltale blemish bestowed by God, the unmistakable mark of the Beast.

The low sky was mottled with gray-black clouds. The air smelled of oncoming rain.

Several peddlers had been allowed to set up business outside the terminal. A few worked from large trunks, others from pushcarts, hawking cigarettes, candy, tourist maps, souvenirs. They were doing a brisk business, and at least some must have been comparatively prosperous, but they were all shabbily dressed. In the old days, prosperity had been an offense requiring prosecution, imprisonment, and occasionally even execution. Many citizens of the new Russia still vividly recalled the former consequences of success and the savage fury of envious bureaucrats.

The Ministry car was immediately in front of the terminal, parked illegally, with the engine running. The moment Gorov and Okudzhava got in the backseat and closed the doors, the driver—a young man in a navy uniform—sped away from the curb.

"What about Nikki?" Gorov demanded.

"He entered the hospital thirty-one days ago with what was first thought to be mononucleosis or influenza. He was dizzy, sweating. So nauseous that he couldn't even take fluids. He was hospitalized for intravenous feeding to guard against dehydration."

In the days of the discredited regime, medical care had been tightly controlled by the state—and had been dreadful even by the standards of Third World countries. Most hospitals had functioned without adequate equipment to maintain sterilized instruments. Diagnostic machines had been in woefully short supply, and health-care budgets had been so pinched that dirty hypodermic needles were regularly reused, often spreading disease. The collapse of the old system had been a blessing; however, the disgraced regime had left the nation deep in bankruptcy, and in recent years the quality of medical care had deteriorated even further.

Gorov shivered at the thought of young Nikki entrusted to the care of physicians who had been trained in medical schools that were no more modern or better equipped than the hospitals in which they subsequently labored. Surely every parent in the world prayed that his children would enjoy good health, but in the new Russia as in the old empire that it replaced, a beloved child's hospitalization was a cause not merely for concern but for alarm, if not quite panic.

"You weren't notified," said Okudzhava, absentmindedly rubbing his facial wart with the tip of his index finger, "because you were on a highly classified mission. Besides, the situation didn't seem all that critical."

"But it wasn't either mononucleosis or influenza?" Gorov asked.

"No. Then there was some thought that rheumatic fever might be to blame."

Having lived so long with the pressure of being a commanding officer in the submarine service, having learned never to appear troubled either by the periodic mechanical difficulties of his boat or by the hostile power of the sea, Nikita Gorov managed to maintain a surface calm even as his mind churned with images of little Nikki suffering and frightened in a cockroach-ridden hospital. "But it wasn't rheumatic fever."

"No," Okudzhava said, still fingering his wart, looking not at Gorov but at the back of the driver's head. "And then there was a brief remission of the symptoms. He seemed in the best of health for four days. When the symptoms returned, new diagnostic tests were begun. And then . . . eight days ago, they discovered he has a cancerous brain tumor."

"Cancer," Gorov said thickly.

"The tumor is too large to be operable, far too advanced for radiation treatments. When it became clear that Nikolai's condition was rapidly deteriorating, we broke your radio silence and called you back. It was the humane thing to do, even if it risked compromising your mission." He paused and finally looked at Gorov. "In the old days, of course, no such risk would have been taken, but these are better times," Okudzhava added with such patent insincerity that he might as well have been wearing the hammer and sickle, emblem of his true allegiance, on his chest.

Gorov didn't give a damn about Boris Okudzhava's nostalgia for the bloody past. He didn't give a damn about democracy, about the future, about himself—only about his Nikki. A cold sweat had sprung up along the back of his neck, as if Death had lightly touched him with icy fingers while on its way to or from the boy's bedside.

"Can't you drive faster?" he demanded of the young officer behind the wheel.

"We'll be there soon," Okudzhava assured him.

"He's only eight years old," Gorov said more to himself than to either of the men with whom he shared the car.

Neither replied.

Gorov saw the driver's eyes in the rearview mirror, regarding him with what might have been pity. "How long does he have to live?" he asked, though he almost preferred not to be answered.

Okudzhava hesitated. Then: "He could go at any time."

Since he had read that decoded message in his quarters aboard the *Ilya Pogodin* thirty-seven hours ago, Gorov had known that Nikki must be dying. The Admiralty was not cruel, but on the other hand it would not have interrupted an important espionage mission on the Mediterranean route unless the situation was quite hopeless. He had carefully prepared himself for this news.

At the hospital, the elevators were out of order. Boris Okudzhava led Gorov to the service stairs, which were dirty and poorly lighted. Flies buzzed at the small, dust-opaqued windows at each landing.

Gorov climbed to the seventh floor. He paused twice when it seemed that his knees might buckle, then each time hurried upward again after only a brief hesitation.

Nikki was in an eight-patient ward with four

other dying children, in a small bed under stained and tattered sheets. No EKG monitor or other equipment surrounded him. Deemed incurable, he had been brought to a terminal ward to suffer through the last of his time in this world. The government was still in charge of the medical system, and its resources were stretched to the limit, which meant that doctors triaged the ill and injured according to a ruthless standard of treatability. No heroic effort was made to save the patient if there was less than a fifty percent chance that he would recover.

The boy was fearfully pale. Waxy skin. A gray tint to his lips. Eyes closed. His golden hair was lank, damp with sweat.

Trembling as though he were an elderly man with palsy, finding it increasingly difficult to maintain a submariner's traditional calm, Gorov stood beside the bed, gazing down at his son, his only child.

"Nikki," he said, and his voice was unsteady, weak.

The boy didn't answer or even open his eyes.

Gorov sat on the edge of the bed. He put one hand over his son's hand. There was so little warmth in the boy's flesh.

"Nikki, I'm here."

Someone touched Gorov's shoulder, and he looked up.

A white-coated physician stood beside the bed. He indicated a woman at the end of the room. "She's the one who needs you now."

It was Anya. Gorov had been so focused on Nikki that he hadn't noticed her. She was standing at a window, pretending to watch the people down on the old Kalinin Prospekt.

Gradually Gorov became aware of the defeat in the slope of his wife's shoulders and the subtle hint of grief in the tilt of her head, and he began to apprehend the full meaning of the doctor's words. Nikki was already dead. Too late to say "I love you" one last time. Too late for one last kiss. Too late to look into his child's eyes and say, "I was always so proud of you," too late to say good-bye.

Although Anya needed him, he couldn't bear to get up from the edge of the bed—as though to do so would ensure that Nikki's death was permanent, while sheer stubborn denial might eventually cause a miraculous resurrection.

He spoke her name, and though it was only a whisper, she turned to him.

Her eyes shimmered with tears. She was biting her lip to keep from sobbing. She said, "I wish you'd been here."

"They didn't tell me until yesterday."

"I've been so alone."

"I know."

"Frightened."

"I know."

"I would have gone in his place if I could," she said. "But there was nothing . . . nothing I could do for him."

At last he found the strength to leave the bed. He went to his wife and held her, and she held him so tightly. So tightly.

All but one of the other four dying children in the ward were comatose, sedated, or otherwise unaware of Gorov and Anya. The sole observer among them was a girl, perhaps eight or nine years old, with chestnut hair and huge solemn eyes. She lay in a bed nearby, propped up on pillows, as frail as an elderly woman who had seen a hundred years of life. "It's okay," she told Gorov. Her voice was musical and sweet in spite of how badly disease had ravaged and weakened her body. "You'll see him again. He's in heaven now. He's waiting for you there."

Nikita Gorov, the product of a strictly materialistic society that had for the better part of a century denied the existence of God, wished that he could find strength in a faith as simple and strong as that revealed by the child's words. He was no atheist. He had seen what monstrous acts the leaders of society would condone when they believed there was no God; he knew that there was no hope for justice in a world where the concepts of divine retribution and life after death had been abandoned. God *must* exist, for otherwise humankind couldn't be prevented from destroying itself. Nevertheless, he lacked a tradition of belief in which to find the degree of hope and reassurance that comforted the dying girl.

Anya wept against his shoulder. He held her and stroked her golden hair.

The bruised sky suddenly ruptured, releasing torrents of rain. Fat droplets snapped against the window and streamed down the pane, blurring the traffic below.

· · ·

During the remainder of that summer, they tried to find things to smile about. They went to the Taganka Theater, the ballet, the music hall, and the circus. They danced more than once at the big pavilion in Gorki Park and exhausted themselves as children might with the amusements at Sokolniki Park. Once a week they ate dinner at Aragvi, perhaps the best restaurant in the city, where Anya learned to smile again when eating the ice cream and jam, where Nikita developed a taste for the spicy chicken *zatsivi* smothered in walnut sauce, and where they both drank too much vodka with their caviar, too much wine with their *sulguni* and bread. They made love every night, urgent and explosive love, as though their passion were a refutation of suffering, cancer, and death.

Although no longer as light-hearted as she had always been, Anya appeared to recover from the loss more quickly and more completely than did Nikita. For one thing, she was thirty-four, ten years younger than he. Her spirit was more resilient than his. Furthermore, she was not burdened with the guilt that he bore like a leaden yoke. He knew that

Nikki had asked for him repeatedly during the last weeks of life and especially during the final few hours. Although aware that he was being foolish and irrational, Gorov felt as if he had deserted the boy, as if he had failed his only son. In spite of uncharacteristic long, thoughtful silences and a new solemnity in her eyes, Anya gradually regained a healthy glow and at least a measure of her former spirit. But Nikita only feigned recovery.

By the first week of September, Anya was back at her job full time. She was a research botanist at a large field laboratory in the deep pine forests twenty miles outside Moscow. Her work soon became one more avenue to forgetfulness; she traveled farther along it every day, arriving early and staying late at the laboratory.

Although they continued to spend the nights and weekends together, Gorov was alone too much now. The apartment was full of memories that had grown painful, as was the dacha they leased in the country. He went for long walks, and almost every time, he ended up at the zoo or the museum, or at some other landmark where he and Nikki had often gone together.

He dreamed ceaselessly of his son and usually woke in the middle of the night with a sick, hollow feeling. In the dreams, Nikki was forever asking why his father had abandoned him.

On the eighth of October, Gorov went to his superiors at the Naval Ministry and requested reassignment to the *Ilya Pogodin*. The boat was in the yards at Kaliningrad for scheduled maintenance and to take on some new state-of-the-art electronic-monitoring gear. He returned to duty, supervised the installation of the surveillance equipment, and took the submarine on a twoweek shakedown cruise in the Baltic during the middle of December.

He was in Moscow with Anya on New Year's Day, but they did not go out into the city. In Russia this was a holiday for the children. Young boys and girls were everywhere: at the lively puppet shows, the ballet, the movies, at the street shows and in the parks. Even the Kremlin grounds were thrown open to them. And at every corner those small ones would be chattering happily about the presents and the gingerbread men that Ded Moroz—Grandfather Frost—had given to them. Although Nikita and Anya were together, each supporting the other, that was one sight they chose not to face. They spent the entire day in their three-room apartment. They made love twice. Anya cooked *chebureki*, Armenian meat pies fried in deep fat, and they washed the food down with a great deal of sweet Algeshat.

He slept on the night train to Kaliningrad. The rocking motion and the rhythmic clatter of the wheels on the rails did not bring him the pure, dreamless sleep that he had expected. He woke twice with his son's name on his lips, his hands fisted, and a chill of sweat on his face.

Nothing is more terrible for a parent to endure than to outlive his child. The natural order seems demolished.

On the second of January, he took the *Ilya Pogodin* to sea on a hundred-day espionage mission. He looked forward to the fourteen weeks beneath the North Atlantic, because that seemed like a good time and place to shrive himself of his remaining grief and of his unshakable guilt.

But at night Nikki continued to visit him, came down through the fathoms, through the dark sea and into the deeper darkness of Gorov's troubled mind, asking the familiar and unanswerable questions: *Why did you abandon me, Father? Why didn't you come to me when I needed you, when I was afraid and calling for you? Didn't you care, Father, didn't you care about me? Why didn't you help me? Why didn't you save me, Father? Why? Why?*

· · ·

Someone rapped discreetly on the cabin door. Like a faint note reverberating in the bronze hollow of a bell, the knock echoed softly in the small room.

Gorov returned from the past and looked up from the silver-framed photograph. "Yes?"

"Timoshenko, sir."

The captain put down the picture and turned away from the desk. "Come in, Lieutenant."

The door opened, and Timoshenko peered in at

him. "We've been intercepting a series of messages you ought to read."

"About what?"

"That United Nations study group. They call their base Edgeway Station. Remember it?"

"Of course."

"Well, they're in trouble."

2:46

Harry Carpenter fixed the steel chain to a carabiner and the carabiner to the frame-mounted tow ring on the back of the snowmobile. "Now we just need a little luck."

"It'll hold," Claude said, patting the chain. He was kneeling on the ice beside Harry with his back to the wind.

"I'm not worried about it breaking," Harry said, getting wearily to his feet and stretching.

The chain looked delicate, almost as if it had been fashioned by a jeweler. But it was four-thousand-pound test, after all. It should be more than strong enough for the task at hand.

The snowmobile was parked virtually on top of the reopened blasting shaft. Inside, behind the slightly misted Plexiglas, Roger Breskin was at the controls, watching the rearview mirror for the go-ahead sign from Harry.

Once he had pulled his snow mask over his

mouth and nose, Harry signaled Breskin to begin. Then he turned into the wind and stared at the small, perfectly round hole in the ice.

Pete Johnson knelt to one side of the shaft, waiting for the snowmobile to get out of his way so he could monitor the progress of the bomb when it began to move. Brian, Fischer, and Lin had returned to the other snowmobiles to get warm.

After he revved the engine several times, Roger slipped the sled into gear. The machine moved less than a yard before the chain held it. The engine noise changed pitch, and gradually its shriek became louder than the wailing wind.

The chain was stretched so tight that Harry imagined it might produce, if plucked, a high note worthy of any operatic soprano.

But the bomb did not move. Not an inch.

The chain appeared to vibrate. Breskin accelerated.

Despite what he had said to Claude, Harry began to think that the chain would snap.

The sled was at peak power, screaming.

With a crack like a rifle shot, the links of the chain broke out of the side of the new shaft in which they had been frozen, and the cylinder tore free of its icy bed. The snowmobile surged forward, the chain remained taut, and in the shaft, the bomb scraped and clattered upward.

Pete Johnson got to his feet and straddled the

hole as Harry and Jobert joined him. Directing a flashlight into the narrow black well, he peered down for a moment and then signaled Breskin to stop. Grasping the chain with both hands, he hoisted the tubular pack of explosives halfway out of the shaft and, with Harry's help, extracted it completely. They laid it on the ice.

One down. Nine to go.

2:58

Gunvald Larsson was adding canned milk to his mug of coffee when the call came through from the United States military base at Thule, Greenland. He put down the milk and hurried to the shortwave set.

"This is Larsson at Edgeway. Reading you clearly. Go ahead, please."

The communications officer at Thule had a strong, mellifluous voice that seemed impervious to static. "Have you heard anything more from your lost sheep?"

"No. They're busy. Mrs. Carpenter has left the radio in the ice cave while she salvages whatever she can from the ruins of their temporary camp. I don't expect her to call unless there's a drastic change in their situation."

"How's the weather at Edgeway?"

"Terrible."

"Here too. And going to get a lot worse before

it gets better. Wind speeds and wave heights are setting storm records on the North Atlantic."

Gunvald frowned at the radio. "Are you trying to tell me the UNGY trawlers are turning back?"

"One has."

"But they headed north only two hours ago!"

"The *Melville* is ten or twelve years older than the *Liberty*. She could probably ride out a storm like this easily enough, but she doesn't have the power or bow construction to plow into it head-on, under power and against the wind. Her captain's afraid she'll break apart if he doesn't turn back now."

"But he's still on the fringe of the storm."

"Even there the seas are bad."

Gunvald wiped one hand across his suddenly damp face and blotted his palm on his pants. "The *Liberty* is continuing?"

"Yes." The American paused. The radio hissed with static, as if it were filled with snakes. "Look, if I were you, I wouldn't pin my hopes on her."

"I've nothing else to pin them on."

"Maybe not. But her skipper really isn't much more confident than the captain of the *Melville*."

"I suppose you still can't get a chopper in the air," Gunvald said.

"Everything's grounded. Will be for days. We're not happy about it, but there's nothing we can do."

Static crackled from the speaker.

Gunvald said nothing.

Finally, sounding embarrassed, the officer at Thule said, "The *Liberty* might just make it, you know."

Gunvald sighed. "I'm not going to tell the others about the *Melville*. Not yet."

"That's up to you."

"If the *Liberty* turns back too, then I'll have to tell them. But there's no sense depressing them with this news while there's still some hope."

The man at Thule said, "We're pulling for them. The story already hit the news in the States. Millions of people are pulling for them."

3:05

The communications center of the *Ilya Pogodin* was full of light and motion as seven radiant video display terminals flickered with decoded messages that had been intercepted by the main surveillance aerial one hundred feet above. The programming consoles were aglow with all the primary colors. Two technicians worked at one end of the cramped chamber, and Timoshenko stood near the entrance with Nikita Gorov.

Among the hundreds of communications being continuously sorted and stored by the *Ilya Pogodin*'s computers, a steady stream of data pertained to the Edgeway crisis. The computer had been instructed to create a special file for any intercepted messages that contained one or more of five key words: Carpenter, Larsson, Edgeway, *Melville*, *Liberty*.

"Is this complete?" Gorov asked when he finished reading the Edgeway material.

Timoshenko nodded. "The computer produces an updated printout every fifteen minutes. This one is only ten minutes old. There may have been a few minor developments. But you have the basics, sir."

"If the weather on the surface is half as bad as they're saying, the *Liberty* will turn back too."

Timoshenko agreed.

Gorov stared at the printout, no longer reading it, not even seeing it. Behind his night-black eyes was the image of a fresh-faced, golden-haired little boy with arms open wide. The son he had been unable to save.

At last he said, "I'll be in the control room until further notice. Let me know at once if there's any important news about this."

"Yes, sir."

Because the *Pogodin* was not actually under way but was hanging motionless in the sea, the control-room watch consisted of only five men in addition to First Officer Zhukov. Three were sitting in the black command chairs, facing the wall of scopes, gauges, graphs, dials, and controls opposite the diving stations. Zhukov was perched on a metal stool in the center of the chamber, reading a novel that he had propped on the big electronic chart table.

Emil Zhukov was the sole potential opposition with which Gorov would have to contend if he were to carry out the plan that he had begun to formulate. Zhukov was the only man aboard the submarine with the authority to relieve the captain of his command if, in Zhukov's opinion, Gorov had lost his senses or had disobeyed a direct order of the Naval Ministry. The first officer would use his power only in an extreme emergency, for he would have to justify his assumption of command when he got back to Russia; nevertheless, he posed a real threat.

Emil Zhukov, at forty-two, was not a great deal younger than his captain, but their relationship had a subtle child-and-mentor quality, primarily because Zhukov placed such a high value on social order and discipline that his respect for authority bordered on an unhealthy reverence. He would have regarded *any* captain as a mentor and a source of wisdom. Tall, lean, with a long narrow face, intense hazel eyes, and thick dark hair, the first officer reminded Gorov of a wolf; he had a lupine grace when he moved, and his direct stare sometimes seemed predatory. In fact, he was neither as impressive nor as dangerous as he appeared to be; he was merely a good man and a reliable though not brilliant officer. Ordinarily, his deference to his captain would ensure his faithful cooperation—but under extreme circumstances, his obedience could not be taken for granted. Emil Zhukov would never lose sight of the fact that there were many men of higher authority than Gorov—and that he owed them greater respect and allegiance than he owed his captain.

At the chart table, Gorov put the printout of Edgeway material on top of the novel that Zhukov was reading. "You better take a look at this."

When he reached the last page of the document, the first officer said, "Quite a trap they've gotten themselves into. But I read a little about this Edgeway Project in the papers, way back when they were still in the planning stages, and these Carpenters sounded like extremely clever people. They might scrape through this."

"It isn't the Carpenters who caught my eye. Another name."

Quickly scanning the printout, Zhukov said, "You must mean Dougherty. Brian Dougherty."

Gorov sat on the only other stool at the Plexiglas-topped, lighted chart table. "Yes. Dougherty."

"Is he related to the assassinated American President?"

"Nephew."

"I much admired his uncle," said Zhukov. "But I suppose you think I'm naïve in that regard."

Gorov's disdain for politics and politicians was well known to his first officer, who quietly disapproved of his attitude. The captain could not convincingly pretend to have had a change of heart just to win Zhukov's backing for the risky operation that he wanted to conduct. Shrugging, he said, "Politics is strictly about power. I admire achievement."

"He was a man of peace," Zhukov said.

"Yes, peace is something they all sell."

Zhukov frowned. "You think he wasn't a great man?"

"A scientist who discovers a cure for disease—that's a great man or woman. But politicians . . ."

Zhukov was not one of those who longed for a return of the old regime, but he had little patience for the series of unstable governments that had afflicted Russia in recent years. He admired strong leaders. He was a man who needed to have someone to whom he could look for direction and purpose—and good politicians were his ultimate heroes, regardless of their nationality.

Gorov said, "No matter what I think of the late President, I'll admit the Dougherty family handled their tragedy with grace and fortitude. Very dignified."

Zhukov nodded solemnly. "An admirable family. Very sad."

Gorov felt as if his first officer were a sophisticated musical instrument. He had just finished tuning Zhukov. Now he was about to attempt a complicated melody with him. "The boy's father is a Senator, isn't he?"

"Yes, and highly regarded," Zhukov said.

"He was also shot, wasn't he?"

"Another assassination attempt."

"After all the American system has done to that family, why do you suppose the Doughertys remain such ardent supporters of it?"

"They're great patriots," Zhukov said.

Pulling thoughtfully at his well-trimmed beard, Gorov said, "How difficult it must be for a family to remain patriotic to a nation that kills its best sons."

"Oh, but it wasn't the country that killed them, sir. Blame a handful of reactionaries. Perhaps even the CIA. But not the American people."

Gorov pretended to think about it for a minute. Then he said, "I suppose you're right. From what I read, Americans seem to have considerable respect and sympathy for the Doughertys."

"Of course. Patriotism in adversity is the only kind that earns respect. It's easy to be patriotic in times of plenty, when no one is asked to make a sacrifice."

The melody that Gorov had hoped to play with his first officer was progressing without a sour note, and the captain almost smiled. Instead, he stared at the Edgeway printout for a long beat, and then he said, "What an opportunity for Russia."

As the captain had expected, Zhukov did not immediately follow the change of thought. "Opportunity?"

"For goodwill."

"Oh?"

"And in a time when Mother Russia desperately needs goodwill more than at any other moment in her history. Goodwill leads to lots of foreign aid, preferential trade treatment, even military cooperation and concessions of strategic importance."

"I don't see the opportunity."

"We're only five hours from their position."

Zhukov raised one eyebrow. "You've plotted it?"

"I'm estimating. But it's a good estimate. And if we were to go to the aid of those miserable people stranded on the iceberg, we'd be heroes. Worldwide heroes. You see? And Russia would be heroic by association."

Blinking in surprise, Zhukov said, "Rescue them?"

"After all, we'd be saving the lives of eight valued scientists from half a dozen countries, including the nephew of the assassinated President. Such an opportunity for propaganda and goodwill comes no more than once a decade."

"But we'd need permission from Moscow."

"Of course."

"To get the quick answer you need, you'll have to send your request by satellite relay. And to use that equipment, we'll have to surface."

"I'm aware of that."

The laser transmission funnel and the collapsible reception dish were mounted atop the submarine's sail, that large finlike projection on the main deck, which also supported the small bridge, radio and radar masts, periscopes, and snorkel. They had to surface before the tracking gear could fix on a series of Russian telecommunications satellites and before the laser could operate properly. But if this breach of secrecy was a disadvantage to a ship like the *Pogodin*, the incredible speed of laser transmission outweighed the negatives. From practically anywhere in the world, one could send a message to Moscow and immediately receive an acknowledgment of its receipt.

Emil Zhukov's long, saturnine face was suddenly lined with anxiety, because he realized that he was going to have to choose to disobey one authority or another—either the captain himself or the captain's superiors in Moscow. "We're on an espionage run, sir. If we surfaced, we'd compromise the entire mission."

With one finger, Gorov traced a painted latitude line on the lighted surface of the electronic chart table. "This far north, in the middle of a raging winter storm, who's to see us? We should be able to go up, send, and receive in total anonymity."

"Yes, all right, but we're under orders to maintain strict radio silence."

Gorov nodded solemnly, as if to say that he had thought about that issue and was conscious of his awesome responsibility. "When my son was dying, Moscow broke our radio silence."

"That was a matter of life and death."

"People are dying here too. Certainly we're

under orders to maintain radio silence. I know how serious a matter it is to set aside such orders. On the other hand, in an emergency, a captain is permitted to disobey the Ministry at his discretion."

Frowning, the lines in his long face cutting so deeply that they began to look like wounds, Zhukov said, "I'm not so sure you could call this an emergency. Not the type of emergency they had in mind when they wrote the rules."

"Well, that's what I'm calling it," Gorov said, issuing a quiet but not particularly subtle challenge.

"You'll have to answer to the Naval Board of Inquiry when it's all over," Zhukov said. "And this is an intelligence mission, so the intelligence services will have some questions."

"Of course."

"And half of them are staffed by former KGB men."

"Perhaps."

"Definitely."

"I'm prepared," Gorov said.

"For an inquiry. But for what the intelligence services might do with you?"

"For both."

"You know what they're like."

"I can be tough. Mother Russia and the navy have taught me endurance." Gorov knew they were approaching the last sixteen bars of the tune. The crescendo was near.

"My head will be on the block too," Zhukov

said morosely as he slid the printout across the table to Gorov.

"No one's head will be on the block."

The first officer was not convinced. If anything, his frown deepened.

"They aren't all fools at the Ministry," Gorov said.

Zhukov shrugged.

"When they weigh the alternatives," Gorov said confidently, "they'll give the permission I want. I'm absolutely positive of it. Clearly, Russia has more to gain by sending us on this rescue mission than she does by insisting upon the continuation of what is, after all, nothing more than another routine surveillance run."

Emil Zhukov still had his doubts.

Getting up from the stool, rolling the printout into a tight tube, Gorov said, "Lieutenant, I want the crew at battle stations in five minutes."

"Is that necessary?"

Except for complicated or dangerous maneuvers, the regular watch could surface or dive the submarine.

"If we're going to break a Ministry rule at our own discretion, we can at least take all precautions," Gorov said.

For a long moment they stared at each other, each trying to read the other's mind, trying to see the future. The first officer's gaze was more penetrating than ever.

Finally Zhukov stood up without breaking eye contact.

He's made his decision, Gorov thought. I hope it's one I can live with.

Zhukov hesitated . . . then saluted. "Yes, sir. It will be done in five minutes."

"We'll surface as soon as the multicommunications aerial has been wound down and secured."

"Yes, sir."

Gorov felt as if hundreds of painful knots were coming untied inside him. He had won. "Go to it, then."

Zhukov left the control room.

Walking to the circular, railed command pad at the end of the control room, Gorov thought about little Nikki and knew that he was doing the right thing. In the name of his dead son, in honor of his lost boy, not for the advantage of Russia, he would save the lives of those stranded people. They must not die on the ice. This time he had the power to thwart death, and he was determined not to fail.

3:46

As soon as the second package of explosives had been hauled out of the ice, Roger, Brian, Claude, Lin, and Fischer moved on to the site of the third sealed shaft.

Harry remained behind with Pete Johnson, who

had yet to disarm the second device. They stood together, their backs to the shrieking wind. The demolitions cylinder lay at their feet, an evil-looking package: sixty inches long and two and a half inches in diameter, black with yellow letters that spelled DANGER. It was encased in a thin, transparent coat of ice.

"You don't have to keep me company," Pete said as he carefully cleaned the snow from his goggles. His vision must be unobstructed when he set to work on the trigger mechanism.

"I thought your people were afraid of being alone in the dark," Harry said.

"My people? You better mean electronic engineers, honky."

Harry smiled. "What else would I mean?"

A strong gust of wind caught them from behind, an avalanche of air that would have knocked them flat if they had not been prepared for it. For a minute they bent with the gale, unable to talk, concerned only about keeping their balance.

When the gust passed and the wind settled down to perhaps forty miles per hour, Pete finished cleaning his goggles and began to rub his hands together to get the snow and ice off his gloves. "I know why you didn't go with the others. You can't deceive me. It's your hero complex."

"Sure. I'm a regular Indiana Jones."

"You've always got to be where the danger is."

"Yeah, me and Madonna." Harry shook his head

sadly. "I'm sorry, but you've got it all wrong, Dr. Freud. I'd much prefer to be where the danger isn't. But it did occur to me the bomb might explode in your face."

"And you'd give me first aid?"

"Something like that."

"Listen, if it does explode in my face but doesn't kill me . . . no first aid, for God's sake. Just finish me off."

Harry winced and started to protest.

"All I'm asking for is mercy," Pete said bluntly.

During the past few months, Harry had come to like and respect this big, broad-faced man. Beneath Pete Johnson's fierce-looking exterior, under the layers of education and training, under the cool competence, there was a kid with a love for science and technology and adventure. Harry recognized much of himself in Pete. "There's really not a great chance of an explosion, is there?"

"Almost none," Pete assured him.

"The casing *did* take a beating coming out of the shaft."

"Relax, Harry. The last one went well, didn't it?"

They knelt beside the steel cylinder. Harry held the flashlight while Pete opened a small plastic box of precision tools.

"Disarming these sonsofbitches is easy enough," Pete said. "That isn't our problem. Our problem is getting eight more of them out of the ice before the clock strikes midnight and the carriage turns back into a pumpkin."

"We're recovering them at the rate of one an hour."

"But we'll slow down," Johnson said. With a small screwdriver he began to remove the end of the cylinder that featured the eye loop. "We needed forty-five minutes to dig out the first one. Then fifty-five for the second. Already we're getting tired, slowing down. It's this wind."

It was a killing wind, pressing and pounding against Harry's back with such force that he felt as though he were standing in the middle of a swollen, turbulent river; the currents in the air were almost as tangible as currents in deep water. The base wind velocity was now forty or forty-five miles an hour, with gusts to sixty-five, steadily and rapidly climbing toward gale force. Later, it would be deadly.

"You're right," Harry said. His throat was slightly sore from the effort required to be heard above the storm, even though they were nearly head-to-head over the package of explosives. "It doesn't do much good to sit ten minutes in a warm snowmobile cabin and then spend the next hour in weather as bad as this."

Pete extracted the last screw and removed a six-inch end piece from the cylinder. "How far has the real temperature fallen? Like to guess?"

"Five degrees above zero. Fahrenheit."

"With the wind-chill factor?"

"Twenty below zero."

"Thirty."

"Maybe." Even his heavy thermal suit could not protect him. The wind's cold blade stabbed continuously at his back, pierced his storm suit, pricked his spine. "I never thought we had much of a chance of getting ten out. I knew we'd slow down. But if we can disarm just five or six, we might have enough room to survive the blowup at midnight."

Pete tipped the six-inch section of casing, and a timer slid out into his gloved hand. It was connected to the rest of the cylinder by four springy coils of wire: red, yellow, green, and white. "I guess it's better to freeze to death tomorrow than be blown to bits tonight."

"Don't you dare do that to me," Harry said.

"What?"

"Turn into another Franz Fischer."

Pete laughed. "Or another George Lin."

"Those two. The Whiner brothers."

"You chose them," Pete said.

"And I take the blame. But, hell, they're good men. It's just that under this much pressure . . ."

"They're assholes."

"Precisely."

"Time for you to get out of here," Pete said, reaching into the tool kit again.

"I'll hold the flashlight."

"The hell you will. Put it down so it shines on this, then go. I don't *need* you to hold the light. What I need you for is to deal out the mercy if it comes to that."

Reluctantly, Harry returned to the snowmobile. He bent down behind the machine, out of the wind. Huddled there, he sensed that all their work and risk-taking was for nothing. Their situation would deteriorate further before it improved. If it ever improved.

4:00

The *Ilya Pogodin* rolled sickeningly on the surface of the North Atlantic. The turbulent sea smashed against the rounded bows and geysered into the darkness, an endless series of waves that sounded like window-rattling peals of summer thunder. Because the boat rode so low in the water, it shuddered only slightly from the impact, but it could not withstand that punishment indefinitely. Gray water churned across the main deck, and foam as thick as pudding sloshed around the base of the huge steel sail. The boat hadn't been designed or built for extended surface runs in stormy weather. Nevertheless, in spite of her tendency to yaw, she could hold her own long enough for Timoshenko to exchange messages with the war room at the Naval Ministry in Moscow.

Captain Gorov was on the bridge with two other men. They were all wearing fleece-lined pea jackets, hooded black rain slickers over the jackets, and gloves. The two young lookouts stood back to back, one facing port and the other starboard. All three men had field glasses and were surveying the horizon.

It's a damned close horizon, Gorov thought as he studied it. And an ugly one.

That far north, the polar twilight had not yet faded entirely from the sky. An eerie greenish glow seeped through the heavy storm clouds and saturated the Atlantic vistas, so Gorov seemed to be peering through a thin film of green liquid. It barely illuminated the raging sea and imparted a soft yellow cast to the foamy crests of the waves. A mixture of fine snow and sleet hissed in from the northwest; the sail, the bridge railing, Gorov's black rain slicker, the laser package, and the radio masts were encrusted with white ice. Scattered formations of fog further obscured the forbidding panorama, and due north the churning waves were hidden by a gray-brown mist so dense that it seemed to be a curtain drawn across the world beyond it. Visibility varied from one half to three quarters of a mile and would have been considerably worse if they had not been using night-service binoculars.

Behind Gorov, atop the steel sail, the satellite tracking dish moved slowly from east to west. Its continuous change of attitude was imperceptible at a glance, but it was locked on to a Soviet telecommunications satellite that was in a tight subpolar orbit high above the masses of slate-colored clouds. Gorov's message had been transmitted by laser four minutes ago. The tracking dish waited to receive Moscow's reply.

The captain had already imagined the worst possible response. He would be ordered to relinquish command to First Officer Zhukov, who would be directed to put him under twenty-four-hour armed guard and continue the mission as scheduled. His court-martial would proceed in his absence, and he would be informed of the decision upon his return to Moscow.

But he expected a more reasoned response than that from Moscow. Certainly the Ministry was always unpredictable. Even under the postcommunist regime, with its greater respect for justice, officers were occasionally court-martialed without being present to defend themselves. But he believed what he had told Zhukov in the control room: They were not *all* fools at the Ministry. They would most likely see the opportunity for propaganda and strategic advantage in this situation, and they would reach the proper conclusion.

He scanned the fog-shrouded horizon.

The flow of time seemed to have slowed almost to a stop. Although he knew that it was an illusion, he saw the sea raging in slow motion, the waves building like ripples in an ocean of cold molasses. Each minute was an hour.

Bang!

Sparks shot out of the vents in the steel-alloy casing of the auxiliary drill. It chugged, sputtered, and cut out.

Roger Breskin had been operating it. "What the hell?" he thumbed the power switch.

When the drill wouldn't start, Pete Johnson stepped in and dropped to his knees to have a look at it.

Everyone crowded around, expecting the worst. They were, Harry thought, like people gathered at an automobile accident—except that the corpses in this wreckage might be their own.

"What's wrong with it?" George Lin asked.

"You'll have to take apart the casing to find the trouble," Fischer told Pete.

"Yeah, but I don't have to take the sucker apart to know I can't repair it."

Brian said, "What do you mean?"

Pointing to the snow and frozen slush around the partially reopened third shaft, Pete said, "See those black specks?"

Harry crouched and studied the bits of metal scattered on the ice. "Gear teeth."

Everyone was silent.

"I could probably repair a fault in the wiring,"

Pete said at last. "But we don't have a set of spare gears for it."

"What now?" Brian asked.

With Teutonic pessimism, Fischer said, "Back to the cave and wait for midnight."

"That's giving up," Brian said.

Getting to his feet, Harry said, "But I'm afraid that's all we can do at the moment, Brian. We lost the other drill when my sled went into that crevasse."

Dougherty shook his head, refusing to accept that they were powerless to proceed. "Earlier, Claude said we could use the ice ax and the power saw to cut some steps in the winter field, angle down to each package—"

The Frenchman interrupted him. "That would only work if we had a week. We'd need six more hours, perhaps longer, to retrieve this one bomb by the step method. It's not worth expending all that energy to gain only forty-five more feet of safety."

"Okay, let's go, let's pack up," Harry said, clapping his hands for emphasis. "No point standing here, losing body heat. We can talk about it back at the cave, out of this wind. We might think of something yet."

But he had no hope.

At 4:02 the communications center reported that a message was coming in from the Naval Ministry.

Five minutes later the decoding sheet was passed up to the bridge, where Nikita Gorov began to read it with some trepidation.

MESSAGE
NAVAL MINISTRY
TIME: 1900 MOSCOW
FROM: DUTY OFFICER
TO: CAPTAIN N. GOROV
SUBJECT: YOUR LAST TRANSMISSION #34-D
MESSAGE BEGINS:
YOUR REQUEST UNDER STUDY BY ADMIRALTY STOP
IMMEDIATE DECISION CANNOT BE MADE STOP SUBMERGE
AND CONTINUE SCHEDULED MISSION FOR ONE HOUR
STOP A CONTINUATION OR NEW ORDERS WILL BE
TRANSMITTED TO YOU AT 1700 HOURS YOUR TIME STOP

Gorov was disappointed. The Ministry's indecision cranked up the level of his tension. The next hour would be more difficult for him than the hour that had just passed.

He turned to the other two men. "Clear the bridge."

They prepared to dive. The lookouts scrambled down through the conning tower and took up stations at the diving wheels. The captain sounded the routine alarm—two short blasts on the electric horns that blared from speakers in the bulkheads of every room on the boat—and then left the bridge, pulling the hatch shut with a lanyard.

The quartermaster of the watch spun the hand-wheel and said, "Hatch secure."

Gorov hurried to the command pad in the control room. On the second blast of the diving klaxon, the air vents in the ballast tanks had been opened, and the sea had roared into the space between the ship's two hulls. Now, to Gorov's right, a petty officer was watching a board that contained one red and several green lights. The green represented hatches, vents, exhausts, and equipment extruders that were closed to the sea. The red light was labeled LASER TRANSMISSION PACKAGE. When the laser equipment settled into a niche atop the sail and an airtight hatch slid over it, the red light blinked off and the safety bulb beneath it lit up.

"Green board!" the petty officer called.

Gorov ordered compressed air released into the submarine, and when the pressure indicator didn't register a fall, he knew the boat was sealed.

"Pressure in the boat," the diving officer called.

In less than a minute they had completed the preparations. The deck acquired an incline, the top of the sail submerged, and they were out of sight of anyone in a ship or aircraft.

"Take her down to one hundred feet," Gorov ordered.

The descent was measured by signifying beeps from the computer.

"At one hundred feet," the diving officer announced.

"Hold her steady."

"Steady, sir."

As the submarine leveled off, Gorov said, "Take over for me, Lieutenant Zhukov."

"Yes, sir."

"You can return the control room to a skeleton watch."

"Yes, sir."

Gorov left the chamber and walked aft to the communications center.

Timoshenko turned toward the door just as the captain entered the room. "Request permission to run up the antenna, sir."

"Denied."

Blinking in surprise, Timoshenko tilted his head to one side and said, "Sir?"

"Denied," Gorov repeated. He surveyed the tele-communications equipment that lined the bulk-heads. He had been given rudimentary training in its use. For security reasons, the telecommunications computer was separate from the ship's main computer, although the keyboards were operated in the same manner as those in the control room with which he was so familiar. "I want to use your coder and the communications computer."

Timoshenko didn't move. He was an excellent technician and a bright young man in some ways. But his world was composed of data banks, programming keys, input, output, and gadgets— and he was not able to deal well with people unless they behaved in a predictable, machinelike manner.

"Did you hear me?" Gorov asked impatiently.

Blushing, embarrassed, and confused, Timoshenko said, "Uh . . . yes. Yes, sir." He directed Gorov to a chair before the primary terminal of the communications computer. "What did you have in mind, sir?"

"Privacy," Gorov said bluntly as he sat down.

Timoshenko just stood there.

"You're dismissed, Lieutenant."

His confusion deepening, Timoshenko nodded, tried to smile, but instead looked as if he had just been jabbed with a long needle. He retired to the other end of the room, where his curious subordinates were unsuccessfully pretending that they had heard nothing.

The coder—or encrypting machine—stood beside Gorov's chair. It was the size and shape of a two-drawer filing cabinet, housed in burnished steel. A keyboard—with all the usual keys plus fourteen with special functions—was built into the top. Gorov touched the ON switch. Crisp yellow paper automatically rolled out of the top of the coder cabinet and onto the platen.

Gorov quickly typed a message. When he was finished, he read it without touching the flimsy paper, then pressed a rectangular red key labeled PROCESS. A laser printer hummed, and the coder produced the encrypted version under the original message. It appeared to be nonsense: clumps of random numbers separated by occasional symbols.

Tearing the paper from the encrypting machine, Gorov swung around in his chair to face the video display terminal. Referring to the encoded version of the message, he carefully typed the same series of numbers and symbols into the communications computer. When that was done, he pressed a special-function key that bore the word DECODE and another labeled PRINTOUT. He did not touch the READOUT tab, because he didn't want his work displayed on the large overhead screen for the benefit of Timoshenko and the other technicians. After dropping the flimsy yellow sheet from the encrypting machine into a paper shredder, he leaned back in his chair.

No more than a minute passed before the communiqué—now decoded and in its original state—was in his hands. He had come full circle in less than five minutes: The printout contained the same fourteen lines that he had composed on the coder, but it was now in the usual type style of the computer. It looked like any other decoded message received from the Ministry in Moscow, which was precisely what he wanted.

He instructed the computer to erase from its memory banks every detail of what he had just done. With that, the printout was the only evidence that remained of the exercise. Timoshenko would not be able to quiz the computer about any of this after Gorov left the cabin.

He got up and went to the open door. From there he said, "Oh, Lieutenant?"

Timoshenko was pretending to study a logbook. He glanced up. "Yes, sir?"

"In those dispatches you intercepted, the ones having to do with the Edgeway group, there was mention of a transmitter on that drift ice with them."

Timoshenko nodded. "They've got a standard shortwave set, of course. But that isn't what you're talking about. There's also a radio transmitter, a tracking beacon, that puts out a two-second signal ten times every minute."

"Have you picked it up?"

"Twenty minutes ago."

"Is it a strong signal?"

"Oh, yes."

"Have you got a bearing?"

"Yes, sir."

"Well, run another check on it. I'll be back to you on the intercom in a few minutes," Gorov said. He returned to the control room for another conversation with Emil Zhukov.

Harry had not yet finished telling Rita how the auxiliary drill had broken down, when she interrupted him. "Hey, where's Brian?"

He turned to the men who had entered the ice cave behind him. Brian Dougherty was not among them.

Harry frowned. "Where's Brian? Why isn't he here?"

"He must be around somewhere. I'll take a look outside," Roger Breskin said.

Pete Johnson left with him.

"He probably just went behind one of the hummocks out there," Fischer said, although he surely knew better than that. "Nothing especially dramatic, I'll wager. Probably just had to go to the john."

"No," Harry disagreed.

Rita said, "He would have told someone."

Out on the icecap, far from the security of Edgeway Station or the inflatable igloos of a temporary camp, no one could afford to be modest even about bladder and bowel habits. When going to the john, they all realized that it was necessary to inform at least one other person as to exactly which hill or pressure ridge would serve as a screen for their toilet. Acutely aware of the vagaries of the icefield and the weather, Brian would have let others know where to start looking if he didn't make a timely return.

Roger and Pete reappeared in less than two minutes, pulling up their goggles, tugging down their ice-veined snow masks.

"He's not at the sleds," Roger said. "Or anywhere else we can see." His gray eyes, usually expressionless, were troubled.

"Who rode back here with him?" Harry asked.

They looked at one another.

"Claude?"

The Frenchman shook his head. "Not me. I thought he rode with Franz."

"I rode with Franz," George Lin said.

Rita was exasperated. Tucking an errant strand of reddish hair back under her hood, she said, "For God's sake, you mean he was left behind in the confusion?"

"No way. He couldn't have been," Harry said.

"Unless that was what he wanted," George Lin suggested.

Harry was perplexed. "Why should he want to be left behind?"

Clearly untouched by their anxiety about Brian, Lin took time to blow his nose, fastidiously fold the handkerchief, and return it to a zippered pocket of his coat before answering the question. "You must have read some of the newspaper stories about him. Spain . . . Africa . . . all over, he's been risking his life for a lark."

"So?"

"Suicidal," Lin said, as though it should have been obvious to them.

Harry was astonished and not a little angry. "You're saying he stayed behind to die?"

Lin shrugged.

Harry didn't even need to think about that. "Good God, George, not Brian. What's the matter with you?"

"He might have been hurt," Pete said. "A fall."

Claude Jobert said, "Fell, hit his head, unable to cry out, and we were so eager to get out of there and back here, we didn't notice."

Harry was skeptical.

"It's possible," Pete insisted.

Dubious, Harry said, "Maybe. All right, we'll go back and look. You and me, Pete. Two snowmobiles."

Roger stepped forward. "I'm going with you."

"Two can handle it," Harry said, quickly fixing his goggles in place.

"I insist," Breskin said. "Look, Brian handled himself damn well out there on the ice today. He didn't hesitate when he had to go over that cliff to get a line around George. I'd have thought about it twice myself. But he didn't. He just went. And if it was me in trouble now, he'd do whatever he could. I know it. So you can count me in on this whether or not you need me."

As far as Harry could remember, that was the longest speech that Roger Breskin had made in months. He was impressed. "Okay, then. You'll come along. You're too damn big to argue with."

The *Ilya Pogodin*'s cook was its greatest treasure. His father had been the head chef at the National Restaurant in Moscow, and from his papa he had learned to perform miracles with food that made the Bible story of loaves and fishes seem like an unremarkable exercise. The fare at his table was the best in the submarine service.

He had already begun to make fish *selianka* for the first course of the evening meal. White fish. Onions. Bay leaves. Egg whites. The aroma drifted from the galley past the communications center, then filled the control room.

When Gorov entered the room, Sergei Belyaev, the diving officer on duty, said, "Captain, will you help me talk sense to Leonid?" He gestured at a young seaman first class who was monitoring the alarm board.

Gorov was in a hurry, but he did not want Belyaev to sense his tension. "What's the trouble?"

Belyaev grimaced. "Leonid's on the first mess shift, and I'm on the fifth."

"Ah."

"I've promised if he'll change shifts with me, I'll fix him up with an absolutely gorgeous blonde in Kaliningrad. This woman is nothing short of spectacular, I swear to you. Breasts like melons. She could arouse a granite statue. But poor, dumb Leonid won't deal with me."

Smiling, Gorov said, "Of course he won't. What woman could be more exciting than the dinner being prepared for us? Besides, who would be simple-minded enough to believe that an absolutely gorgeous blonde with breasts like melons would have anything to do with you, Sergei Belyaev?"

Laughter echoed in the low-ceilinged chamber.

Grinning broadly, Belyaev said, "Perhaps I should offer him a few rubles instead."

"Much more realistic," Gorov said. "Better yet, U.S. dollars if you have any." He walked to the chart table, sat on one of the stools, and put a folded printout in front of Emil Zhukov. It was the message that he had run through the coder and communications computer only a few minutes ago. "Something else for you to read," he said quietly.

Zhukov pushed aside his novel and adjusted his wire-rimmed eyeglasses, which had slid down on his long nose. He unfolded the paper.

MESSAGE
NAVAL MINISTRY
TIME: 1900 MOSCOW
FROM: DUTY OFFICER
TO: CAPTAIN N. GOROV
SUBJECT: YOUR LAST TRANSMISSION #34-D
MESSAGE BEGINS:
YOUR REQUEST UNDER CONSIDERATION BY ADMIRALTY
STOP CONDITIONAL PERMISSION GRANTED STOP MAKE
NECESSARY COURSE CHANGES STOP CONFIRMATION OR
CANCELLATION OF PERMISSION WILL BE TRANSMITTED
TO YOU AT 1700 HOURS YOUR TIME STOP

After he had chewed on his lower lip for a moment, Zhukov turned his intense stare on Gorov and said, "What's this?"

Gorov kept his voice low, but he tried not to seem secretive to any crewmen who might be watching. "What is it? I think you can see what it is, Emil. A forgery."

The first officer didn't know what to say.

Gorov leaned toward him. "It's for your protection."

"My protection?"

Gorov plucked the printout from his first officer's hands and carefully refolded it. He put it in his shirt pocket. "We're going to plot a course and set out at once for that iceberg." He tapped the chart table between them. "We're going to rescue those Edgeway scientists and Brian Dougherty."

"You don't actually have Ministry permission. A forgery won't stand up to—"

"Does one need permission to save lives?"

"Please, sir. You know what I mean."

"Once we're under way, I'll give you the forged communiqué that you just read. It will be yours to keep, your protection if there's ever an inquiry."

"But I saw the real message."

"Deny it."

"That might not be easy."

Gorov said, "I am the only one aboard this ship who knows that you saw it. I will tell any court-martial magistrate that I showed you the forgery and nothing else."

"If I'm ever interrogated, there's a chance drugs

would be used. Besides, I just don't like going against orders when—"

"One way or another, you'll be going against orders. Mine or theirs. Now, listen to me, Emil. This is right. This is the thing we should do. And I will protect you. You do feel I'm a man of my word, I hope?"

"I have no doubt," Zhukov said immediately and finally broke eye contact, as though embarrassed by the thought that he should ever doubt his captain in any way.

"Then? Emil?" When the first officer remained silent, Gorov said quietly but forcefully, "Time is wasting, Lieutenant. If we're going after them, then for God's sake let's not wait until they're dead."

Zhukov took off his glasses. He closed his eyes and pressed his fingertips to them. "I've served with you how long?"

"Seven years."

"There have been tense moments," Zhukov said.

Like this one, Gorov thought.

Zhukov lowered his hands from his face but didn't open his eyes. "That time the Norwegian corvette dropped depth charges on us when it caught us in Oslo Fjord."

"Tense indeed."

"Or that cat-and-mouse game with the American submarine off the coast of Massachusetts."

"We made fools of them, didn't we?" Gorov said. "We've been a good team."

184 · *Dean Koontz*

"Never once have I seen you panic or issue orders that I thought were inappropriate."

"Thank you, Emil."

"Until now."

"Not now either."

Zhukov opened his eyes. "With all due respect, this isn't like you, sir. It's reckless."

"I disagree. It's not reckless. Not at all. As I told you earlier, I'm quite certain the Admiralty will approve of the rescue mission."

"Then why not wait for the transmission at 1700 hours?"

"We can't waste time. The bureaucratic pace of the Ministry just isn't good enough in this case. We've got to reach that iceberg before too many more hours have passed. Once we've located it, we'll need a lot of time just to get those people off the ice and aboard with us."

Zhukov consulted his watch. "It's twenty minutes past four. We've only got to wait another forty minutes to hear the Admiralty's decision."

"But on a rescue mission like this, forty minutes could be the difference between success and failure."

"You're adamant?"

"Yes."

Zhukov sighed.

"You could relieve me of my command," Gorov said. "Right now. You have reason. I wouldn't hold it against you, Emil."

Staring at his hands, which were trembling slightly, Zhukov said, "If they deny you the permission you want, will you turn back and continue the surveillance run?"

"I would have no choice."

"You would turn back?"

"Yes."

"You wouldn't disobey them?"

"No."

"Your word?"

"My word."

Zhukov thought about it.

Gorov rose from the stool. "Well?"

"I must be crazy."

"You'll agree to this?"

"As you know, I named my second son after you. Nikita Zhukov."

The captain nodded. "I was honored."

"Well, if I've been wrong about you, if I shouldn't have named him Nikita, I won't be able to forget it now. He'll be around as a reminder of how wrong I was. I don't need that thorn in my side. So I'll have to give you one more chance to prove I've been right all along."

Smiling, Gorov said, "Let's get a new bearing on that iceberg and plot a course, Lieutenant."

After returning to the third blasting shaft, Pete and Roger left the two snowmobiles in park, with engines running and headlights blazing. Exhaust fumes plumed in brilliant crystalline columns. They set out in different directions, and Harry set out in a third to search for Brian Dougherty in the drifts, waist-high pressure ridges, and low ice hummocks around the site.

Cautious, aware that he could be swallowed by the storm as quickly and completely as Brian had been, Harry probed the black-and-white landscape before he committed himself to it. He used his flashlight as if it were a machete, sweeping it from side to side. The insubstantial yellowish beam slashed through the falling snow, but the white jungle was undisturbed by it. Every ten steps, he looked over his shoulder to see if he was straying too far from the snowmobiles. He was already well out of the section of the icefield that was illuminated by the headlights, but he knew that he must not lose sight of the sleds altogether. If he got lost, no one would hear his cries for help above the screeching, hooting wind. Although it was diffused and dimmed by the incredibly heavy snowfall, the glow from the snowmobiles was his only signpost to safety.

Even as he searched assiduously behind every drift and canted slab of ice, he nurtured only a slim hope that he would ever locate Dougherty. The wind was fierce. The snow was mounting at the rate of two inches an hour or faster. In those brief moments when he stopped to take a closer look into especially long, deep shadows, drifts began to form against his boots. If Brian had lain on the ice, unconscious or somehow stricken and unable to move, for the past fifteen minutes, maybe longer . . . Well, by this time the kid would be covered over, a smooth white lump like any hummock or drift, frozen fast to the winter field.

It's hopeless, Harry thought.

Then, not forty feet from the blasting shaft, he stepped around a monolith of ice as large as a sixteen-wheel Mack truck and found Brian on the other side. The kid was on his back, laid out flat, one arm at his side and the other across his chest. He still wore his goggles and snow mask. At a glance he appeared to be lolling there, merely taking a nap, in no trouble whatsoever. Because the upturned slab of ice acted as a windbreak, the snow had not drifted over him. For the same reason, he'd been spared the worst of the bitter cold. Nevertheless, he didn't move and was most likely dead.

Harry knelt beside the body and pulled the snow mask from the face. Thin, irregularly spaced puffs of vapor rose from between the parted lips. Alive. But for how long? Brian's lips were thin and bloodless. His skin was no less white than the snow around him. When pinched, he didn't stir. His eyelids didn't flutter. After lying motionless on the ice for at least a quarter of an hour, even if he had been out of the wind for the entire time and even though he was wearing full survival gear, he would already be suffering from exposure. Harry adjusted the snow mask to re-cover the pale face.

He was deciding how best to get Brian out of there when he saw someone approaching through the turbulent gloom. A shaft of light appeared in the darkness, hazy at first, getting sharper and brighter as it drew nearer.

Roger Breskin staggered through a thick curtain of snow, holding his flashlight before him as a blind man held a cane. Apparently he had become disoriented and wandered out of his assigned search area. He hesitated when he saw Brian.

Harry gestured impatiently.

Pulling down his snow mask, Breskin hurried to them. "Is he alive?"

"Not by much."

"What happened?"

"I don't know. Let's get him into one of the snowmobile cabins and let the warm air work on him. You take his feet and I'll—"

"I can handle him myself."

"But—"

"It'll be easier and quicker that way."

Harry accepted the flashlight that Roger passed to him.

The big man bent down and lifted Brian as if the kid weighed no more than ten pounds.

Harry led the way back through the drifts and hummocks to the snowmobiles.

❄

At 4:50 the Americans at Thule radioed Gunvald Larsson with more bad news. Like the *Melville* before her, the trawler *Liberty* had found the storm to be an irresistible force against which only big warships and fools tried to stand. She simply could not head straightaway into the massive, powerful waves that surged across nearly all of the North Atlantic and the unfrozen portions of the Greenland Sea. She had turned back five minutes ago when a seaman discovered minor buckling of the starboard bow plates. The American radioman repeatedly assured Gunvald that everyone stationed at Thule was praying for those poor bastards on the iceberg. Indeed, prayers were no doubt being said for them all over the world.

No number of prayers would make Gunvald feel better. The cold, hard fact was that the captain of the *Liberty*, although certainly of necessity and only with great remorse, had made a decision which virtually sentenced eight people to death.

Gunvald couldn't bring himself to pass on the news to Rita. Not right away, not that minute. Maybe on the hour—or at a quarter past. He wanted time to get in control of himself. These were his friends, and he cared about them. He didn't want to be the one who delivered their death notice. He was trembling. He had to have time to think about how he would tell them.

He needed a drink. Although he was not a man who usually sought to relieve tension with liquor, and in spite of being known for his steely nerves, he poured himself a shot of vodka from the three-bottle store in the communications-hut pantry. When he had finished the vodka, he was still unable to call Rita. He poured another shot, hesitated, then made it a double, before putting the bottle away.

Although the snowmobiles were stationary, the five small engines rumbled steadily. On the icecap, in the middle of a fierce storm, the machines must never be switched off, because the batteries would go dead and the lubricants in the engines would freeze up within two or three minutes. The unrelenting wind was growing colder as the day wore on; it could kill men and machines with ease.

Harry came out of the ice cave and hurried to the nearest snowmobile. When he was settled in the warm cabin, he screwed off the top of the Thermos bottle that he'd brought with him. He took several quick sips of the thick, fragrant vegetable soup. It had been brewed from freeze-dried mix and brought to the boiling point on the hot plate that they had used earlier to melt snow at the open blasting shafts. For the first time all day, he was able to relax, though he knew this was a temporary state of peace.

In the three snowmobiles to his left, George Lin, Claude, and Roger were eating dinner in equal privacy. He could barely see them: dim shapes inside the unlighted cabins.

Everyone had been given three cups of soup. At this rate, they had enough supplies for only two more meals. Harry had decided against rationing the remaining food, for if they were not well fed, the cold would kill them that much sooner.

Franz Fischer and Pete Johnson were in the ice cave. Harry could see them clearly, for his machine's headlamps shone through the entrance and provided the only light in there. The two men were pacing, waiting for their turn at warm cabins and Thermos bottles full of hot soup. Franz moved briskly, agitatedly, almost as if marching back and forth. In perfect contrast, Pete ambled from one end of the cave to the other, loose-jointed, fluid.

Rita knocked and opened the cabin door, startling Harry.

Swallowing a mouthful of soup, he said, "What's wrong?"

She leaned inside, using her body to block out the wind and its gibberous voice. "He wants to talk to you."

"Brian?"

"Yes."

"He's still improving?"

"Oh, yes. Nicely."

"Does he remember what happened?"

"Let him tell you," she said.

In the fifth snowmobile, the one parked farthest from the cave, Brian was slowly recuperating. Rita had been in the cabin with him for the past twenty minutes, massaging his chilled fingers, feeding him soup, and making sure that he didn't lapse into a dangerous sleep. He had regained consciousness during the ride back from the third demolition shaft, but he had been in too much agony to talk. When he first woke, he'd been racked with pain as his numbed nerve endings belatedly responded to the severe cold that had nearly killed him. The kid would not feel half normal for at least another hour.

Harry capped his Thermos bottle. Before he pulled his goggles in place, he kissed Rita.

"Mmmmm," she said. "More."

This time her tongue moved between his lips. Snowflakes swept past her head and danced across his face, but her breath was hot on his greased skin. He was flushed with a poignant concern for her. He wanted to protect her from all harm.

When they drew apart she said, "I love you."

"We *will* go back to Paris. Somehow. When we get out of this."

"Well, if we don't get out of it," she said, "we haven't been short-changed. We've had eight good years together. We've had more fun and love than most people get in a lifetime."

He felt powerless, up against impossible odds. All his life he had been a man who took charge in a crisis. He had always been able to find solutions to even the most difficult problems. This new sense of impotency enraged him.

She kissed him lightly on one corner of his mouth. "Hurry now. Brian's waiting for you."

The snowmobile cabin was uncomfortably cramped. Harry sat backward on the narrow passenger bench, facing the rear of the machine, where Brian Dougherty was facing forward. The handlebars pressed into his back. His knees were jammed against Brian's knees. Only a vague, amber radiance from the headlamps filtered through the Plexiglas, and the darkness made the tiny enclosure seem even tinier than it was.

Harry said, "How do you feel?"

"Like hell."

"You will for a while yet."

"My hands and feet sting. And I don't mean they're just numb. It's like someone's jabbing lots of long needles into them." His voice was shaded with pain.

"Frostbite?"

"We haven't looked at my feet yet. But they feel about the same as my hands. And there doesn't seem to be any frostbite on my hands. I think I'm safe. But—" He gasped in pain, and his face contorted. "Oh, Jesus, that's bad."

Opening his Thermos, Harry said, "Soup?"

"No, thanks. Rita pumped a quart of it into me. One more drop, and I'll float away." He rubbed his hands together, apparently to ease another especially sharp prickle of pain. "By the way, I'm head over heels in love with your wife."

"Who isn't?"

"And I want to thank you for coming after me. You saved my life, Harry."

"Another day, another act of heroism," Harry said. He took a mouthful of soup. "What happened to you out there?"

"Didn't Rita tell you?"

"She said I should hear it from you."

Brian hesitated. His eyes glittered in the shadows. At last he said, "Someone clubbed me."

Harry almost choked on his soup. "Knocked you out?"

"Hit me on the back of the head."

"That can't be right."

"I've got the lumps to prove it."

"Let me see."

Brian leaned forward, lowered his head.

Harry stripped off his gloves and felt the boy's head. The two lumps were prominent and easy to find, one larger than the other, both on the back of the skull and one slightly higher and to the left of the other. "Concussion?"

"None of the symptoms."

"Headache?"

"Oh, yeah. A real bastard of a headache."

"Double vision?"

"No."

"Any slurred speech?"

"No."

"You're certain you didn't faint?"

"Positive," Brian said, sitting up straight again.

"You could have taken a nasty bump on the head if you'd fainted. You might have fallen against a projection of ice."

"I distinctly remember being struck from behind." His voice was hard with conviction. "Twice. The first time he didn't put enough force into it. My hood cushioned the blow. I stumbled, kept my balance, started to turn around—and he hit me a lot harder the next time. The lights went out but good."

"And then he dragged you out of sight?"

"Before any of you saw what was happening, evidently."

"Not very damned likely."

"The wind was gusting. The snow was so thick I couldn't see more than two yards. He had excellent cover."

"You're saying someone tried to murder you."

"That's right."

"But if that's the case, why did he drag you behind a windbreak? You would have frozen to death in fifteen minutes if he'd left you in the open."

"Maybe he thought the blow killed me. Anyway,

he did leave me in the open. But I came to after you'd all left. I was dizzy, nauseated, cold. I managed to drag myself out of the wind before I passed out again."

"Murder . . ."

"Yes."

Harry didn't want to believe it. He had too much on his mind as it was. He didn't have the capacity to deal with yet another worry.

"It happened as we were getting ready to leave the third site." Brian paused, hissed in pain. "My feet. God, like hot needles, hot needles dipped in acid." His knees pressed more forcefully against Harry's knees, but after half a minute or so, he gradually relaxed. He was tough; he continued as if there had been no interruption. "I was loading some equipment into the last of the cargo trailers. Everyone was busy. The wind was gusting especially hard, the snow was falling so heavily I'd lost sight of the rest of you, then he hit me."

"But who?"

"I didn't see him."

"Not even from the corner of your eye?"

"No. Nothing."

"Did he speak to you?"

"No."

"If he wanted you dead, why wouldn't he wait for midnight? The way it looks now, you'll die then with the rest of us. Why would he feel he had to hurry you along? Why not wait for midnight?"

"Well, maybe . . ."

"What?"

"This sounds crazy . . . but, well, I *am* a Dougherty."

Harry understood at once. "To a certain breed of maniac, yes, that would make you an appealing victim. Killing a Dougherty, any Dougherty— there's a sense of history involved. I suppose I can see a psychopath getting a real thrill out of that."

They were silent.

Then Brian said, "But who among us is psychotic?"

"Seems impossible, doesn't it?"

"Yeah. But you do believe me?"

"Of course. I can't make myself believe you knocked yourself unconscious with two blows to the back of the head, then dragged yourself out of sight."

Brian sighed with relief.

Harry said, "This pressure we're under . . . If one of us was a borderline case, potentially unstable but functional, maybe the stress was all that was needed to push him over the edge. Like to take a guess?"

"Guess who it was? No."

"I expected you to say George Lin."

"For whatever reasons, George doesn't care for me or my family. He's sure made that abundantly clear. But whatever's wrong with him, whatever bee he's got up his ass, I still can't believe he's a killer."

"You can't be sure. You don't know what's going on inside his head any more than I do. There're few people in this life we can ever really know. With me . . . Rita's the only person I'd ever vouch for and have no doubts."

"Yes, but I saved his life today."

"If he's psychotic, why would that matter to him? In fact, in his twisted logic, for some reason we'd never be able to grasp, that might even be why he wants to kill you."

The wind rocked the snowmobile. Beads of snow ticked and hissed across the cabin roof.

For the first time all day, Harry was on the verge of despair. He was exhausted both physically and mentally.

Brian said, "Will he try again?"

"If he's nuts, obsessed with you and your family, then he's not going to give up easily. What does he have to lose? I mean, he's going to die at midnight anyway."

Looking out the side window into the churning night, Brian said, "I'm afraid, Harry."

"If you weren't afraid right now, kid, then *you'd* be psychotic."

"You're afraid too?"

"Scared out of my wits."

"You don't show it."

"I never do. I just pee my pants and hope nobody'll notice."

Brian laughed, then winced at another spasm of

stinging pain in his extremities. When he recovered, he said, "Whoever he is, at least I'll be prepared for him now."

"You won't be left alone," Harry said. "Either Rita or I will stay with you at all times."

Rubbing his hands together, massaging his still cold fingers, Brian said, "Are you going to tell the others?"

"No. We'll say you don't remember what happened, that you must have fallen and hit your head on an outcropping of ice. Better that your would-be killer thinks we don't know about him."

"I had the same thought. He'll be especially cautious if he knows we're waiting for his next move."

"But if he thinks we don't know about him, he might get careless the next time he tries for you."

"If he's a lunatic because he wants to murder me even though I'll probably die at midnight anyway . . . then I guess I must be nuts too. Here I am worrying about being murdered even though midnight's only seven hours away."

"No. You've got a strong survival instinct, that's all. It's a sign of sanity."

"Unless the survival instinct is so strong that it keeps me from recognizing a hopeless situation. Then maybe it's a sign of lunacy."

"It isn't hopeless," Harry said. "We've got seven hours. Anything could happen in seven hours."

"Like what?"

"Anything."

5:00

Like a whale breaching in the night sea, the *Ilya Pogodin* surfaced for the second time in an hour. Glistening cascades of water slid from the boat's dark flanks as it rolled in the storm waves. Captain Nikita Gorov and two seamen scrambled out of the conning-tower hatch and took up watch positions on the bridge.

In the past thirty minutes, cruising at its maximum submerged speed of thirty-one knots, the submarine had moved seventeen miles north-northeast of its assigned surveillance position. Timoshenko had taken a bearing on the Edgeway group's radio beacon, and Gorov had plotted a perfectly straight course that intersected with the estimated path of the drifting iceberg. On the surface, the *Pogodin* was capable of twenty-six knots; but because of the bad seas, it was only making three quarters of that speed. Gorov was anxious to take the boat down again, to three hundred feet this time, where it would glide like any other fish, where the turbulence of the storm could not affect it.

The satellite tracking gear rose from the sail behind the bridge and opened like spring's first blossom. The five petal-form radar plates, which quickly joined together to become a dish, were already beginning to gleam and sparkle with ice as the snow and sleet froze to them; nevertheless, they diligently searched the sky.

At three minutes past the hour, a note from Timoshenko was sent up to the bridge. The communications officer wished to inform the captain that a coded message had begun to come in from the Ministry in Moscow.

The moment of truth had arrived.

Gorov folded the slip of paper, put it in a coat pocket, then kept his eyes to the night glasses. He scanned ninety degrees of the storm-swept horizon, but it was not waves and clouds and snow that he saw. Instead, two visions plagued him, each more vivid than reality. In the first, he was sitting at a table in a conference room with a gilt-trimmed ceiling and a chandelier that cast rainbows on the walls; he was listening to the state's testimony at his own court-martial, and he was forbidden to speak in his own defense. In the second vision, he stared down at a young boy who lay in a hospital bed, a dead boy rank with sweat and urine. The night glasses seemed to be a conduit to both the past and the future.

At 5:07 the decoded message was passed through the conning-tower hatch and into the captain's hands. Gorov skipped the eight lines of introductory material and got straight to the body of the communiqué.

YOUR REQUEST GRANTED STOP MAKE ALL SPEED TO
RESCUE MEMBERS EDGEWAY EXPEDITION STOP WHEN
FOREIGN NATIONALS ABOARD TAKE ALL PRECAUTIONS

AGAINST COMPROMISE OF CLASSIFIED MATERIAL STOP
SECURE ALL SENSITIVE AREAS OF YOUR COMMAND STOP
EMBASSY OFFICIALS IN WASHINGTON HAVE INFORMED
AMERICAN GOVERNMENT OF INTENT TO RESCUE
EDGEWAY GROUP STOP

At the bottom of the decoding sheet, Timoshenko had written two words in pencil: RECEIPT ACKNOWLEDGED. There was nothing to do now but act upon their new orders—which they had been doing anyway for the past half an hour.

Although he was not at all sure that sufficient time remained in which to get those people off the iceberg, Gorov was happier than he had been in a long time. At least he was *doing* something. At least he had a chance, however slim, of reaching the Edgeway scientists before they were all dead.

He stuffed the decoded message into a coat pocket and sounded two brief blasts on the electric diving horns.

By 5:30 Brian had been in the snowmobile nearly an hour. He was suffering from claustrophobia. "I'd like to go out and walk."

"Don't rush yourself." Rita switched on a flashlight, and the sudden brightness made her eyes water. She studied his hands. "Numb? Tingling?"

"No."

"A burning sensation?"

"Not much any more. And my feet feel a lot better." He saw that Rita still had her doubts. "My legs are cramped. I really need to exercise them. Besides, it's too warm in here."

She hesitated. "Your face *does* have some color now. I mean, other than the attractive blue it was. And your hands don't look translucent any more. Well . . . all right. But when you've stretched your muscles, if you still feel any tingling, any numbness, you've got to come back here right away."

"Good enough."

She pulled on her felt boots and then worked her feet into her outer boots. She picked up her coat from the bench between them. Afraid of working up a sweat in the warm air, she hadn't been wearing all of her gear. If she perspired in her suit, the moisture against her skin would leach away her body heat, which would be an invitation to death.

For the same reason, Brian wasn't wearing his coat, gloves, or either pair of boots. "I'm not as limber as you are. But if you'll step outside and give me more room, I think I'll manage."

"You must be too stiff and sore to do it yourself. I'll help."

"You're making me feel like a child."

"Rubbish." She patted her lap. "Put your feet up here, one at a time."

He smiled. "You'd make a wonderful mother for someone."

"I already am a wonderful mother for someone. Harry."

She worked the outer boot onto his somewhat swollen foot. Brian grunted with pain when he straightened his leg; his joints felt as if they were popping apart like a string of decorative plastic beads.

While Rita threaded the laces through the eyelets and drew them tight, she said, "Well, if nothing else, you've a wealth of material for those magazine pieces."

He was surprised to hear himself say, "I've decided not to write them. I'm going to do a book instead." Until that moment his obsession had been a private matter. Now that he had revealed it to someone he respected, he had forced himself to regard it less as an obsession and more as a commitment.

"A book? You'd better think twice about that."

"I've thought about it a thousand times the last few weeks."

"Writing a book is an ordeal. I've done three, you know. You may have to write thirty magazine articles to get the same word count as a book, but if I were you, I'd write articles and forget about being an 'author.' There isn't half so much agony in the shorter work as there is in the writing of a book."

"But I've been swept along by the idea."

"Oh, I know how it is. Writing the first third of

the book, you're almost having a sexual experience. But you lose that feeling. Believe me, you do. In the second third, you're just trying to prove something to yourself. And when you get to the last third, it's simply a matter of survival."

"But I've figured out how to make everything hang together in the narrative. I've got my theme."

Rita winced and shook her head sadly. "So you're too far gone to respond to reason." She helped him get his right foot into the sealskin boot. "What *is* your theme?"

"Heroism."

"Heroism?" She grimaced as she worked with the laces. "What in the name of God does heroism have to do with the Edgeway Project?"

"I think maybe it has everything to do with it."

"You're daft."

"Seriously."

"I never noticed any heroes here."

Brian was surprised by her apparently genuine astonishment. "Have you looked in a mirror?"

"Me? A hero? Dear boy, I'm the furthest thing from it."

"Not in my view."

"I'm scared sick half the time."

"Heroes can be scared and still be heroes. That's what makes them heroes—acting in spite of fear. This is heroic work, this project."

"It's work, that's all. Dangerous, yes. Foolish, perhaps. But heroic? You're romanticizing it."

He was silent as she finished lacing his boots. "Well, it's not politics."

"What isn't?"

"What you're doing here. You're not in it for power, privilege, or money. You're not out here because you want to control people."

Rita raised her head and met his gaze. Her eyes were beautiful—and as deep as the clear Arctic sea. He knew that she understood him, in that moment, better than anyone ever had, perhaps even better than he knew himself. "The world thinks your family is full of heroes."

"Well."

"But you don't."

"I know them better."

"They've made sacrifices, Brian. Your uncle was killed. Your father took a bullet of his own."

"This will sound meanspirited, but it wouldn't if you knew them. Rita, neither of them *expected* to have to make a sacrifice like that—or any sacrifice at all. Getting shot or killed isn't an act of bravery—any more than it is for some poor bastard who gets gunned down unexpectedly while he's withdrawing money from an automatic teller machine. He's a victim, not a hero."

"Some people get into politics to make a better world."

"Not anyone I've known. It's dirty, Rita. It's all about envy and power. But out here, everything's so clean. The work is hard, the environment is hostile—but *clean*."

She had never taken her eyes from his. He couldn't recall anyone ever having met his gaze as unwaveringly as she did. After a thoughtful silence, she said, "So you're not just a troubled rich boy out for thrills, the way the media would have it."

He broke eye contact first, taking his foot off the bench and contorting himself in the small space in order to slip his arms into the sleeves of his coat. "Is that what you thought I was like?"

"No. I don't let the media do my thinking for me."

"Of course, maybe I'm deluding myself. Maybe that's just what I am, everything they write in the papers."

"There's precious little truth in the papers," she said. "In fact, you'll only find it one place."

"Where's that?"

"You know."

He nodded. "In myself."

She smiled. Putting on her coat, she said, "You'll be fine."

"When?"

"Oh, in twenty years maybe."

He laughed. "Good God, I hope I'm not going to be screwed up that long."

"Maybe longer. Hey, that's what life's all about: little by little, day by day, with excruciating stubbornness, each of us learning how to be less screwed up."

"You should be a psychiatrist."

"Witch doctors are more effective."

"I've sometimes thought I've needed one."

"A psychiatrist? Better save your money. Dear boy, all you need is time."

When he followed Rita out of the snowmobile, Brian was surprised by the bitter power of the storm wind. It took his breath away and almost drove him to his knees. He gripped the open cabin door until he was certain of his balance.

The wind was a reminder that his unknown assailant, the man who had struck him on the head, was not the only threat to his survival. For a few minutes he'd forgotten that they were adrift, had forgotten about the time bombs ticking toward midnight. The fear came back to him like guilt to a priest's breast. Now that he had committed himself to writing the book, he wanted *very* much to live.

The headlamps on one of the snowmobiles shone through the mouth of the cave. In places, the fractured ice deconstructed the beams into glimmering prisms of light in all the primary colors, and those geometric shapes shimmered jewellike in the walls of the otherwise white chamber. The eight distorted shadows of the expedition members rippled and slid across that dazzling backdrop, swelled and shrank, mysterious but perhaps no more so than the people who cast them—five of whom were suspects and one of whom was a potential murderer.

Harry watched Roger Breskin, Franz Fischer, George Lin, Claude, and Pete as they argued about the options open to them, about how they should spend the six hours and twenty minutes remaining before midnight. He ought to have been leading the discussion or at the very least contributing to it, but he couldn't keep his mind on what the others were saying. For one thing, no matter how they spent their time, they could not escape from the iceberg or retrieve the explosives, so their discussion could resolve nothing. Furthermore, although trying to be discreet, he couldn't prevent himself from studying them intensely, as though psychotic tendencies ought to be evident in the way a man walked, talked, and gestured.

His train of thought was interrupted by a call from Edgeway Station. Gunvald Larsson's voice, shot through with static, rattled off the ice walls.

The other men stopped talking.

When Harry went to the radio and responded to the call, Gunvald said, "Harry, the trawlers have turned back. The *Melville* and the *Liberty*. Both of them. Some time ago. I've known, but I couldn't bring myself to tell you." He was unaccountably buoyant, excited, as if that bad news should have brought smiles to their faces. "But now it doesn't matter. It doesn't matter, Harry!"

Pete, Claude, and the others had crowded around the radio, baffled by the Swede's excitement.

Harry said, "Gunvald, what in the hell are you talking about? What do you mean, it doesn't matter?"

Static shredded the airwaves, but then the frequency cleared as Larsson said, ". . . just got word from Thule. Relayed from Washington. There's a submarine in your neighborhood, Harry. Do you read me? A Russian submarine."

Four

❄

NIGHT

8:20
DETONATION IN THREE HOURS
FORTY MINUTES

Gorov, Zhukov, and Seaman Semichastny clambered onto the bridge and faced the port side. The sea was neither calm nor as tumultuous as it had been when they had surfaced earlier to receive the message from the Naval Ministry. The iceberg lay off to port, sheltering them from some of the power of the storm waves and the wind.

They couldn't see the berg, even though the radar and sonar images had indicated that it was massive both above and below the water line. They were only fifty to sixty yards from the target, but the darkness was impenetrable. Instinct alone told Gorov that something enormous loomed over them, and the awareness of being in the shadow of an invisible colossus was one of the eeriest and most disconcerting feelings that he had ever known.

They were warmly dressed and wore goggles. Riding in the lee of the iceberg, however, made it possible to go without snow masks, and conversation was not as difficult as when they'd been running on the surface a few hours previously.

"It's like a windowless dungeon out there," Zhukov said.

No stars. No moon. No phosphorescence on the waves. Gorov had never seen such a perfectly lightless night.

Above and behind them on the sail, the hundred-watt bridge lamp illuminated the immediate steel-work and allowed the three men to see one another. Clotted with scattered small chunks of ice, choppy waves broke against the curved hull, reflecting just enough of that red light to give the impression that the *Pogodin* was sailing not on water but on an ocean of wine-dark blood. Beyond that tiny illumined circle lay an unrelieved blackness so flawless and deep that Gorov's eyes began to ache when he stared at it too long.

Most of the bridge rail was sheathed in ice. Gorov gripped it to steady himself as the boat yawed, but he happened to take hold of a section of bare metal. His glove froze to the steel. He ripped it free and examined the palm: The outer layer of leather was torn, and the lining was exposed. If he had been wearing sealskin gloves, he would not have stuck fast, and he should have remembered to get that particular item of arctic gear out of the storage locker. If he hadn't been wearing gloves at all, his hand would have been welded instantly to the railing, and when he pulled loose, he would have lost a substantial patch of flesh.

Staring in amazement at the captain's shredded glove, Seaman Semichastny exclaimed: "Incredible!"

Zhukov said, "What a miserable place."

"Indeed."

The snow that swept across the bridge was not in the form of flakes. The subzero temperatures and the fierce wind conspired to produce hard beads of snow—what a meteorologist would call "gravel," like millions of granules of white buckshot, the next worst thing to a storm of ice spicules.

Tapping the bridge anemometer, the first officer said, "We've got wind velocity of thirty miles an hour, even leeward of the iceberg. It must be blowing twice to three times that hard on top of the ice or on the open sea."

With the wind factored in, Gorov suspected that the subjective temperature atop the iceberg had to be at least minus sixty or minus seventy degrees. Rescuing the Edgeway scientists under those hideous conditions was a greater challenge than any he had ever faced in his entire naval career. No part of it would be easy. It might even be impossible. And he began to worry that, once again, he had arrived too late.

"Let's have some light," Gorov ordered.

Semichastny immediately swung the floodlight to port and closed the switch.

The two-foot-diameter beam pierced the darkness as if a furnace door had been thrown open in an unlighted basement. Canted down on its gimbal ring, the big floodlight illuminated a circular swatch of sea only ten yards from the submarine:

churning waves filigreed with icy foam, a seething maelstrom but one that was not too difficult to ride. Sheets of spray exploded into the bitter air as the waves met the boat, froze instantly into intricate and glittering laces of ice, hung suspended for a timeless time, and then fell back into the water, their strange beauty as ephemeral as that of any moment in a perfect sunset.

The ocean temperature was a few degrees above freezing, but the water retained sufficient heat and was in such turmoil—and was sufficiently salty, of course—that the only ice it contained was that which had broken off from the polar cap, fifteen miles to the north. Mostly small chunks, none larger than a car, which rode the waves and crashed into one another.

Grasping the pair of handles on the back of the floodlight, Semichastny tilted it up, swung it more directly toward port. The piercing beam bore through the polar blackness and the seething snow—and blazed against a towering palisade of ice, so enormous and so close that the sight of it made all three men gasp.

Fifty yards away, the berg drifted slowly east-southeast in a mild winter current. Even with the storm wind pretty much behind it, the massive island of ice was able to make no more than two or three knots; most of it lay under the water, and it was driven not by the surface tempest but by deeper influences.

Semichastny moved the floodlight slowly to the right, then back to the left.

The cliff was so long and high that Gorov could not get an idea of the overall appearance of it. Each brilliantly lighted circle of ice, although visible in considerable detail from their front-row seat, seemed disassociated from the one that had come before it. Comprehending the whole of the palisade was like trying to envision the finished image of a jigsaw puzzle merely by glancing at five hundred jumbled, disconnected pieces.

"Lieutenant Zhukov, put up a flare."

"Yes, sir."

Zhukov was carrying the signal gun. He raised it—a stubby pistol with a fat, extralong barrel and a two-inch muzzle—held it at arm's length, and fired up into the port-side gloom.

The rocket climbed swiftly through the falling snow. It was visible for a moment as it trailed red sparks and smoke, but then it vanished into the blizzard as though it had passed through a veil into another dimension.

Three hundred feet . . . four hundred feet . . . five hundred . . .

High above, the rocket burst into a brilliant incandescent moon. It didn't immediately begin to lose altitude, but drifted southward on the wind.

Beneath the flare, three hundred yards in every direction, the ocean was painted with cold light that revealed its green-gray hue. The arrhythmic ranks of choppy waves cast jagged, razor-edged shadows that fluttered like uncountable flocks of frantic dark birds feeding on little fishes in the shallow troughs.

The iceberg loomed: a daunting presence, at least one hundred feet high, disappearing into the darkness to the right and left, a huge rampart more formidable than the fortifications of any castle in the world. During their radar- and sonar-guided approach to the site, they had discovered that the berg was four fifths of a mile long. Rising dramatically from the mottled green-gray-black sea, it was curiously like a totem, a man-made monolith with mysterious religious significance. It soared, glass-smooth, gleaming, marred by neither major outcroppings nor indentations: vertical, harsh, forbidding.

Gorov had hoped to find a ragged cliff, one that shelved into the water in easy steps. The sea was not discouragingly rough there in the leeward shadow, and a few men might be able to get across to the ice. But he saw no place for them to land.

Among the submarine's equipment stores were three inflatable, motorized rubber rafts and a large selection of the highest-quality climbing gear. On fifteen separate occasions in the past seven years, the *Ilya Pogodin* had carried top-secret passengers—mostly special-forces operatives from the army's Spetsnaz division, highly trained saboteurs, assassins, reconnaissance teams—and had put them ashore at night on rugged coastlines in seven Western countries. Furthermore, in the event of war, the boat could carry a nine-member commando team in addition to her full crew and could put them safely ashore in less than five minutes, even in bad weather.

But they had to find a place to land the rafts. A small shelf. A tiny cove. A niche above the water line. *Something.*

As if reading the captain's mind, Zhukov said, "Even if we could land men over there, it would be one hell of a climb."

"We could do it."

"It's as straight and smooth as a hundred-foot sheet of window glass."

"We could chop footholds out of the ice," Gorov said. "We have the climbing picks. Axes. Ropes and pitons. We've got the climbing boots and the grappling hooks. Everything we need."

"But these men are submariners, sir. Not mountain climbers."

The flare was high over the *Ilya Pogodin* now, still drifting southward. The light was no longer either fierce or white; it had taken on a yellowish tint and was dwindling. Smoke streamed around the flare and threw bizarre shadows that curled and writhed across the face of the iceberg.

"The right men could make it," Gorov insisted.

"Yes, sir," Zhukov said. "I know they could. I could even make it myself if I had to, and *I'm* afraid of heights. But neither I nor the men are very experienced at this sort of thing. We don't have a single man aboard who could make that climb in even half the time it would take a trained mountaineer. We'd need hours, maybe three or four, maybe even five hours, to get to the top and to rig a system for bringing the Edgeway scientists down to the rafts. And by the time—"

"—by the time we've worked out a way to land them on the ice, they'll be lucky to have even an hour left," Gorov said, finishing the first officer's argument for him.

Midnight was fast approaching.

The flare winked out.

Semichastny still trained the floodlight on the iceberg, moving it slowly from left to right, focusing at the water line, hopefully searching for a shelf, a fissure, a flaw, anything that they had missed.

"Let's have a look at the windward flank," Gorov said. "Maybe it'll have something better to offer."

In the cave, waiting for more news from Gunvald, they were exhilarated by the prospect of rescue—but sobered by the thought that the submarine might not arrive quickly enough to take them off the iceberg before midnight. At times, they were all silent, but at other times, they all seemed to be talking at once.

After waiting until the chamber was filled with excited chatter and the others were particularly distracted, Harry quietly excused himself to go to the latrine. Passing Pete Johnson, he whispered, "I want to talk to you alone."

Pete blinked in surprise.

Not even breaking stride as he spoke, barely glancing at the engineer, Harry put his goggles in place and pulled up his snow mask and walked out of the cave. He bent into the wind, switched on his flashlight, and trudged past the rumbling snowmobiles.

He doubted that much fuel remained in their tanks. The engines would conk out soon. No more light. No more heat.

Past the snowmobiles, the area that they had used for the temporary-camp lavatory lay on the far side of a U-shaped, ten-foot-high ridge of broken ice and drifted snow, twenty yards beyond the inflatable igloos that now lay in ruins. Harry actually had no need to relieve himself, but the call of nature provided the most convenient and least suspicious excuse for getting out of the cave and away from the others. He reached the opening in the crescent ridge that formed the windbreak, shuffled through drifted snow to the rear of that pocket of relative calm, and stood with his back to the ridge wall.

He supposed he might be making a big mistake with Pete Johnson. As he'd told Brian, no one could ever be entirely sure what might lie within the mind of another human being. Even a friend or loved one, well known and trusted, might harbor some unspeakable dark urge and despicable desire. Everyone was a mystery within a mystery, wrapped in an enigma. In his lifelong quest for adventure, Harry had settled by chance into a line of work that brought him into contact with fewer people on a daily basis than he would have met in virtually any other profession, and each time he took on a new challenge, the adversary was never another person but always Mother Nature herself. Nature could be hard but never treacherous, powerful and uncaring but never consciously cruel; in any contest with her, he didn't have to worry about losing because of deceit or betrayal. Nevertheless, he had decided to risk confronting Pete Johnson alone.

He wished that he had a gun.

Considering the assault on Brian, it seemed criminally stupid of Harry to have come to the ice-cap without a large-caliber personal weapon holstered under his parka at all times. Of course, in his experience, geological research had never before required him to shoot anyone.

In a minute, Pete arrived and joined him at the back wall of the U-shaped, roofless shelter.

They faced each other, snow masks pulled down and goggles up on their foreheads, flashlights aimed at their boots. The light bounced back up at them, and Pete's face glowed as if irradiated. Harry knew that his own countenance looked much the same: brightest around the chin and mouth, darker toward the forehead, eyes glittering from the depths of what appeared to be dark holes in his skull—as spooky as any Halloween mask.

Pete said, "Are we here to gossip about someone? Or have you suddenly taken a romantic interest in me?"

"This is serious, Pete."

"Damn right it is. If Rita finds out, she'll beat the crap out of me."

"Let's get right to the point. I want to know . . . why did you try to kill Brian Dougherty?"

"I don't like the way he parts his hair."

"Pete, I'm not joking."

"Well, okay, it was because he called me a darky."

Harry stared at him but said nothing.

Above their heads, at the crest of the sheltering ridge, the storm wind whistled and huffed through the natural crenelations in the tumbled-together slabs of ice.

Pete's grin faded. "Man, you *are* serious."

"Cut the bullshit, Pete."

"Harry, for God's sake, what's going on here?"

Harry watched him for long seconds, using silence to disconcert him, waiting either to be attacked—or not. Finally, he said, "Maybe I believe you."

"Believe me about what?" The bafflement on the big man's broad, black face seemed as genuine as any lamb's sweet look of innocence; the only hint of evil was entirely the theatrical effect from the upwash of the flashlight beams. "Are you saying somebody actually *did* try to kill him? When? Back at the third blasting site, when he got left behind? But he fell, you said. *He* said. He told us that he fell and hit his head. Didn't he?"

Harry sighed, and some of the tension went out of his neck and shoulders. "Damn. If you *are* the one, you're good. I believe you really don't know."

"Hey, I *know* I really don't know."

"Brian didn't fall and knock himself unconscious, and he wasn't left behind by accident. Someone struck him on the back of the head. Twice."

Pete was speechless. His line of work didn't usually require him to carry a sidearm, either.

As quickly as he could, Harry recounted the conversation that he'd had with Brian in the snowmobile cabin a few hours ago.

"Jesus!" Pete said. "And you thought I might be the one."

"Yeah. Although I didn't suspect you as much as I do some of the others."

"You thought I might go for your throat a minute ago."

"I'm sorry. I like you a hell of a lot, Pete. But I've known you only eight or nine months, after all. There could be things you've hidden from me, certain attitudes, prejudices—"

Pete shook his head. "Hey, you don't have to explain yourself. You had no reason to trust me further than you did the others. I'm not asking for an apology. I'm just saying you've got guts. You aren't exactly a little guy, but physically I'm more than a match for you."

Harry had to look up to see Pete's face, and suddenly his friend seemed more of a giant than ever before. Shoulders almost too broad for a conventional doorway. Massive arms. If he had accepted those offers to play pro football, he would have been a formidable presence on the field, and if a polar bear showed up now, he might be able to give it a good fight.

"If I'd been this psycho," Pete said, "and if I'd decided to kill you here and now, you wouldn't have had much chance."

"Yeah, but I didn't have any choice. I needed one more ally, and you were the best prospect. By the way, thanks for not tearing my head off."

Pete coughed and spat in the snow. "I've changed my mind about you, Harry. You don't have a hero complex after all. This is just perfectly natural for you, this kind of courage. You're built this way. This is how you came into the world."

"I only did what I had to do," Harry said impatiently. "So long as we were stranded on this iceberg, so long as it appeared that we were all going to die at midnight, I thought Rita and I could watch over Brian. I figured our would-be killer might take advantage of any opening we gave him at the boy, but I didn't think he'd bother to engineer any opportunities. But with this submarine on the way . . . Well, if he thinks Brian will be rescued, he might do something bold. He might make another attempt on the boy's life, even if he has to reveal himself to do it. And I need someone besides Rita and me to help stop him when the time comes."

"And I've been nominated."

"Congratulations."

A whirl of wind crested the ridge and swooped down on them. They lowered their heads while a column of spinning snow passed over them, so dense that it seemed almost like an avalanche. For a few seconds they were blinded and deafened. Then the squall-within-a-storm passed out of the open end of the crescent ridge.

Pete said, "So far as you're concerned, is there any one of them we should watch more closely than the others?"

"I ought to have asked you that question. I already know what Rita, Brian, and I think. I need a fresh perspective."

Pete didn't have to ponder the question to come up with an answer. "George Lin," he said at once.

"That was my own first choice."

"Not first and last? So you think he's too obvious?"

"Maybe. But that doesn't rule him out."

"What's wrong with him, anyway? I mean, the way he acts with Brian, the anger—what's that all about?"

"I'm not sure," Harry said. "Something happened to him in China when he was a child, very young. It must've been in the last days of Chiang's rule, something traumatic. He seems to connect Brian to that, because of his family's politics."

"And the pressure we've been under these past nine hours might have snapped him."

"I suppose it's possible."

"But it doesn't feel right."

"Not quite."

They thought about it.

Pete Johnson started walking in place to keep his feet from getting chilled. Harry followed suit, stepping smartly up and down, going nowhere.

After a minute or so, still exercising, Pete said, "What about Franz Fischer?"

"What about him?"

"He's cool toward you. And toward Rita. Not cool toward *her* exactly . . . but there's sure something odd in the way he looks at her."

"You're observant."

"Maybe it's professional jealousy because of all these science awards the two of you have piled up the last few years."

"He's not that petty."

"What then?" When Harry hesitated, Pete said, "None of my business?"

"He knew her when."

"Before she married you?"

"Yes. They were lovers."

"So he *is* jealous, but not because of the awards."

"Apparently, yeah."

"She's a terrific lady," Pete said. "Anybody who lost her to you would not be likely to think you're such a great guy. You ever think maybe that should have been a reason not to bring Franz onto this team?"

"If Rita and I could put that part of the past behind us, why couldn't he?"

"Because he's not you and Rita, man. He's a self-involved science nerd, for one thing. He may be good-looking and smart and sophisticated in some ways, but he's basically insecure. Probably accepted the invitation to join the expedition just so Rita would have a chance to compare him and you under extreme conditions. He probably thought you'd stumble around like a dweeb here on the ice, while he'd be Nanook of the North, larger than life, a macho man by comparison. From day one, of course, he must have realized it wasn't going to work out that way, which explains why he's been so bitchy."

"Doesn't make sense."

"Does to me."

Harry stopped exercising, afraid of working up a chilling sweat. "Franz might hate me and perhaps even Rita, but how do his feelings toward *us* translate into an attack on Brian?"

After a dozen more steps, Pete also quit walking in place. "Who knows how a psychopath's mind works?"

Harry shook his head. "It might be Franz. But not because he's jealous of me."

"Breskin?"

"He's a cipher."

"He strikes me as *too* self-contained."

"We always tend to suspect the loner," Harry said, "the quiet man who keeps to himself. But that's no more logical than suspecting Franz merely because he had a relationship with Rita years ago."

"Why did Breskin emigrate to Canada from the U.S.?"

"I don't recall. Maybe he never said."

"Could have been for political reasons," Pete suggested.

"Yeah, maybe. But Canada and the U.S. have basically similar politics. I mean, if a man leaves his homeland and takes citizenship in a new country, you'd expect him to go somewhere that was radically different, a whole other system of government, economics." Harry sniffed as he felt his nose beginning to run. "Besides, Roger had a chance to kill the kid early this afternoon. When Brian was dangling over the cliff, trying to reach George, Roger could have cut the rope. Who would have been the wiser?"

"Maybe he doesn't want to kill anyone but Brian. Maybe that's his only obsession. If he had cut the rope, he wouldn't have been able to save Lin all by himself."

"He could have cut it after Lin was brought up."

"But then George would have been a witness."

"What psychopath has that degree of self-control? Besides, I'm not sure that George was in any condition to be a witness, little more than half conscious at that point."

"But like you said, Roger's a cipher."

"We're going in circles."

As they breathed, the vapor they expelled crystallized between them. The cloud had become so thick that they could not see each other clearly, though they were no more than two feet apart.

Waving the fog out of their way and far enough from the sheltering ridge wall for a draft to catch it, Pete said, "We're left with Claude."

"He seems the least likely of the lot."

"How long have you known him?"

"Fifteen years. Sixteen. Thereabouts."

"You've been on the ice with him before?"

"Several times," Harry said. "He's a wonderful man."

"He often talks about his late wife. Colette. He still gets teary about it, shaky. When did she die?"

"Three years ago this month. Claude was on the ice, his first expedition in two and a half years, when she was murdered."

"*Murdered?*"

"She'd flown from Paris to London on a holiday. She was in England just three days. The IRA had planted a bomb in a restaurant where she went for lunch. She was one of the eight killed in the blast."

"Good God!"

"They caught one of the men involved. He's still in prison."

Pete said, "And Claude took it very hard."

"Oh, yes. Colette was great. You'd have liked her. She and Claude were as close as Rita and I."

For a moment neither of them spoke.

At the top of the ridge, the wind moaned like a revenant trapped between this world and the next. Again, the ice reminded Harry of a graveyard. He shuddered.

Pete said, "If a man is deeply in love with a woman, and she's taken from him, blown to pieces by a bomb—he might be twisted by the loss."

"Not Claude. Broken, yes. Depressed, yes. But not twisted. He's the kindest—"

"His wife was killed by Irishmen."

"So?"

"Dougherty is Irish."

"That's a stretch, Pete. Irish-American, actually. And third generation."

"You said one of these bombers was apprehended?"

"Yeah. They never nailed any of the others."

"Do you remember his name?"

"No."

"Was it Dougherty, anything like Dougherty?"

Harry grimaced and waved one hand dismissively. "Come on now, Pete. You've stretched it to the breaking point."

The big man began to walk in place once more. "I guess I have. But you know . . . both Brian's uncle and his father have been accused of playing favorites with their Irish-American constituencies at the expense of other groups. And some people say they sympathized with the IRA's leftward tilt to the extent that for years they secretly funneled donations to them."

"I've heard it all too. But it was never proved. Political slander, as far as we know. The actual fact is . . . we have four suspects, and none of them looks like a sure bet."

"Correction."

"What?"

"Six suspects."

"Franz, George, Roger, Claude . . ."

"And me."

"I've ruled you out."

"Not at all."

"Now pull the other leg."

"I'm serious," Pete said.

"After the conversation we've just had, I know you can't—"

"Is there a law that says a psychopathic killer can't be a good actor?"

Harry stared at him, trying to read his expression. Suddenly the malevolence in Johnson's face didn't seem to be entirely a trick played by the peculiar backwash of light. "You're making me edgy, Pete."

"Good."

"I know you told me the truth, you're not the guy. But what you're saying is that I mustn't trust anyone, not even for a moment, not even if I think I know him like a brother."

"Precisely. And it goes for both of us. That's why the sixth name on the list of suspects is yours."

"What? *Me?*"

"You were at the third blasting shaft with the rest of us."

"But I'm the one who found him when we went back."

"And you were the one who assigned search areas. You could have given yourself the right one, so you'd make sure he was dead before you 'found' him. Then Breskin stumbled on you before you had a chance to deal Brian the coup de grâce."

Harry gaped at him.

"And if you're twisted enough," Pete said, "you might not even realize there's a killer inside you."

"You don't really think I'm capable of murder?"

"It's a chance in a million. But I've seen people win on much longer odds."

Although he knew that Pete was giving him a taste of his own medicine, letting him know what it was like to be treated as a suspect, Harry felt a tension ache return to his neck and shoulders. "You know what's wrong with you Californians?"

"Yeah. We make you Bostonians feel inferior, because we're so self-aware and mellow, but you're so repressed and uptight."

"Actually, I'd been thinking that all the earthquakes and fires and mudslides and riots and serial killers out there have made you paranoid."

They smiled at each other.

Harry said, "We'd better be getting back."

Two flares floated five hundred feet apart in the night sky, and the floodlight swept back and forth along the base of the gleaming ice cliffs.

The windward flank of the iceberg was not as forbidding as the featureless, vertical leeward wall had been. Three rugged shelves stepped back and up from the water line. Each appeared to be between eight and ten yards deep, and together they jutted twenty or twenty-five feet above the sea. Beyond the shelves, the cliff rose at an angle for fifty feet or more and then broke at a narrow ledge. Above the ledge was a sheer face of about twenty feet of vertical ice, and then the brink.

"Rafts could land on those shelves," Zhukov

said, examining the ice through his binoculars. "And even untrained men could climb that cliff. But not in this weather."

Gorov could barely hear him above the raucous voice of the storm and the boat's rhythmic collisions with the high waves.

The sea was remarkably more violent on the windward flank than it had been on the protected leeward side. Huge waves crashed across the steps at the base of the iceberg. They would overturn a medium-size lifeboat and tear one of the *Pogodin*'s motorized rubber rafts to pieces. Even the submarine, with its forty-thousand-horsepower turbines and sixty-five-hundred-ton surface displacement, was having some difficulty making way properly. Frequently the bow was underwater, and when it did manage to nose up, it resembled an animal fighting quicksand. Waves slammed into the superstructure deck with shocking fury, sent protracted shudders through the hull, exploded against the sail, washed onto the bridge, cast spray higher than Gorov's head. All three men were wearing suits of ice: ice-covered boots, ice-rimed trousers, ice-plated coattails.

The brutal wind registered seventy-two miles per hour on the bridge anemometer, with gusts half again as strong. The pellets of snow were like swarming bees; they stung Gorov's face and brought tears to his eyes.

"We'll go around to leeward again," the captain

shouted, though standing virtually shoulder-to-shoulder with his subordinates on the small bridge.

He remembered too vividly the smooth hundred-foot cliff that awaited them on the other side, but he had no choice. The windward flank offered them no hope at all.

"And on the other side—what then?" Zhukov asked.

Gorov hesitated, thinking about it. "We'll shoot a line across. Get a man over there. Rig a breeches buoy."

"Shoot a line?" Zhukov was doubtful. He leaned closer, face-to-face with his captain, and shouted out his concern: "Even if that works, even if it holds in the ice, can it be done from one moving object to another?"

"In desperation, perhaps. I don't know. Got to try it. It's a place to start."

If a few men with enough equipment could be gotten from the sub to the leeward face of the iceberg by means of a breeches buoy, they could blast out a landing shelf to allow the rafts to follow them. Then they might be able to shoot a line to the top. With that, they could ascend the cliff as easily as flies walking on walls.

Zhukov glanced at his watch. "Three and a half hours!" he shouted above the Armageddon wind. "We better begin."

"Clear the bridge!" Gorov ordered. He sounded the diving alarm.

When he reached the control room half a minute later, he heard the petty officer say, "Green board!"

Zhukov and Semichastny had already gone to their quarters to get into dry clothes.

As Gorov stepped off the conning-tower ladder, shedding brittle jackets of ice as he moved, the diving officer turned to him and said, "Captain?"

"I'm going to change clothes. Take us down to seventy-five feet and get back into the leeward shadow of the iceberg."

"Yes, sir."

"I'll take over in ten minutes."

"Yes, sir."

· · ·

In his quarters, after he had changed out of his sodden and frozen gear into a dry uniform, Gorov sat at the corner desk and picked up the photograph of his dead son. Everyone in the picture was smiling: the piano-accordion player, Gorov, and Nikki. The boy's smile was the broadest of the three—genuine, not assumed for the camera. He was gripping his father's hand. In his other hand, he held a large, two-scoop cone of vanilla ice cream that was dripping onto his fingers. Ice cream frosted his upper lip. His thick, windblown golden hair fell across his right eye. Even on the flat, two-dimensional surface of the photo, one could sense the aura of delight, love, and pleasure that the child had always radiated in life.

"I swear I came as quickly as I could," Gorov murmured to the photograph.

The boy stared, smiling.

"I'm going to get those people off the iceberg before midnight." Gorov hardly recognized his own voice. "No more putting assassins and saboteurs ashore. Saving lives now, Nikki. I know I can do it. I'm not going to let them die. That's a promise."

He was squeezing the photograph so tightly that his fingers were pale, bloodless.

The silence in the cabin was oppressive, for it was the silence of the other world to which Nikki had gone, the silence of lost love, of a future that would never happen, of stillborn dreams.

Someone walked by Gorov's door, whistling.

As if the whistle were a slap in the face, the captain twitched and sat up straight, suddenly aware of how maudlin he had become. He was privately humiliated. Sentimentalism would not help him adjust to his loss; sentimentality was a corruption of the legacy of good memories and laughter that this honest and good-hearted boy had left behind.

Annoyed with himself, Gorov put down the photograph. He got to his feet and left the cabin.

• • •

Lieutenant Timoshenko had been off duty for the past four hours. He had eaten dinner and napped for two hours. Now, at eight-forty-five, fifteen minutes ahead of schedule, he had returned to the communications center once more, preparing to take the last watch of the day, which would end at one o'clock in the morning. One of his subordinates manned the equipment while Timoshenko sat at a corner work desk, reading a magazine and drinking hot tea from an aluminum mug.

Captain Gorov stepped in from the companionway. "Lieutenant, I believe it's time to make direct radio contact with those people on the iceberg."

Timoshenko put down his tea and got up. "Will we be surfacing again, sir?"

"In a few minutes."

"Do you want to talk to them?"

"I'll leave that to you," Gorov said.

"And what should I tell them?"

Gorov quickly explained what they had found on their trip around the huge island of ice—the hopelessly stormy seas on the windward side, the sheer wall on the leeward side—and outlined his plans for the breeches buoy. "And tell them that from here on out, we'll keep them informed of our progress, or lack of it, every step of the way."

"Yes, sir."

Gorov turned to go.

"Sir? They're certain to ask—do you think we've a good chance of saving them?"

"Not good, no. Only fair."

"Should I be honest with them?"

"I think that's best."

"Yes, sir."

"But also tell them that if it's at all humanly possible, we'll do it, one way or the other. No matter what the odds against, by God, we'll try our damnedest to get them off. I'm more determined about this than I've been about anything else in my life. Tell them that, Lieutenant. Make sure you tell them that."

8:57

Harry was surprised to hear his mother tongue spoken so fluently by a Russian radio operator. The man sounded as though he had taken a degree at a good middle-level university in Britain. English was the official language of the Edgeway expedition, as it was of nearly every multinational scientific study group. But somehow it seemed *wrong* for a Russian submariner to speak it so flawlessly. Gradually, however, as Timoshenko explained why the leeward flank was the only avenue of approach to the iceberg worth investigating, Harry became accustomed to the man's fluency and to his decidedly English accent.

"But if the berg is five hundred yards wide," Harry said, "why couldn't your men come on from one end or the other?"

"Unfortunately, the sea is as stormy at either end as it is on the windward side."

"But a breeches buoy," Harry said doubtfully. "It

can't be easy to rig one of those between two moving points, and in this weather."

"We can match speeds with the ice pretty much dead on, which makes it almost like rigging between two stationary points. Besides, a breeches buoy is only one of our options. If we're unable to make it work, we'll get to you some other way. You needn't worry about that."

"Wouldn't it be simpler to send divers across to the ice? You must have scuba equipment aboard."

"And we've a number of well-trained frogmen," Timoshenko said. "But even the leeward sea is much too rough for them. These waves and currents would carry them away as quickly as if they leaped into a waterfall."

"We certainly don't want anyone put at too great a risk on our behalf. It wouldn't make sense to lose some people to save others. From what you said, your captain sounds confident. So I guess we're better off leaving all the worrying to you. Have you anything else to tell me?"

"That's all for the moment," Timoshenko said. "Stay by your radio. We'll keep you informed of developments."

· · ·

Everyone except Harry and George had something to say about the call from the *Ilya Pogodin*'s communications officer—suggestions about preparations to be made for the rescue party, ideas about how they might be able to help the Russians scale

the leeward wall—and everyone seemed determined to say it first, now, instantly. Their voices,
echoes of their voices, and echoes of the echoes
filled the ice cave.

Harry acted as a moderator and tried to keep
them from jabbering on to no point.

When George Lin saw that their excitement had
begun to abate and that they were growing quieter,
he finally joined the group and faced Harry. He had
something to say after all, and he had only been
waiting until he was certain he would be heard.
"What was a Russian submarine doing in this part
of the world?"

"This part of the world?"

"You know what I mean."

"I'm afraid I don't, George,"

"It doesn't belong here."

"But these are international waters."

"They're a long way from Russia."

"Not all that far, actually."

Lin's face was distorted by anger, and his voice
was strained. "But how did they learn about us?"

"From monitoring radio reports, I suppose."

"Exactly. Precisely," Lin said, as if he had
proved a point. He looked at Fischer and then at
Claude, searching for a supporter. "Radio reports.
Monitoring." He turned to Roger Breskin. "And
why would the Russians be monitoring communications in this part of the world?" When Breskin
shrugged, Lin said, "I'll tell you why. For the same

reason this Lieutenant Timoshenko speaks English so well: The *Pogodin* is on a surveillance mission. It's a goddamned spy ship, that's what it is."

"Most likely," Claude agreed, "but that's hardly a startling revelation, George. We may not like it much, but we all know how the world works."

"Of course it's a spy ship," Fischer said. "If it had been a nuclear-missile sub, one of their doomsday boats, they wouldn't even let us know they were in the area. They wouldn't allow one of those to break security. We're *lucky* it's a spy ship, actually, something they're willing to compromise."

Lin was clearly baffled by their lack of outrage, but he was determined to make them see the situation with the same degree of alarm that he himself obviously felt. "Listen to me, think about this: It isn't *just* a spy ship." His voice rose on the last few words. His hands were at his sides, opening and closing repeatedly, almost spastically. "It's carrying motorized rafts, for God's sake, and the equipment to rig a breeches buoy to a point on land. That means it puts spies ashore in other countries, saboteurs and maybe even assassins, probably puts them ashore in our own countries."

"Assassins and saboteurs may be stretching it," Fischer said.

"Not stretching it at all!" Lin responded ardently. His face was flushed, and his sense of urgency grew visibly by the moment, as if the greatest threat were not the deadly cold or the sixty time bombs buried in the ice, but the Russians who proposed to rescue them. "Assassins and saboteurs. I'm sure of it, positive. These communist bastards—"

"They aren't communists any more," Roger noted.

"Their new government's riddled with the old criminals, the same old criminals, and when the moment's right, they'll be back. You'd better believe it. And they're barbarians, they're capable of anything. *Anything.*"

Pete Johnson rolled his eyes for Harry's benefit. "Listen, George, I'm sure the U.S. does some of the same things. It's a fact of life, standard international relations. The Russians aren't the only people who spy on their neighbors."

Trembling visibly, Lin said, "It's *more* than spying. Anyway, goddammit, that's no reason for us to legitimize the *Ilya Pogodin!*" He slammed his left fist into the open palm of his right hand.

Brian winced at the gesture and glanced at Harry.

Harry wondered if that might be the same hand—and the same violent temper—that had turned against Brian out on the ice.

Gently putting one hand on Lin's shoulder, Rita said, "George, calm down. What do you mean, 'legitimize' it? You aren't making a great deal of sense."

Whipping around to face her as though she had

threatened him, Lin said, "Don't you realize why these Russians want to rescue us? They aren't really concerned about whether we live or die. We don't matter to them. We're *nothing* to them. They aren't acting out of any humanitarian principles. It's strictly the propaganda value of the situation that interests them. They're going to use us. At best, we're pawns to them. They're going to use us to generate pro-Russian sentiment in the world press."

"That's certainly true," Harry said.

Lin turned to him again, hopeful of making a convert. "Of course it's true."

"At least in part."

"No, Harry. Not partly true. It's *entirely* true. Entirely. And we can't let them get away with it!"

"We're in no position to reject them," Harry said.

"Unless we stay here and die," Roger Breskin said. His deep voice, although devoid of emotion, gave his simple statement the quality of an ominous prophecy.

Pete's patience with Lin had been exhausted. "Is that what you want, George? Have you taken leave of your senses altogether? Do you want to stay here and die?"

Lin was flustered. He shook his head: no. "But you've got to see—"

"No."

"Don't you understand . . . ?"

"What?"

"What they are, what they want?" the Chinese said with such misery that Harry felt sorry for him. "They're . . . they're . . ."

Pete pressed his point. "Do you want to stay here and die? That's the only question that matters. That's the bottom line. Do you want to die?"

Lin fidgeted, searched their faces for a sign of support, and then looked down at the floor. "No. Of course not. Nobody wants to die. I'm just . . . just . . . Sorry. Excuse me." He walked to the far end of the cave and began to pace as he had done earlier, when he had been embarrassed about the way he had treated Brian.

Leaning close to Rita, Harry whispered, "Why don't you go talk to him?"

"Sure," she said with a big, theatrical smile. "We can discuss the international communist conspiracy."

"Ho ho."

"He's such a charming conversationalist."

"You know what I'm asking," Harry murmured conspiratorially. "Lift his spirits."

"I don't think I'm strong enough."

"If you aren't, then nobody is. Go on, tell him about your own fear, how you deal with it every single day. None of them know how difficult it is for you to be here, what a challenge it is for you every day. Hearing about that might give George the courage to face up to what *he* fears."

"If he's the one who clubbed Brian, I don't *care* what he fears."

"We don't know it was George."

"He's a better bet than the Loch Ness monster."

"Please, Rita."

She sighed, relented, and went to have a word with George Lin at the back of the ice cave.

Harry joined the others, nearer the entrance.

Roger Breskin had taken his watch from a zippered pocket in his parka. "Five after nine."

"Less than three hours," Claude said.

"Can it be done in three hours?" Brian wondered. "Can they get to us and take us off the ice in just three hours?"

"If they can't," Harry said, trying to lighten the moment, "I'm going to be really pissed."

9:10

Emil Zhukov climbed onto the bridge with a Thermos of hot tea and three aluminum mugs. "Have they assembled the gun?"

"A few minutes yet," Gorov said. He held one of the mugs while the first officer poured the tea.

Suddenly the night smelled of herbs and lemons and honey, and Nikita Gorov's mouth watered. Then the wind caught the fragrant steam rising from the mug, crystallized it, and carried it away from him. He sipped the brew and smiled. Already the tea was growing cool, but sufficient heat remained to put an end to the chills that had been racing along his spine.

Below the bridge, on the forward section of the main deck, framed by four emergency lights, three crewmen were busy assembling the special gun that would be used to shoot a messenger line to the iceberg. All three wore black, insulated wet suits, with heat packs at their waists, and their faces were covered by rubber hoods and large diving masks. Each man was secured by a steel-link tether that was fixed to the forward escape hatch; the tethers were long enough to allow them to work freely, but not long enough to let them fall overboard.

Although it was not a weapon, the gun looked so wicked that an uninformed observer might have expected it to fire nuclear mortar rounds. Nearly as tall as any of the men assembling it, weighing three hundred fifty pounds, it consisted of just three primary components that were now pretty much locked together. The square base contained the motor that operated the pulleys for the breeches buoy, and it was fastened to four small steel rings recessed in the deck. The rings had been a feature of the boat ever since the *Pogodin* had begun putting special-forces agents ashore in foreign lands. The blocklike middle component of the gun fitted into a swivel mount on the base and contained the firing mechanism, the gunman's handgrips, and a large drum of messenger line. The final piece was a four-foot-long barrel with a five-inch-diameter bore, which the three-man team had just inserted in its socket; an any-light scope was mounted at the base of the barrel. The device appeared capable of blowing a hole through a tank; on a battlefield, however, it would have been every bit as ineffective as a child's peashooter.

At times the runneled deck was nearly dry, but that wasn't the typical condition, and it lasted only briefly. Every time the bow dipped and a wave broke against the hull, the forward end of the boat was awash. Brightened by chunks of ice and cottony collars of frozen foam, the frigid dark sea rushed onto the deck, sloshed between the crewmen's legs, battered their thighs, and surged to their waists before gushing away. If the *Ilya Pogodin* had been on the windward side of the iceberg, the towering waves of the storm would have overwhelmed the men and knocked them about mercilessly. In the sheltered lee, however, as long as they anticipated and prepared for each downward arc of the bow, they were able to stay on their feet and perform their tasks even when the sea swirled around them; and in those moments when the deck was free of water, they worked at top speed and made up for lost time.

The tallest of the three crewmen stepped away from the gun, glanced up at the bridge, and signaled the captain that they were ready to begin.

Gorov threw out the last of his tea. He gave the mug to Zhukov. "Alert the control room."

If his risky plan to use the breeches buoy was to have any chance to succeed, the submarine had to match speeds perfectly with the iceberg. If the boat outpaced the ice, or if the ice surged ahead by even a fraction of a knot, the messenger line might pull taut, stretch, and snap faster than they could reel out new slack.

Gorov glanced at his watch. A quarter past nine. The minutes were slipping away too quickly.

One of the men on the forward deck uncapped the muzzle of the gun, which had been sealed to keep out moisture. Another man loaded a shell into the breech at the bottom.

The projectile, which would tow the messenger line, was simple in design. It looked rather like a fireworks rocket: two feet long, nearly five inches in diameter. Trailing the nylon-and-wire line, it would strike the face of the cliff, explode on impact, and fire a four-inch bolt into the ice.

That bolt, to which the messenger line was joined, could slam eight to twelve inches into a solid rockface, essentially fusing with the natural material around it, extruding reverse-hooked pins to prevent extraction. Welded to granite or limestone—or even to shale if the rock strata were tight enough—the bolt was a reliable anchor. Certain that the far point was securely fixed, a man could travel to shore on the messenger line if necessary, climbing hand over hand. Depending on the angle of approach, he could even convey himself in a simple sling suspended from a pair of small Teflon-coated steel wheels with deep concavities in which the line traveled, propelled by a vertical hand crank. Either way, he could take with him the heavy-duty pulley and a stronger line to rig an even more reliable system from the other end.

Unfortunately, Gorov thought, they were not dealing with granite or limestone or hard shale. A large element of the unknown had been introduced. The anchor might not penetrate the ice properly or fuse with it as it did with most varieties of stone.

One of the crewmen took hold of the handgrips, in one of which the trigger was seated. With the help of the other two men, he got a range fix and a wind reading. The target area was thirty feet above the water line. Semichastny had marked it with the floodlight. Compensating for the wind, the shooter aimed to the left of the mark.

Zhukov put up two flares.

Gorov lifted his night glasses. He focused on the circle of light on the face of the cliff.

A heavy *whump!* was audible above the wind.

Even before the sound of the shot faded, the rocket exploded against the iceberg fifty yards away.

"Direct hit!" Zhukov said.

With cannonlike volleys of sound, the cliff fractured. Cracks zigzagged outward in every direction from the tow rocket's point of impact. The ice shifted, rippled like jelly at first, then shattered as completely as a plate-glass window. A prodigious wall of ice—two hundred yards long, seventy or eighty feet high, and several feet thick—slid away from the side of the berg, collapsed violently into the sea, and sent shimmering fountains of dark water more than fifty feet into the air.

The messenger line went down with the ice.

Like a great amorphous, primordial beast, a twenty-foot-high tidal wave of displaced water surged across the fifty yards of open sea toward the port flank of the submarine, and there was no time to take evasive action. One of the three crewmen on the deck cried out as the small tsunami crashed across the main deck with enough power to rock the *Pogodin* to starboard. With the messenger-line gun, all three vanished under that black tide. Cold brine exploded against the sail, and drenching geysers shot high into the night air, hung for a moment in defiance of gravity, and then collapsed across the bridge. Carried on the flood, hundreds of fragments of ice, some as large as a man's fist, rained down against the steel and pummeled Gorov, Zhukov, and Semichastny.

The water poured away through the bridge scuppers, and the boat wallowed back to port. A secondary displacement wave hit them with only a small fraction of the force of the first.

On the main deck, the three crewmen had been

knocked flat. If they hadn't been tethered, they would have been washed overboard and possibly lost.

As the crewmen struggled to their feet, Gorov turned his field glasses on the iceberg again.

"It's still too damned sheer."

The tremendous icefall had done little to change the vertical topography of the leeward flank of the berg. A two-hundred-yard-long indentation marked the collapse, but even that new feature was a sheer plane, uncannily smooth, unmarked by ledges or projections or wide fissures that might have been of use to a climber. The cliff dropped straight into the water, much as it had before the rocket was fired; there was still no shelf or sheltering niche where a motorized raft could put in and tie up.

Gorov lowered his night glasses. Turning again toward the three men on the forward main deck, he signaled them to dismantle the gun and get below.

Dispirited, Zhukov said, "We could edge closer, then send two men across on a raft. They could match speeds with the berg, ride close to it, somehow anchor themselves to it, and just let it tow them along. Then the raft itself might be able to serve as the platform for the climbers to—"

"No. Too unsteady," Gorov said.

"Or they could take explosives over in the raft and blast out a landing shelf and operations platform."

Gorov shook his head. "No. That would be an

extremely risky proposition. Like riding a bicycle alongside a speeding express train and trying to grab on for a free trip. The ice isn't moving as fast as an express train, of course. But there's the problem of the rough seas, the wind. No, I'm not sending anyone out on a suicide mission. The landing shelf must already be there when the rafts reach the ice."

"What now?"

Gorov wiped his goggles with the back of one ice-crusted glove. He studied the cliff through the binoculars. At last he said, "Tell Timoshenko to put through a call to the Edgeway group."

"Yes, sir. What should he say to them?"

"Find out where their cave is located. If it's near the leeward side . . . Well, this might not be necessary, but if it *is* near the leeward side, they ought to move out of there altogether, right now."

"Move?" Zhukov said.

"I'm going to see if I can create a landing shaft if I torpedo the base of the cliff."

"The rest of you go ahead," Harry insisted. "I've got to let Gunvald know what's happening here. As soon as I've talked to him, I'll bring out the radio."

"But surely Larsson's been monitoring every conversation you've had with the Russians," Franz said.

Harry nodded. "Probably. But if he hasn't been, he has a right to know about this."

"You've only got a few minutes," Rita said worriedly. She reached for his hand, as if she might pull him out of the cave with her, whether he wanted to go or not. But then she seemed to sense that he had another and better reason for calling Gunvald, a reason that he preferred to conceal from the others. Their eyes met, and understanding passed between them. She said, "A few minutes. You remember that. Don't you start chatting with him about old girlfriends."

Harry smiled. "I never had any."

"Just young ones, right?"

Claude said, "Harry, I really think it's foolish to—"

"Don't worry. I promise I'll be out of here long before the shooting starts. Now the rest of you get moving. Go, go."

The ice cave was neither along the leeward flank of the berg nor near the midpoint of its length, where the Russian radioman had said the torpedo would strike. Nevertheless, they had unanimously decided to retreat to the snowmobiles. The concussion from the torpedo would pass through the berg from one end to the other. And the hundreds of interlocking slabs of ice that formed the ceiling of the cave might succumb to the vibrations.

As soon as he was alone, Harry knelt in front of the radio and called Larsson.

"I read you, Harry." Gunvald's voice was distant, faint, and overlaid with static.

Harry said, "Have you been listening in to my conversations with the Russians?"

"What I could hear of them. This storm is beginning to generate a hell of a lot of interference, and you're drifting farther away from me by the minute."

"At least you've got a general idea of the situation here," Harry said. "I haven't time to chat about that. I'm calling to ask you to do something important for me. Something you may find morally repugnant."

As succinctly as he could, Harry told Gunvald Larsson about the attempt to kill Brian Dougherty and then quickly explained what he wanted done. Although shocked by the attack on Brian, the Swede appreciated the need for haste and didn't waste time asking for more details. "What you want me to do isn't especially pleasant," he agreed. "But under the circumstances it—"

Static blotted out the rest of the sentence.

Harry cursed, glanced at the entrance of the cave, turned to the microphone again, and said, "Better repeat that. I didn't read you."

Through crackling atmospherics: ". . . said under the circumstances . . . seems necessary."

"You'll do it, will you?"

"Yes. At once."

"How long will you need?"

"If I'm to be thorough ..." Gunvald faded out. Then in again: "... if I can expect that what I'm searching for will be hidden ... half an hour."

"Good enough. But hurry. Do it."

As Harry put down the microphone, Pete Johnson entered the cave. "Man, are you suicidal? Maybe I was wrong about you being a natural-born hero. Maybe you're just a natural-born masochist. Let's get the hell out of here before the roof falls in."

Unplugging the microphone and handing it to Pete, Harry said, "That wouldn't faze me. I'm a Bostonian, remember. Let the roof fall in. I couldn't care less."

"Maybe you aren't a masochist, either. Maybe you're just flat-out crazy."

Picking up the radio by the thick, crisscrossing leather straps atop the case, Harry said, "Only mad dogs and Englishmen go out in the midnight sun."

He didn't mention what he had asked Gunvald to do, because he had decided to take Pete's advice to heart. He wasn't going to trust anyone. Except himself. And Rita. And Brian Dougherty.

Stepping out of the cave into the wildly howling night, Harry discovered that the snow had at last given way entirely to an ice storm. The tiny spicules were harder than mere sleet, needle-sharp, glittering in the headlamps, coming along like great clouds of diamond dust, on a course nearly horizontal to the ground, hissing abrasively across every surface they encountered. They stung the exposed sections of Harry's face and began immediately to plate his storm suit with transparent armor.

The supply shed at Edgeway Station was a pair of joined Nissen huts, in which the expedition stored tools, spare parts, any equipment that wasn't in use, comestibles, and the other provisions. Just inside the door, Gunvald stripped out of his heavy coat and hung it on a wooden rack near one of the electric heaters. The coat was sheathed in ice, and water began to stream from it by the time he had taken off his outer boots.

Although the trip from the communications shack to the supply shed was a short one, he had been chilled as he'd shuffled through deep drifts of snow and prickling clouds of wind-driven ice spicules. Now he reveled in the blessed warmth.

As he walked to the back of the long hut in his felt boots, he didn't make a sound. He had an unpleasant but unshakable image of himself: a thief in a strange house, prowling.

The rear half of the supply shed lay in velvety darkness. The only light was the small bulb at the door, where he had come inside. For a moment he had the eerie notion that someone was waiting for him in the shadows.

He was alone, of course. His uneasiness arose

from guilt. He didn't like having to do what he was there to do, and he felt as if he deserved to be caught in the act.

Reaching overhead in the blackness, he located the light chain and tugged it. A naked hundred-watt bulb blinked on, shedding cold white light. When he let go of the chain, the bulb swung back and forth on its cord, and the supply shed was filled with leaping shadows.

Along the back wall, nine metal lockers stood like narrow, upright caskets. A name was stenciled on the gray door of each, white letters above the set of three narrow ventilation slits: H. CARPENTER, R. CARPENTER, JOHNSON, JOBERT, and so forth.

Gunvald went to the tool rack and took down a heavy hammer and an iron crowbar. He was going to have to force open five of those lockers. He intended to breach them one after the other, as quickly as possible, before he had any second thoughts that might deter him.

Previous expeditions onto the icecap had learned that every man needed a private space, no matter how small, even a few cubic feet, that he could regard as his and his alone, where he could keep personal belongings and where inadvertent trespass wasn't possible. In the cramped environment of an Arctic research station, especially in one established with minimum funding in an age of tight money and especially during particularly extended tours of duty, the average person's natural prefer-

260 * Dean Koontz

ence for privacy could rapidly degenerate into a craving for it, a debilitating obsession.

There were no private quarters at Edgeway Station, no bedrooms where one could sleep alone. Most huts housed two, in addition to various pieces of equipment. And the vast, empty land beyond the camp offered no refuge for anyone in need of solitude. If one valued his life, he simply didn't go out there alone, not ever.

Often, the only way to have solitude and actually ensure it for a few minutes was to visit one of the two heated toilet stalls that were attached to the supply shed. But it wasn't practical to cache personal effects in the toilet.

After all, everyone had at least a handful of items that he preferred to keep private: love letters, photographs, mementos, a personal journal, whatever. Nothing shameful was likely to be hidden in the lockers, nothing that would shock Gunvald or embarrass its owner; scientists like themselves, perhaps excessively rational and all but compulsively dedicated to their work, were a bland lot, not the sort to have terrible dark secrets to conceal. The purpose of the lockers was merely to maintain a totally personal space as a way to preserve each person's necessary sense of identity in a claustrophobic and communal environment where, in time, it was easy to feel absorbed into a group identity and thereby become psychologically disassociated and quietly depressed.

Stashing one's most personal belongings under the bed was an unsatisfactory solution, even if it was understood that the space beneath a mattress was sacrosanct. This was not to say that members of any expedition automatically distrusted one another. Trust had nothing to do with it. The need for a secure private space was a deep and perhaps even irrational psychological need, and only those locked metal cabinets could satisfy it.

Gunvald used the hammer to smash combination dials from five of the lockers, one after the other. The shattered parts clattered across the floor, pinged off the walls, and the supply shed sounded like a busy foundry.

If a psychopathic killer was a member of the Edgeway expedition, if one of the apparent lambs of science was a wolf in disguise, and if evidence existed to identify that man, then the lockers were the logical—the sole—place to look. Harry had been certain of that. Reluctantly, Gunvald agreed with him. It seemed reasonable to suppose that in his personal effects, even a sociopath who could easily pass for normal might possess something revealingly different from the usual items that sane men treasured and carried with them to the top of the world. Something indicative of a bizarre fixation or obsession. Perhaps something horrifying. Something unexpected and so unusual that it would say at once, *This belongs to a dangerously disturbed person.*

Wedging the hook of the crowbar into the round hole where the combination dial had been, Gunvald pulled backward with all his might and tore the lock from the first locker. The metal squealed and bent, and the door popped open. He didn't pause to look inside but quickly proceeded to wrench open the other four: *bang, bang, bang, bang!* Done.

He threw the crowbar aside.

His hands were sweating. He wiped them on his insulated vest and then on his quilted trousers.

After he had taken half a minute to catch his breath, he picked up a wooden crate full of freeze-dried food from the large stacks of supplies along the right-hand wall. He put the crate in front of the first locker and sat on it.

He reached to a zippered vest pocket for his pipe, but decided against it. He touched the bowl, but his fingers twitched, and he withdrew his hand. The pipe relaxed him. It had pleasant associations. And this search definitely was not a high point of pleasure in his life. If he used the pipe, if he puffed away on it while he poked through the contents of his friends' lockers, then . . . Well, he had a hunch that he would never be able to enjoy a good smoke again.

All right then. Where should he start?

Roger Breskin.

Franz Fischer.

George Lin.

Claude Jobert.

Pete Johnson.

Those were the five suspects. All were good men, as far as Gunvald was aware, although some were friendlier and easier to get to know than others. They were smarter and more well-balanced than the average person on the street; they *had* to be so, in order to have successful research careers in the Arctic or Antarctic, where the arduousness of the job and the unusual pressures quickly eliminated those who weren't self-reliant and exceptionally stable. None was a likely candidate for the tag "psychopathic killer," not even George Lin, who had revealed aberrant behavior only on this expedition and only recently, after having participated in many other projects on the ice during a long and admirable career.

He decided to begin with Roger Breskin because Roger's locker was the first in line. All the shelves were bare except the top one, on which was a cardboard box. Gunvald lifted the box out and put it between his feet.

As he had expected, the Canadian traveled light. The box contained only four items. A laminated eight-by-ten color photograph of Roger's mother: a strong-jawed woman with a winning smile, curly gray hair, and black-rimmed glasses. One silver brush-and-comb set: tarnished. A rosary. And a scrapbook filled with photographs and newspaper clippings, all concerned with Breskin's career as an amateur weight lifter.

Gunvald left everything on the floor and moved the wooden crate two feet to the left. He sat in front of Fischer's locker.

The submarine was submerged again, holding steady just below the surface, at its highest periscope depth. It was lying in wait along the iceberg's projected course.

On the conning-tower platform in the control room, Nikita Gorov stood at the periscope, his arms draped over the horizontal "ears" at the base of it. Even though the top of the scope was eight or nine feet above sea level, the storm waves exploded against it and washed over it, obscuring his view from time to time. When the upper window was out of the water, however, the night sea was revealed, dimly lighted by four drifting, dying flares.

The iceberg had already begun to cross their bow, three hundred yards north of their position. That gleaming white mountain was starkly silhouetted against the black night and sea.

Zhukov stood next to the captain. He was wearing headphones and listening on an open line that connected him to the petty officer in the forward torpedo room. He said, "Number one tube ready."

To Gorov's right, a young seaman was monitoring a backup safety board full of green and red lights that represented equipment and hatches in the torpedo room. When Zhukov, relaying the torpedo-room report, said that the breach door was secure, the seaman at the backup board confirmed: "Green and check."

"Tube flooded."

From the backup board: "Flood indicated."

"Muzzle door open."

"Red and check."

"Tube shutters open."

"Red and check."

The *Ilya Pogodin* was not primarily a warship, but an information gatherer. It didn't carry nuclear missiles. However, the Russian Naval Ministry had planned that every submarine should be prepared to bring the battle to the enemy in the event of a non-nuclear war. Therefore, the boat was carrying twelve electric torpedoes. Weighing over a ton and a half, packed with seven hundred pounds of high explosives, each of those steel sharks had huge destructive potential. The *Ilya Pogodin* was not primarily a warship, but if so ordered, it could have sunk a considerable tonnage of enemy ordnance.

"Number one tube ready," Zhukov said again as the officer in the torpedo room repeated that announcement over the headset.

"Number one tube ready," said the enunciator.

Nikita Gorov realized for the first time that the process of readying and launching a torpedo had a ritualistic quality that was oddly similar to a religious service. Perhaps because worship and war

266 · Dean Koontz

both dealt in different ways with the subject of death.

At the penultimate moment of the litany, the control room behind him fell into silence, except for the soft hum of machinery and the electronic muttering of computers.

After a protracted and almost reverent silence, Nikita Gorov said, "Match bearings . . . and . . . *shoot!*"

"Fire one!" Zhukov said.

The young seaman glanced at his fire-control panel as the torpedo was let go. "One gone."

Gorov squinted through the eyepiece of the periscope, tense and expectant.

The torpedo had been programmed to seek a depth of fifteen feet. It would strike the cliff exactly that far below the water line. With luck, the configuration of the ice after the explosion would be more amenable than it was now to the landing of a couple of rafts and the establishment of a base platform for the climbers.

The torpedo hit its mark.

Gorov said, "Strike!"

The black ocean swelled and leaped at the base of the cliff, and for an instant the water was full of fiery yellow light, as if sea serpents with radiant eyes were surfacing.

Echoes of the concussion vibrated through the submarine's outer hull. Gorov felt the deck plates *thrum.*

The bottom of the white cliff began to dissolve. A house-size chunk of the brittle palisade tumbled into the water and was followed by an avalanche of broken ice.

Gorov winced. He knew that the explosives were not powerful enough to do major damage to the iceberg, let alone blast it to pieces. In fact, the target was so enormous that the torpedo could do little more than take a chip out of it. But for a few seconds, there was an illusion of utter destruction.

The petty officer in the forward torpedo room told Zhukov that the breach door was shut, and the first officer passed the word to the technicians.

"Green and check," one of them confirmed.

Lifting the headset from one ear, Zhukov said, "How's it look out there, sir?"

Keeping his eye to the periscope, Gorov said, "Not much better than it did."

"No landing shelf?"

"Not really. But the ice is still falling."

Zhukov paused, listening to the petty officer at the other end of the line. "Muzzle door shut."

"Green and check."

"Blowing number one tube."

Gorov wasn't listening closely to the series of safety checks, because his full attention was riveted on the iceberg. Something was wrong. The floating mountain had begun to act strangely. Or was it his imagination? He squinted, trying to get a better view of the ice behemoth between the high waves, which still continued to wash rhythmically over the upper window of the periscope. The target seemed not to be advancing eastward any longer. Indeed, he thought the "bow" of it was even beginning to swing around to the south. Ever so slightly toward the south. No. Absurd. Couldn't happen. He closed his eyes and told himself that he was seeing things. But when he looked again, he was even more certain that—

The radar technician said, "Target's changing course!"

"It can't be," Zhukov said, startled. "Not all that quickly. It doesn't have any power of its own."

"Nevertheless, it's changing," Gorov said.

"Not because of the torpedo. Just one torpedo— even *all* our torpedoes—couldn't have such a profound effect on an object that large."

"No. Something else is at work here," Gorov said worriedly. The captain turned away from the periscope. From the ceiling, he pulled down a microphone on a steel-spring neck and spoke both to the control room around him and to the sonar room, which was the next compartment forward in the boat. "I want an all-systems analysis of the lower fathoms to a depth of seven hundred feet."

The voice that issued from the overhead squawk box was crisp and efficient. "Commencing full scan, sir."

Gorov put his eye to the periscope again.

The purpose of the scan was to look for a major ocean current that was strong enough to affect an object as large as the iceberg. Through the use of limited-range sonar, thermal-analysis sensors, sophisticated listening devices, and other marine-survey equipment, the *Ilya Pogodin*'s technicians were able to plot the movements of both warm- and cold-blooded forms of sea life beneath and to all sides of the boat. Schools of small fish and millions upon millions of krill, shrimplike creatures upon which many of the larger fish fed, were swept along by the more powerful currents or lived in them by choice, especially if those oceanic highways were warmer than the surrounding water. If masses of fish and krill—as well as thick strata of plankton—were found to be moving in the same direction, and if several other factors could be correlated with the movement, they could identify a major current, lower a current meter, and get a reasonable indication of the water's velocity.

Two minutes after Gorov had ordered the scan, the squawk box crackled again. "Strong current detected, traveling due south, beginning at a depth of three hundred forty feet."

Gorov looked away from the scope and pulled down the overhead microphone again. "How deep does it run below three forty?"

"Can't tell, sir. It's choked with sea life. Probing it is like trying to see through a wall. We *have* gotten readings as deep as six hundred sixty feet, but that's not the bottom of it."

"How fast is it moving?"

"Approximately nine knots, sir."

Gorov blanched. "Repeat."

"Nine knots."

"Impossible!"

"Have mercy," Zhukov said.

Gorov released the microphone, which sprang up out of the way, and with a new sense of urgency, he returned to the periscope. They were in the path of a juggernaut. The massive island of ice had been swinging slowly, ponderously into the new current, but now the full force of the fast-moving water was squarely behind it. The berg was still turning, bringing its "bow" around, but it was mostly sideways to the submarine and would remain like that for several minutes yet.

"Target closing," the radar operator said. "Five hundred yards!" He read off the bearing that he had taken.

Before Gorov could reply, the boat was suddenly shaken as if a giant hand had taken hold of it. Zhukov fell. Papers slid off the chart table. The event lasted only two or three seconds, but everyone was rattled.

"What the hell?" Zhukov asked, scrambling to his feet.

"Collision."

"With what?"

The berg was still five hundred yards away.

"Probably a small floe of ice," Gorov said. He ordered damage reports from every part of the boat.

He knew that they hadn't collided with a large object, for if they had done so, they would already be sinking. The submarine's hull wasn't tempered, because it required a degree of flexibility to descend and ascend rapidly through realms of varying temperatures and pressures. Consequently, even a single ton of ice, if moving with sufficient velocity to have substantial impact energy, would cave in the hull as if crashing into a cardboard vessel. Whatever they had encountered was clearly of limited size; nevertheless, it must have caused at least minor damage.

The sonar operator called out the position of the iceberg: "Four hundred fifty yards and closing!"

Gorov was in a bind. If he didn't take the boat down, they would collide with that mountain of ice. But if he dived before he knew what damage had been sustained, they might never be able to surface again. There simply wasn't enough time to bring the big boat around and flee either to the east or to the west; because the iceberg was rushing at them sideways, it stretched nearly two fifths of a mile both to port and starboard. The nine-knot, deepwater current, which began at a depth of three hundred forty feet, would not manage to turn the narrow profile of the berg toward them for another few minutes, and Gorov could not escape the full width of it before it reached them.

He snapped up the horizontal bar on the periscope and sent it into its hydraulic sleeve.

"Four hundred twenty yards and closing!" called the sonar operator.

"Dive!" Gorov said, even as the first damage reports were being made. *"Dive!"*

The diving klaxons blasted throughout the boat. Simultaneously the collision alarm wailed.

"We're going under the ice before it hits us," Gorov said.

Zhukov paled. "It must ride six hundred feet below the damn water line!"

Heart racing, mouth dry, Nikita Gorov said, "I know. I'm not certain we'll make it."

A fierce gale relentlessly hammered the Nissen huts. The rivets in the metal walls creaked. At the two small, triple-pane windows, ice spicules tapped like the fingernails of ten thousand dead men wanting in, and great rivers of subzero air moaned and keened as they rushed over the Quonset-shaped structures.

In the supply shed, Gunvald had discovered nothing of interest, though he had pored through the lockers belonging to Franz Fischer and George Lin. If either man had murderous tendencies or was in any way less than entirely stable and normal, nothing in his personal effects gave him away.

Gunvald moved on to Pete Johnson's locker.

Gorov knew that, among men of other nations, Russians were often perceived as dour, somber, determinedly gloomy people. Of course, in spite of a dismaying historical tendency to afflict themselves with brutal rulers and with tragically flawed ideologies, that stereotype was as empty of truth as any other. Russians laughed and partied and made love and got drunk and made fools of themselves, as did people everywhere. Most university students in the West had read Feodor Dostoyevsky and had tried to read Tolstoy, and it was from those few pieces of literature that they had formed their opinions of modern-day Russians. Yet, if there had been any foreigners in the control room of the *Ilya Pogodin* at that moment, they would have seen precisely the Russians that the stereotype described: somber-faced men, all frowning, all with deeply beetled brows, all weighed down with a profound respect for fate.

The damage reports had been made: No bulkheads had buckled; no water was entering the boat. The shock had been worse in the forward quarters than anywhere else, and it had been especially unsettling to the men in the torpedo room, two decks below the control room. Though the safety-light boards registered no immediate danger, the boat had apparently sustained some degree of exterior hull damage immediately aft and starboard of the bow, just past the diving planes, which did not themselves seem to have been affected.

If the outer skin had only been scraped, or if it had suffered only a minor dent, the boat would survive. However, if the hull had sustained even moderate compaction at any point—and worst of all, distortion that lay across welded seams—they might not live through a deep dive. The pressure on the submarine would not be uniformly resisted by the damaged areas, which could cause severe strain, and the boat might fail them, implode, and sink straight to the ocean floor.

The young diving officer's voice was loud but, in spite of the circumstances, not shaky. "Two hundred feet and descending."

The sonar operator reported: "The profile of the target is narrowing. She's continuing to come bow-around in the current."

"Two hundred fifty feet," said the diving officer.

They had to get down at least six hundred feet. Approximately a hundred feet of ice had been visible above the water line, and only one seventh of an iceberg's mass rode above the surface. To be safe, Gorov preferred to descend to seven hundred feet, though the speed of the target's approach reduced their chances of attaining even six hundred in time to avoid it.

The sonar operator called the distance: "Three hundred eighty yards and closing."

"If I weren't an atheist," Zhukov said, "I'd start praying."

No one laughed. At that moment none of them was an atheist—not even Emil Zhukov, in spite of what he'd said.

Even though everyone appeared cool and confident, Gorov could smell the fear in the control room. That was neither an exaggeration nor a theatrical conceit. Fear *did* have a pungent odor of its own: the tang of an unusually acrid sweat. Cold sweat. Virtually every man in the control chamber was perspiring. The place was redolent of fear.

"Three hundred twenty feet," the diving officer announced.

The sonar operator reported on the iceberg as well: "Three hundred fifty yards and closing fast."

"Three hundred sixty feet."

They were in a crash dive. Going down fast. A lot of strain on the hull.

Even as each man monitored the equipment at his station, he found time to glance repeatedly at the diving stand, which suddenly seemed to have become the very center of the room. The needle on the depth gauge was falling rapidly, far faster than they had ever seen it drop before.

Three hundred eighty feet.

Four hundred.

Four hundred twenty feet.

Everyone aboard knew that the boat had been designed for sudden and radical maneuvers, but that knowledge did not relieve anyone's tension. In recent years, as the country had struggled to rise out of the impoverishment in which decades of totalitarianism had left it, defense budgets had been trimmed—except in the nuclear-weapons development program—and systems maintenance had been scaled back, delayed, and in some instances postponed indefinitely. The *Pogodin* was not in the best shape of its life, an aging fleet submarine that *might* have years of faithful service in it—or that might be running with a stress crack serious enough to spell doom at any moment.

"Four hundred sixty feet," said the diving officer.

"Target at three hundred yards."

"Depth at four hundred eighty feet."

With both hands, Gorov gripped the command-pad railing tightly and resisted the pull of the inclined deck until his arms ached. His knuckles were as sharp and white as bare bones.

"Target at *two* hundred yards!"

Zhukov said, "It's picking up speed like it's going downhill."

"Five hundred twenty feet."

Their descent was accelerating, but not fast enough to please Gorov. They would need to get down at least another hundred and eighty feet until they were without a doubt safely under the iceberg—and perhaps, a great deal more than that.

"Five hundred forty feet."

"I've only been this deep twice before in ten years of service," Zhukov said.

"Something to write home about," Gorov said.

"Target at one hundred sixty yards. Closing fast!" called the sonar operator.

"Five hundred sixty feet," the diving officer said, although he must have known that everyone was watching the platter-size depth gauge.

One thousand feet was the official maximum operating depth for the *Ilya Pogodin*, because she wasn't one of the very-deep-running nuclear-war boats. Of course, if its outer skin had suffered a loss of integrity in the earlier collision, the thousand-foot figure was meaningless, and all bets were off. The starboard-bow damage might have rendered the boat vulnerable to implosion at considerably less depth than that stated in the official manual.

"Target at one hundred twenty yards and closing."

Gorov was contributing his share to the stench within the small chamber. His shirt was sweat-stained down the middle of the back and under the arms.

The diving officer's voice had softened almost to a whisper, yet it carried clearly through the control room. "Six hundred feet and descending."

Emil Zhukov's face was as gaunt as a death mask.

Still bracing himself against the railing, Gorov said, "We've got to risk another eighty feet or a hundred, anyway. We've got to be well under the ice."

Zhukov nodded.

"Six hundred twenty feet."

The sonar operator struggled to control his voice. Nevertheless, a faint note of distress colored his next report: "Target at sixty yards and closing fast. Dead ahead of the bow. It's going to hit us!"

"None of that!" Gorov said sharply. "We'll make it."

"Depth at six hundred seventy feet."

"Target at thirty yards."

"Six hundred eighty feet."

"Twenty yards."

"Six hundred ninety."

"Target lost," the sonar operator said, his voice rising half an octave on the last word.

They froze, waiting for the grinding impact that would smash the hull.

I've been a fool to jeopardize my own and seventy-nine other lives just to save one tenth that number, Gorov thought.

The technician who was monitoring the surface fathometer cried, "Ice overhead!"

They were under the berg.

"What's our clearance?" Gorov asked.

"Fifty feet."

No one cheered. They were still too tense for that. But they indulged in a modest, collective sigh of relief.

"We're under it," Zhukov said, amazed.

"Seven hundred feet and descending," the diving officer said worriedly.

"Blow negative to the mark," Gorov said. "Stabilize at seven hundred forty."

"We're safe," Zhukov said.

Gorov pulled on his neatly trimmed beard and found it wet with perspiration. "No. Not entirely safe. Not yet. No iceberg will have a flat bottom. There'll be scattered protrusions below six hundred feet, and we might even encounter one that drops all the way down to our running depth. Not safe until we're completely out from under."

A few minutes after the concussion from the torpedo had rumbled through the ice, Harry and Pete cautiously returned to the cave from the snowmobiles, in which the others were still taking shelter. They proceeded only as far as the entrance, where they stood with their backs to the furious wind.

They needed to take the radio, which Harry was carrying, to the deepest and quietest part of the cave in order to contact Lieutenant Timoshenko aboard the *Pogodin* and find out what would happen next. Outside, the wind was a beast of a thousand voices, all deafeningly loud, and even in the cabins of the sleds, the roaring-shrieking-whistling gale made it impossible to hear one's own voice, let alone comprehend what was being said by anyone on the radio.

With his flashlight beam, Pete worriedly probed the jumbled slabs in the ceiling.

"Looks okay!" Harry shouted, though his mouth was no more than an inch from the other man's head.

Pete looked at him, not sure what he'd said.

"Okay!" Harry bellowed, and he made a thumbs-up sign.

Pete nodded agreement.

They hesitated, however, because they didn't know if the Russian submarine was going to launch another torpedo.

If they reentered the cave with the radio and then the Russians fired on the ice again, the concussion might bring the ceiling down this time. They would be crushed or buried alive.

The malevolent wind at their backs was so powerful and fearfully cold, however, that Harry felt as though someone had dropped several ice cubes down his back, under his storm suit. He knew they dared not stand there much longer, paralyzed by indecision, so at last he stepped inside. Pete followed with the flashlight, and together they hurried toward the rear of the chamber.

The cacophony of the storm diminished drastically as they went deeper into the cave, though even against the back wall there was so much noise that they would need to turn the receiver volume all the way to its maximum setting.

The orange utility cord still trailed inside from one of the snowmobile batteries. Harry plugged in the radio. He preferred to power it from the sled as long as possible and save the batteries in the set, in case they were needed later.

As they worked, Pete said, "You've noticed the wind direction?"

They still had to raise their voices to hear each other, but it wasn't necessary to shout. Harry said, "Fifteen minutes ago it was blowing from another quarter of the compass."

"The iceberg changed direction again."

"What do you make of that?"

"Damned if I know."

"You're the demolitions expert. Could the torpedo have been powerful enough to push the whole berg temporarily off its previous course?"

Shaking his head emphatically, Pete said, "No way."

"I don't think so, either."

Suddenly Harry was desperately weary and oppressed by a sense of utter helplessness. It seemed as if Mother Nature herself had set out to get them. The odds against their survival were growing by the minute and would soon be insurmountable—if they weren't already. In spite of the

Vaseline that coated his face and the knitted snow mask that was usually so effective, in spite of layers of Gore-Tex and Thermolite insulation, in spite of having been able to shelter in the cave for part of the night and periodically in the comparative warmth of the heated snowmobile cabins, he was succumbing to the unyielding, merciless, thermometer-bursting cold. His joints ached. Even in gloves, his hands felt as cold as if he had been arranging things in a refrigerator for half an hour. And an unnerving numbness was gradually creeping into his feet. If the fuel tanks on the sleds ran dry, denying them periodic sessions in the fifty-degree air of the cabins, frostbite of the face was a real danger, and what little energy they still possessed would be sapped quickly, leaving them too exhausted to stay either on their feet or awake, unable to meet the Russians halfway.

But no matter how heavily weariness and depression weighed on him, he could not buckle, for he had Rita to think about. She was his responsibility, because she was not as comfortable on the ice as he was; she was frightened of it even in the best of times. Come what may, he was determined to be there when she needed him, till the last minute of her life. And because of her, he had something to live for: the reward of more years together, more laughter and love, which ought to be enough to sustain him no matter how fierce the storm became.

"The only other explanation," Harry said as he switched on the radio and turned up the volume, "is that maybe the iceberg was picked up by a new current, something a whole lot stronger that pulled it out of its previous course and got it moving due south."

"Is that going to make it easier or harder for the Russians to climb up here and get us?"

"Harder, I think. If the ice is heading south, and if the wind is coming pretty much from the north, then the only leeward area is at the bow. They can't put men onto the ice as it's rushing straight at them."

"And it's nearly ten o'clock."

"Exactly," Harry said.

"If they can't get us off in time . . . if we have to stay here through midnight, will we come out of this alive? Don't bullshit me now. What's your honest opinion?"

"I should ask you. You're the man who designed those bombs. You know better than I what damage they'll do."

Pete looked grim. "What I think is . . . the shock waves are going to smash up most of the ice we're standing on. There's a chance that five or six hundred feet of the berg will hold together, but not the entire length from the bow of it to the first bomb. And if only five or six hundred feet are left, do you know what's going to happen?"

Harry knew too well. "The iceberg will be five

hundred feet long and *seven* hundred feet from top to bottom."

"And it can't float that way."

"Not for a minute. The center of gravity will be all wrong. It'll roil over, seek a new attitude."

They stared at each other as the open radio frequency produced squeals and hisses that competed with the wind beyond the cave entrance.

At last Pete said, "If only we'd been able to dig out ten of the bombs."

"But we weren't." Harry picked up the microphone. "Let's see if the Russians have any good news."

Gunvald found nothing incriminating in the lockers that belonged to Pete Johnson and Claude Jobert.

Five suspects. No sinister discoveries. No clues.

He got up from the wooden crate and went to the far end of the room. At that distance from the violated lockers—although distance itself didn't make him any less guilty—he felt that he could fill and light his pipe. He needed the pipe to calm him and to help him think. Soon the air was filled with the rich aroma of cherry-flavored tobacco.

He closed his eyes and leaned against the wall and thought about the numerous items that he had taken from the lockers. At a glance he had seen nothing *outré* in those personal effects. But it was possible that the clues, if any existed, would be subtle. He might discover them only on reflection. Therefore, he carefully recalled each of the things that he had found in the lockers, and he held it before his mind's eye, searching for some anomaly that he might have overlooked when he'd had the real object in his hand.

Roger Breskin.

Franz Fischer.

George Lin.

Claude Jobert.

Pete Johnson.

Nothing.

If one of those men was mentally unbalanced, a potential killer, then he was damned clever. He had hidden his madness so well that no sign of it could be found even in his most personal, private effects.

Frustrated, Gunvald emptied his pipe into a sand-filled waste can, put the pipe in his vest pocket, and returned to the lockers. The floor was littered with the precious detritus of five lives. As he gathered up the articles and put them back where he had found them, his guilt gave way to shame at the violation of privacy that he had committed, even though it had been necessitated by the events of the day.

And then he saw the envelope. Ten by twelve inches. About one inch thick. At the very bottom of the locker, against the back wall.

In his haste, he had overlooked it, largely

because it was a shade of gray similar to that of the metal against which it stood and because it was in the lowest part of the locker, at foot level, tucked back at the rear of the twelve-inch-high space under the lowest shelf. Indeed, he was surprised that he'd noticed it even now. The instant he spotted the envelope, he was overcome by a vivid premonition that it contained the damaging evidence for which he had been searching.

It was stuck firmly to the locker wall. When he tore it free, he saw that six loops of electrician's tape had held it fast, so it had been placed there with considerable deliberation, in hope of keeping it a secret even if the locker was violated.

The flap was held shut only by a metal clasp, and Gunvald opened it. The envelope contained only a spiral-bound notebook with what appeared to be newspaper and magazine clippings interlarded among the pages.

Reluctantly but without hesitation, Gunvald opened the notebook and began to page through it. The contents hit him with tremendous force, shocked him as he had never imagined that he could be shocked. Hideous stuff. Page after page of it. He knew at once that the man who had compiled this collection, if not a raving maniac, was at least a seriously disturbed and dangerous individual.

He closed the book, yanked the chain to turn out the light at the back of the room, and hurriedly pulled on his coat and outer boots. Kicking through snowdrifts, head tucked down to protect his face from a savage wind filled with flaying specks of ice, he ran back to the telecommunications hut, frantic to let Harry know what he had found.

"Ice overhead. One hundred feet."

Gorov left the command pad and stood behind the technician who was reading the surface Fathometer.

"Ice overhead. One hundred twenty feet."

"How can it be receding?" Gorov frowned, reluctant to believe the proof provided by the very technology that he had always before trusted. "By now the iceberg's turned its narrow profile to us, so we can't have passed under even half its length. There's still a huge, long mountain hanging over us."

The technician frowned too. "I don't understand it, sir. But now it's up to a hundred and forty feet and still rising."

"A hundred and forty feet of clear water between us and the bottom of the iceberg?"

"Yes, sir."

The surface Fathometer was a sophisticated version of the echo sounder that had been used for decades to find the floor of the ocean beneath a submarine. It broadcast high-frequency sound waves upward in a tightly controlled spread, bounced an echo off the underside of the ice—if any actually lay overhead—and determined the distance between the top of the sail and the frozen ceiling of the sea. It was standard equipment on every ship that might possibly be called upon—on rare occasions, if ever—to pass under the icecap in order to fulfill its duties or to escape an enemy vessel.

"One hundred sixty feet, sir."

The stylus on the surface Fathometer wiggled back and forth on a continuous drum of graph paper. The black band that it drew was steadily growing wider.

"Ice overhead. One hundred eighty feet."

The ice continued to recede above them.

It made no sense.

The squawk box above the command pad hissed and crackled. The voice that issued from it was gruff by nature and metallic, as all voices were that passed through the intercom. The torpedo officer reported news that Nikita Gorov had hoped never to hear at *any* depth, let alone at seven hundred forty feet: "Captain, our forward bulkhead is sweating."

Everyone in the control room stiffened. Their attention had been riveted on the ice reports and on the sonar readings, because the greatest danger had seemed to be that they would ram into a long stalactite of ice hanging from the bottom of the berg. The torpedo officer's warning was an unnerving reminder that they had collided with an unknown mass of drift ice before initiating a crash dive and that they were more than seven hundred feet beneath the surface, where every square inch of the hull was under brutal pressure. Millions upon millions of tons of seawater lay between them and the world of sky and sun and open air that was their true home.

Pulling down an overhead microphone, Gorov said, "Captain to torpedo room. There's dry insulation behind that bulkhead."

The squawk box was now the center of interest, as the diving gauge had been a moment ago. "Yes, sir. But it's sweating just the same. The insulation behind it must be wet now."

Evidently they had sustained a dangerous amount of damage when they had collided with that floe ice. "Is there much water?"

"Just a sweat, sir. Just a film."

"Where did you find it?"

The torpedo officer said, "Along the weld between number four tube and number five tube."

"Any buckling?"

"No, sir."

"Watch it closely," Gorov said.

"I've got eyes for nothing else, sir."

Gorov let go of the microphone, and it sprang back up out of the way.

Zhukov was at the command pad. "We could change course, sir."

"No."

Gorov knew what his first officer was thinking. They were passing under the length of the iceberg, with half of it—at least two fifths of a mile—still ahead of them. To port and starboard, however, open water could be found in two or three hundred yards, for the width of the berg was substantially less than its length. Changing course seemed reasonable, but it would be a waste of effort.

Gorov said, "By the time we could bring the boat around and to port or starboard, we'd have passed under the iceberg's stern and would be in open water anyway. Hold tight, Lieutenant."

"All right, sir."

"Rudder amidships, and keep it that way unless this current begins to push us around."

The operator seated at the surface Fathometer announced, "Ice overhead. Two hundred fifty feet."

The mystery of the receding ice again.

They were not descending. And Gorov knew damned well that the iceberg above them was not magically levitating out of the sea. So why was the distance between them steadily widening?

"Should we take her up, sir?" Zhukov suggested. "A little closer to the ice. If we ascend even to just six hundred feet, that torpedo-room bulkhead might stop sweating. The pressure would be considerably less."

"Steady at seven hundred forty," Gorov said shortly.

He was more worried about his sweating crew than he was about the sweating bulkhead. They were good men, and he'd had many reasons to be proud of them during the time that they had served under him. They'd been in numerous tight spots before, and without exception they had remained calm and professional. On every previous occasion, however, they had needed nothing but nerve and skill to see them through. This time a big measure of good luck was needed as well. No amount of nerve and skill could save them if the hull cracked under the titanic pressure to which it was currently being subjected. Unable to rely solely on themselves, they were forced to trust also in the faceless engineers who had designed the boat and the shipyard workers who had built it. Perhaps that would not have been too much to ask if they had not been acutely aware that the country's troubled economy had led to a reduction in the frequency and extent of dry-dock maintenance of the vessel. *That* was enough to make them a bit crazy—and perhaps careless.

"We can't go up," Gorov insisted. "There's still all that ice above us. I don't know what's happening here, how the ice can be receding like this, but we'll be cautious until I understand the situation."

"Ice overhead. Two hundred eighty feet."

Gorov looked again at the surface-Fathometer graph.

"Three hundred feet, sir."

Abruptly the stylus stopped jiggling. It produced a straight, thin, black line down the center of the drum.

"Clear water!" the technician said with obvious astonishment. "*No* ice overhead."

"We're out from under?" Zhukov asked.

Gorov said, "Impossible. That's a monster berg, at least four fifths of a mile long. No more than half of it has passed over us. We can't—"

"Ice overhead again!" the surface-Fathometer operator called out. "Three hundred feet. Ice at three hundred feet and *falling* now."

Gorov watched the stylus closely. The channel of open water between the top of the *Pogodin*'s sail and the bottom of the iceberg narrowed steadily, rapidly.

Two hundred sixty feet. Two hundred twenty.

One hundred eighty. One forty. One hundred.

Eighty. Sixty.

Separation held at fifty feet for a few seconds but then began to fluctuate wildly: fifty feet, a hundred and fifty feet, fifty feet again, a hundred feet, eighty, fifty feet, two hundred feet, up and down, up and down, in utterly unpredictable peaks and troughs. Then it reached fifty feet of clearance once more, and at last the stylus began to wiggle less erratically.

"Holding steady," the surface-fathometer technician reported. "Fifty to sixty feet. Minor variations. Holding steady . . . still holding . . . holding . . ."

"Could the Fathometer have been malfunctioning back there?" Gorov asked.

The technician shook his head. "No, sir. I don't think so, sir. It seems fine now."

"Then do I understand what just happened? Did we pass under a *hole* in the middle of the iceberg?"

The technician kept a close watch on the graph drum, ready to call out if the ceiling of ice above them began to drop lower than the fifty-foot mark. "Yes. I think so. From every indication, a hole. Approximately in the middle."

"A funnel-shaped hole."

"Yes, sir. It began to register as an inverted dish. But when we were directly under, the upper two thirds of the cavity narrowed drastically."

With growing excitement, Gorov said, "And it went all the way to the top of the iceberg?"

"I don't know about that, sir. But it went up at least to sea level."

The surface Fathometer, of course, couldn't take readings farther up than the surface of the sea.

"A hole," Gorov said thoughtfully. "How in the name of God did it get there?"

No one had an answer.

Gorov shrugged. "Perhaps one of the Edgeway people will know. They've been studying the ice. The important thing is that it's *there*, however it came to be."

"Why is this hole so important?" Zhukov asked.

Gorov had a seed of an idea, the germ of an outrageously daring plan to rescue the Edgeway scientists. If the hole was—

"Clear water," the technician announced. "No ice overhead."

Emil Zhukov pressed a few keys on the command-pad console. He looked up at the computer screen to his right. "It checks. Taking into account the southward current and our forward speed, we should be entirely out from under. This time the berg's really gone."

"Clear water," the technician repeated.

Gorov glanced at his watch: 10:02. Less than two hours remained until the sixty explosive charges would shatter the iceberg. In that length of time, the crew of the *Pogodin* could not possibly mount a conventional rescue attempt with any hope of success. The unorthodox scheme that the captain had in mind might seem to some to border on outright lunacy, but it had the advantage of being a plan that could work within the limited time they had left.

Zhukov cleared his throat. No doubt with a vivid mental image of that sweating bulkhead in the torpedo room, the first officer was waiting for orders to take the boat up to a less dangerous depth.

Pulling down the steel-spring microphone, Gorov said, "Captain to torpedo room. How's it look there?"

From the overhead speaker: "Still sweating, sir. It's not any better, but it's not any worse, either."

"Keep watching. And stay calm." Gorov released the microphone and returned to the command pad. "Engines at half speed. Left full rudder."

Astonishment made Emil Zhukov's long face appear even longer. He opened his mouth to speak, but he couldn't make a sound. He swallowed hard. His second attempt was successful: "You mean we aren't going up?"

"Not this minute," Gorov said. "We've got to make another run under that behemoth. I want to have another look at the hole in the middle of it."

The volume on the shortwave radio was at its maximum setting, so the Russian communications officer aboard the *Pogodin* could be heard over the roar of the storm beast that prowled at the entrance to the cave and above the roof of interlocking slabs of ice. Hard shatters of static and electronic squeals of interference echoed off the ice walls, rather like the enormously amplified sound of fingernails being dragged across a blackboard.

The others had joined Harry and Pete in the ice cave to hear the astounding news firsthand. They were crowded together near the back wall.

When Lieutenant Timoshenko had described the hole and the large area of dramatically scalloped ice on the bottom of their floating prison, Harry had explained the probable cause of it. The iceberg had been broken off the cap by a tsunami, and the tsunami had been generated by a seabed earthquake almost directly beneath them. In this part of the world, in association with this chain of fractures, volcanic activity was *de rigueur*, as witness the violent Icelandic eruptions a few decades ago. And if ocean-floor volcanic activity had been associated with the recent event, enormous quantities of lava could have been discharged into the sea, flung upward with tremendous force. Spouts of white-hot lava could have bored that hole, and the millions of gallons of boiling water that it produced could easily have sculpted the troughs and peaks that marked the bottom of the iceberg just past the hole.

Although it originated from a surfaced submarine only a fraction of a mile away, Timoshenko's voice was peppered with static, but the transmission didn't break up. "As Captain Gorov sees it, there are three possibilities. First, the hole in the bottom of your berg might end in solid ice above the water line. Or second, it might lead into a cavern or to the bottom of a shallow crevasse. Or third, it might even continue for another hundred feet above sea level and open at the top of the iceberg. Does that analysis seem sound to you, Dr. Carpenter?"

"Yes," Harry said, impressed by the captain's reasoning. "And I think I know which of the three it is." He told Timoshenko about the crevasse that had opened midway in the iceberg's length when the gigantic seismic waves had passed under the edge of the winter field. "It didn't exist when we went out to position the explosives, but there it was, waiting for us, on our way back to the temporary camp. I nearly drove straight into it, lost my snowmobile."

"And the bottom of this crevasse is open all the way down to the sea?" Timoshenko asked.

"I don't know, but now I suspect it is. As near as I'm able to calculate, it must lie directly above the hole you've found on the underside. Even if the lava spout didn't punch through the entire hundred feet of ice above the water line, the heat needed to bore upward through all that underwater mass would at least have *cracked* the ice above the surface. And those cracks are sure to lead all the way down to the open water that your Fathometer operator detected."

"If the hole is at the bottom of the crevasse—I suppose we should call it a shaft or tunnel, rather than a hole—would you be willing to try to reach it by climbing down *into* the crevasse?" Timoshenko inquired.

The question seemed bizarre to Harry. He could not see the point of going down into that chasm where his snowmobile had vanished. "If we had to do it, I suppose we could improvise some climbing equipment. But what would be the point? I don't understand where you're going with this."

"That's how we're going to try to take you off the ice. Through that tunnel and out from underneath the berg."

In the cave behind Harry, the seven others responded to that suggestion with noisy disbelief.

He gestured at them to be quiet. To the Russian radioman, he said, "Down through this hole, this tunnel, and somehow into the submarine? But how?"

Timoshenko said, "In diving gear."

"We haven't any."

"Yes, but *we* have." Timoshenko explained how the gear would be gotten to them.

Harry was more impressed than ever with the Russians' ingenuity but still doubtful. "I've done some diving in the past. I'm not an expert at it, but I know a man can't dive that deep unless he's trained and has special equipment."

"We've got the special equipment," Timoshenko said. "I'm afraid you'll have to do without the special training." He spent the next five minutes outlining Captain Gorov's plan in some detail.

The scheme was brilliant, imaginative, daring, and well thought out. Harry wanted to meet this Captain Nikita Gorov, to see what kind of man could come up with such a stunningly clever idea. "It might work, but it's risky. And there's no guarantee that the tunnel from your end actually opens into the bottom of the crevasse at our end. Maybe we won't be able to find it."

"Perhaps," Timoshenko agreed. "But it's your best chance. In fact, it's your only chance. There's

just an hour and a half until those explosives detonate. We can't get rafts across to the iceberg, climb
up there, and bring you down as we'd planned. Not
in ninety minutes. The wind is coming from the
stern of the iceberg now, blowing hard along *both*
flanks. We'd have to land the rafts at the bow, and
that's impossible with the whole mountain of ice
rushing down on us at nine knots."

Harry knew that was true. He had said as much
to Pete just half an hour ago. "Lieutenant Timoshenko, I need to discuss this with my colleagues.
Give me a minute, please." Still hunkering before
the radio, he turned slightly to face the others and
said, "Well?"

Rita would have to control her phobia as never
before, because she would have to go down *inside*
the ice, be entirely surrounded by it. Yet she was
the first to speak in favor of the plan: "Let's not
waste time. Of course we'll do it. We can't just sit
here and wait to die."

Claude Jobert nodded. "We haven't much
choice."

"We've got one chance in ten thousand of getting through alive," Franz estimated. "But it's not
altogether hopeless."

"Teutonic gloom," Rita said, grinning.

In spite of himself, Fischer managed a smile.
"That's what you said when I was worried that an
earthquake might strike before we got back to base
camp."

"Count me in," Brian said.

Roger Breskin nodded. "And me."

Pete Johnson said, "I joined up for the adventure. Now I'm sure as hell getting more of it than I bargained for. If we ever get out of this mess, I swear I'll be content to spend my evenings at home with a good book."

Turning to Lin, Harry said, "Well, George?"

With his goggles up and his snow mask pulled down, Lin revealed his distress in every line and aspect of his face. "If we stayed here, if we didn't leave before midnight, isn't there a chance we'd come through the explosions on a piece of ice large enough to sustain us? I was under the impression that we were counting on that before this submarine showed up."

Harry put it bluntly: "If we've only one chance in ten thousand of living through the escape Captain Gorov has planned for us, then we've no better than one chance in a million of living through the explosions at midnight."

Lin was biting his lower lip so hard that Harry would not have been surprised to see blood trickle down his chin.

"George? Are you with us or not?"

Finally Lin nodded.

Harry picked up the microphone again. "Lieutenant Timoshenko?"

"I read you, Dr. Carpenter."

"We've decided that your captain's plan makes

sense if only because it's a necessity. We'll do it—if it can be done."

"It can be done, Doctor. We're convinced of it."

"We'll have to move quickly," Harry said. "There isn't any hope in hell of our reaching the crevasse much before eleven o'clock. That leaves just one hour for the rest of it."

Timoshenko said, "If we all keep in mind a vivid image of what's going to happen at midnight, we should be able to hustle through what needs to be done in the time we have. Good luck to all of you."

"And to you," Harry said.

• • •

When they were ready to leave the cave a few minutes later, Harry had still not heard from Gunvald regarding the contents of those five lockers. When he tried to raise Edgeway Station on the radio, he could get no response except squalls of static and the hollow hiss of dead air.

Apparently, they were going to have to descend into that deep crevasse and go down the tunnel beneath it without knowing which of them was likely to make another attempt on Brian Dougherty's life if the opportunity arose.

Even the most sophisticated telecommunications equipment was unable to cope with the interference that accompanied a storm in polar latitudes in the bitter heart of winter. Gunvald could no longer pick up the powerful transmissions emanating from the U.S. base at Thule. He tried every frequency band, but across all of them, the storm reigned. The only scraps of man-made sound that he detected were fragments of a program of big-band music that faded in and out on a five-second cycle. The speakers were choked with static: a wailing, screaming, screeching, hissing, crackling concert of chaos unaccompanied by even a single human voice.

He returned to the frequency where Harry was supposed to be awaiting his call, leaned toward the set, and held the microphone against his lips, as if he could *will* the connection to happen. "Harry, can you read me?"

Static.

For perhaps the fiftieth time, he read off his call numbers and their call numbers, raising his voice as if trying to shout above the interference.

No response. It wasn't a matter of hearing them or being heard through the static. They simply weren't receiving him at all.

He knew that he ought to give up.

He glanced at the spiral-bound notebook that lay open on the table beside him. Although he had looked at the same page a dozen times already, he shuddered.

He *couldn't* give up. They had to know the nature of the beast in their midst.

He called them again.

Static.

Five

❅

TUNNEL

10:45
DETONATION IN ONE HOUR
FIFTEEN MINUTES

Dressed in heavy winter gear and standing on the bridge of the *Pogodin,* Nikita Gorov methodically searched one third of the horizon with his night glasses, alert for drift ice other than the iceberg that was carrying the Edgeway group. That formidable white mountain lay directly ahead of the submarine, still driven by the deep current that originated three hundred forty feet below the surface and extended to about seven hundred eighty feet.

The storm-tossed sea, which churned on all sides of the boat, exhibited none of its familiar, rhythmic motion. It affected the ship in an unpredictable fashion, so Gorov couldn't prepare for its next attack. Without warning, the boat rolled to port so violently that everyone on the bridge was thrown sideways; the captain collided with Emil Zhukov and Semichastny. He disentangled himself from them and gripped an ice-sheathed section of the railing just as a wall of water burst across the sail and flooded the bridge.

As the ship righted itself, Zhukov shouted, "I'd rather be down at seven hundred feet!"

"Ah! You see?" Gorov shouted. "You didn't know when you were well off!"

"I'll never complain again."

The iceberg no longer provided a leeward flank in which the *Ilya Pogodin* could take shelter. The full force of the storm assaulted the berg from behind, and both of its long flanks were vulnerable to the pitiless wind. The boat was forced to endure on the open surface, pitching and heaving, rocking and falling and rising and wallowing as though it were a living creature in its death throes. Another of the monumental waves battered the starboard hull, roared up the side of the sail, and cast Niagaras of spray down the other side, repeatedly drenching everyone on the bridge. Most of the time, the submarine listed heavily to port on the back of a monstrous black swell that was simultaneously monotonous and terrifying. All the men on the bridge were jacketed in thick ice, as was the metalwork around them.

Where it was not covered by goggles or protected by his hood, Gorov's face was heavily smeared with lanolin. Although his post did not require him to confront the fiendish wind directly, his nose and cheeks had been cruelly bitten by the viciously cold air.

Emil Zhukov had been wearing a scarf over the bottom half of his face, and it had come undone. At his assigned post, he had to stare directly into the storm, and he could not be without some protection, because his skin would be peeled from his face by the spicules of ice that were like millions of needles on the hundred-mile-an-hour wind. He quickly twisted and squeezed the scarf in both hands, cracking the layer of ice that encrusted it, then hastily retied it over his mouth and nose. He resumed his watch on one third of the murky horizon, miserable but stoical.

Gorov lowered his night glasses and turned to look back and up at the two men who were working on top of the sail just aft of the bridge. They were illuminated by the red bridge bulb to some extent and by a portable arc light. Both cast eerie, twisted shadows like those of demons toiling diligently over the bleak machinery of Hell.

One of those crewmen was standing atop the sail, wedged between the two periscopes and the radar mast, which must have been either immeasurably more terrifying *or* more exhilarating than riding a wild horse in a Texas rodeo, depending on the man's tolerance for danger, even though a safety line encircled his waist and secured him to the telecommunications mast. He presented one of the strangest sights that Captain Gorov had ever seen. He was swathed in so many layers of waterproof clothes that he had difficulty moving freely, but in his dangerously exposed position, he needed every layer of protection to avoid freezing to death where he stood. Like a human lightning rod at the pinnacle of the submarine superstructure, he was a target for the hurricane-force winds, the ceaseless barrage of sleet, and the cold sea spray. *His* suit of ice was extremely thick and virtually without chink or rent. At his neck, shoulders, elbows, wrists, hips, and knees, the encasing ice was marred by well-delineated cracks and creases, but even at those joints, the cloth under the glistening storm coat was not visible. Otherwise, from head to foot, the poor devil glittered, sparkled, gleamed. He reminded Gorov of the cookie men, coated with sweet white icing, that were sometimes among the treats given to children in Moscow on New Year's Day.

The second seaman was standing on the short ladder that led from the bridge to the top of the sail. Tied fast to one of the rungs in order to free his hands for work, he was locking several water-tight aluminum cargo boxes to a length of titanium-alloy chain.

Satisfied that the job was nearly completed, Gorov returned to his post and raised the night glasses to his eyes.

10:56
DETONATION IN ONE HOUR
FOUR MINUTES

Because the rampaging wind was behind them, they were able to proceed to the crevasse in their snowmobiles. If they had been advancing into the teeth of the storm, they would have had to cope with near zero visibility, and in that case they would have done as well or better on foot, though they would have to have been tied together to prevent one of them from being bowled over by the wind and carried away. Driving *with* the wind, however, they could often see ten to fifteen yards ahead, although visibility was decreasing by the minute. Soon they would be in a full-fledged whiteout.

When they were in the vicinity of the chasm, Harry brought his sled to a full stop and, with a measure of reluctance, climbed out. Though he held tightly to the door handle, a hundred-mile-per-hour gust immediately knocked him to his knees. When the murderous velocity declined enough, he got up, though not without considerable effort, and hung on to the door, cursing the storm.

The other snowmobiles pulled up behind him. The last vehicle in the train was only thirty yards from him, but he could see nothing more than vague yellow aureoles where the headlights should have been. They were so dim that they might have been merely a trick of his bleary vision.

Daring to let go of the handle on the cabin door, hunching low to present the smallest possible profile to the wind, he hurried forward with his flashlight, scouting the ice, until he ascertained that the next hundred feet were safe. The air was bone-freezing, so cold that breathing it even through his snow mask hurt his throat and made his lungs ache. He scrambled back to the comparative warmth of his snowmobile and cautiously drove thirty yards before getting out to conduct further reconnaissance.

Again he had found the crevasse, although this time he had avoided nearly driving over the brink. The declivity was ten or twelve feet wide, narrowing toward the bottom, filled with more darkness than his flashlight could dispel.

As far as he could see through his frosted goggles—which were speckled with new ice the instant that he wiped them—the wall along which he would have to descend was pretty much a flat, unchallenging surface. He couldn't be entirely sure of what he was seeing: The angle at which he was able to look into the chasm, the curious way in which the deep ice refracted and reflected the light, the shadows that cavorted like demon dancers at the slightest movement of his flashlight, the wind-blown snow that spumed over the brink and then spiraled into the depths—all conspired to prevent him from getting a clear view of what lay below. Less than a hundred feet down was what appeared to be a floor or a wide ledge, which he thought he could reach without killing himself.

Harry turned his sled around and gingerly backed it to the edge of the chasm, a move that might reasonably have been judged suicidal; however, considering that barely sixty precious minutes remained to them, a certain degree of recklessness seemed not only justifiable but essential. Except for professional mannequins and British Prime Ministers, no one ever accomplished anything by standing still. That was a favorite maxim of Rita's, herself a British citizen, and Harry usually smiled when he thought of it. He wasn't smiling now. He was taking a calculated risk, with a greater likelihood of failure than success. The ice might collapse under him and tumble into the pit, as it had done earlier in the day.

Nevertheless, he was prepared to trust to luck and put his life in the hands of the gods. If there was justice in the universe, he was about to benefit from a change of fortune—or at least he was overdue for one.

By the time the others parked their snowmobiles, got out, and joined him near the brink of the crevasse, Harry had fixed two one-thousand-pound-test, ninety-strand nylon lines to the tow hitch of his sled. The first rope was an eighty-foot safety line that would bring him up short of the crevasse floor if he fell. He knotted it around his waist. The second line, the one that he would use to attempt a measured descent, was a hundred feet long, and he tossed the free end into the ravine.

Pete Johnson arrived at the brink and gave Harry his flashlight.

Harry had already snapped his own flashlight to the tool belt at his waist. It hung at his right hip, butt up and lens down. Now he clipped Pete's torch at his left hip. Twin beams of yellow light shone down his quilted pants legs.

Neither he nor Pete attempted to speak. The wind was shrieking like something that had crawled out of the bowels of Hell on Judgment Day. It was so loud that it was stupefying, louder than it had been earlier. They couldn't have heard each other even if they had screamed at the top of their lungs.

Harry stretched out on the ice, flat on his stomach, and took the climbing line in both hands.

Bending down, Pete patted him reassuringly on the shoulder. Then he slowly pushed Harry backward, over the ledge, into the crevasse.

Harry thought he had a firm grip on the line and was certain that he could control his descent, but he was mistaken. As though greased, the line slipped through his hands, and he dropped unchecked into the gap. Maybe it was the crust of ice on his gloves, maybe the fact that the leather was soft with Vaseline from all the times in recent days when he had unconsciously touched his grease-protected face. Whatever the reason, the rope was like a live eel in his hands, and he plunged into the abyss.

A wall of ice flashed past him, two or three inches from his face, flickering with the reflections of the two flashlight beams that preceded him. He clenched the rope as tightly as he could and also tried to pin it between his knees, but he was in what amounted to freefall.

In the whirl of blown snow and the peculiar prismatic refraction of the light in the deep ice, Harry had thought that the wall was a flat and relatively smooth surface, but he hadn't been entirely sure. Now the shorter safety line wouldn't save him if he encountered a sharp spike of ice that projected from the wall of the crevasse. If he dropped at high speed onto a jagged outcropping, it could rip even his heavy storm suit, tear him open from crotch to throat, impale him—

The rope burned through the surface slickness of his gloves, and abruptly he was able to stop himself, perhaps seventy feet below the brink of the crevasse. His percussive heart was pounding out a score for kettledrums, and every muscle in his body was knotted tighter than the safety line around his waist. Gasping for breath, he swung back and forth on the oscillating line, banging painfully—and then more gently—against the chasm wall while shadows and frantic flares of reflected light swarmed up from below like flocks of spirits escaping from Hades.

He dared not pause to settle his nerves. The timers on those packages of explosives were still ticking.

After easing down the rope another fifteen or twenty feet, he reached the bottom of the crevasse. It proved to be about ninety feet deep, which was fairly close to the estimate he had made when he had studied it from above.

He unclipped one of the flashlights from his tool

belt and began to search for the entrance to the tunnel that Lieutenant Timoshenko had described. He remembered from his first encounter with the chasm earlier in the day that it was forty-five or fifty feet long, ten or twelve feet wide at the midpoint but narrower at both ends. At the moment he did not have a view of the entire floor of the crevasse. When part of one wall had collapsed under his snowmobile, it had tumbled to the bottom; now it constituted a ten-foot-high divider that partitioned the chasm into two areas of roughly equal size. The badly charred wreckage of the sled was strewn over the top of that partition.

The section into which Harry had descended was a dead end. It contained no side passages, no deeper fissures large enough to allow him to descend farther, and no sign of a tunnel or open water.

Slipping, sliding, afraid that the jumbled slabs of ice would shift and catch him like a bug between two bricks, he climbed out of the first chamber. At the top of that sloped mound, he picked his way through the smashed and burned ruins of the snowmobile and through more slabs of ice, which shifted treacherously under his feet, then slid down the far side.

Beyond that partition, in the second half of the chasm, he found a way out, into deeper and more mysterious realms of ice. The right-hand wall offered no caves or fissures, but the left-hand wall didn't come all the way to the floor. It ended four feet above the bottom of the crevasse.

Harry dropped flat on his stomach and poked his flashlight into that low opening. The passageway was about thirty feet wide and no higher than four feet. It appeared to run straight and level for six or seven yards under the crevasse wall, sideways into the ice, before it curved sharply downward and out of sight.

Was it worth exploring?

He looked at his watch. 11:02.

Detonation in fifty-eight minutes.

Holding the light in front of him, Harry quickly wriggled into the horizontal passage. Although he was squirming on his stomach, the ceiling of the crawl space was so low in some places that it brushed the back of his head.

He wasn't claustrophobic, but he had a logical and healthy fear of being confined in an extremely cramped place ninety feet beneath the ice, in the Arctic wilderness, while surrounded by fifty-eight enormous packages of explosives that were ticking rapidly toward detonation. He was funny that way.

Nevertheless, he twisted and writhed and pulled himself forward with his elbows and his knees. When he'd gone twenty-five or thirty feet, he discovered that the passageway led into the bottom of what seemed to be a large open space, a hollow in the heart of the ice. He moved the flashlight to the left and right, but from his position, he was unable to get a clear idea of the cavern's true size. He slid out of the crawl space, stood up, and unclipped the second flashlight from his belt.

He was in a circular chamber one hundred feet in diameter, with dozens of fissures and culs-de-sac and passageways leading from it. Apparently the ceiling had been formed by a great upward rush of hot water and steam: a nearly perfect dome, too smooth to have been formed by any but the most exceptional phenomenon—such as freakish volcanic activity. That vault, marked only by a few small stalactites and spider-web cracks, was sixty feet high at the apex and curved to thirty feet where it met the walls. The floor descended toward the center of the room in seven progressive steps, two or three feet at a time, so the overall effect was of an amphitheater. At the nadir of the cavern, where the stage would have been, was a forty-foot-diameter pool of thrashing sea water.

The tunnel.

Hundreds of feet below, that wide tunnel opened into a hollow in the bottom of the iceberg, to the lightless world of the deep Arctic Ocean, where the *Ilya Pogodin* would be waiting for them.

Harry was as mesmerized by the dark pool as he would have been by a gate between this dimension and the next, by a door in the back of an old wardrobe that led to the enchanted land of Narnia, by any tornado that could spin a child and a dog to Oz.

"I'll be damned." His voice echoed back to him from the dome.

He was suddenly energized by hope.

In the back of his mind, he had harbored some doubt about the very existence of the tunnel. He had been inclined to think that the *Pogodin*'s surface Fathometer was malfunctioning. In those frigid seas, how could a long tunnel through solid ice remain open? Why hadn't it frozen over and closed up again? He hadn't asked the others if they could explain it to him. He hadn't wanted to worry them. They would pass the last hour of their lives more easily with hope than without it. Nonetheless, it had been a riddle for which he saw no solution.

Now he had the answer to that riddle. The water inside the tunnel continued to be affected by tremendous tidal forces in the sea far below. It was not stagnant or even calm. It welled up and fell away forcefully, rhythmically, surging as high as six or eight feet into the cavern, churning and sloshing, then draining back swiftly until it was level with the lip of the hole. Swelling and falling away, swelling and falling away ... The continuous movement prevented the opening from freezing over, and it inhibited the development of ice within the tunnel itself.

Of course, over an extended period of time, say two or three days, the tunnel would most likely grow steadily narrower. Gradually new ice would build up on the walls, regardless of the tidal motion, until the passageway became impassable or closed altogether.

But they didn't need the tunnel two or three days in the future. They needed it *now.*

Nature had been set firmly against them for the past twelve hours. Perhaps now she was working for them and ready to show them a little mercy.

Survival.

Paris. The Hôtel George V.

Moët & Chandon.

The Crazy Horse Saloon.

Rita . . .

Escape was possible. Just barely.

Harry clipped one of the flashlights to his belt. Holding the other light in front of him, he wriggled back through the crawl space between the domed cavern and the bottom of the open crevasse, eager to signal the others to descend and begin their tortuous escape from that prison of ice.

11:06
DETONATION IN FIFTY-FOUR MINUTES

At the command pad, Nikita Gorov monitored a series of five video display terminals arrayed on the ceiling. With little strain, he was simultaneously tracking the computations—some expressed in dimensional diagrams—provided by five different programs that were constantly collecting data regarding the boat's and the iceberg's positions, relative attitudes, and speeds.

"Clear water," said the technician who was operating the surface Fathometer. "No ice overhead."

Gorov had jockeyed the *Ilya Pogodin* under the quarter-mile-long, disc-shaped concavity in the bottom of the iceberg. The sail of the submarine was directly below the forty-foot-wide tunnel in the center of that concavity. Essentially, they were holding steady under an inverted funnel of ice and had to remain there for the duration of the operation.

"Speed matched to target," Zhukov said, repeating the report that had come over his headset from the maneuvering room.

One of the technicians along the left-hand wall said, "Speed matched and check."

"Rudder amidships," Gorov said.

"Rudder amidships, sir."

Unwilling to look away, Gorov scowled at the VDTs as though speaking to them rather than to the control-room team. "And keep a damned close watch on the drift compass."

"Clear water. No ice overhead."

An enormous structure of ice *was* overhead, of course, a huge island, but not *directly* above the surface-Fathometer package on the sail. They were sounding straight up into the forty-foot-wide tunnel at the top of the cavity, and the return signal showed clearance all the way to the surface, six hundred feet above, where the tunnel terminated in the bottom of the crevasse that Dr. Carpenter had described to Timoshenko.

The captain hesitated, reluctant to act until he was absolutely certain that they were properly positioned. He studied the five screens for another half minute. When he was satisfied that the speed of the boat was as closely coordinated with the iceberg's progress as was humanly possible, he pulled down a microphone and said, "Captain to communications center. Release the aerial at will, Lieutenant."

Timoshenko's voice grated from the overhead speaker. "Aerial deployed."

Topside, eight watertight, aluminum cargo boxes nestled among the masts and periscopes and snorkels on the *Pogodin*'s sail. They were held in place by multiple lengths of nylon cord, some of which had no doubt snapped, as expected, during the submarine's second descent to seven hundred feet.

When Timoshenko released the aerial, a helium balloon had been ejected in a swarm of bubbles from a pressurized tube on top of the sail. If it was functioning properly—as it always had before—the balloon was now rising rapidly in the dark sea, trailing the multicommunications wire behind it. As an intelligence-gathering boat, the *Ilya Pogodin* had deployed that aerial in the same fashion on thousands of occasions over the years.

The eight watertight boxes fastened atop the sail, however, were not a standard feature. They were secured to the communications wire with a fine-link titanium-alloy chain and spring locks. When the rising helium balloon was twenty feet above the sail, it should jerk the chain tight and draw the boxes upward, pulling hard enough against the remaining nylon restraining lines to cause them to slip their knots. Because the aluminum boxes were buoyant, they would then rise instantly from the sail and would not be a drag on the balloon.

In seconds, that helium-filled sphere was up to six hundred feet, then five hundred fifty feet, and then five hundred—well into the bowl of the inverted funnel above the boat. Four hundred feet and rising. The cargo boxes should be soaring upward in its wake. Three hundred fifty feet. The air bubbles from the pressure tube would fall behind the aerial and the boxes almost from the start, because the helium in the balloon expanded and rose much faster than did the oxygen in the bubbles. At approximately four hundred feet, the balloon would slide smoothly into the entrance to the long tunnel and continue to rise effortlessly, towing the boxes higher, higher, faster, faster. . . .

Bending over the graph of the surface Fathometer, the operator said, "I'm registering a fragmented obstruction in the tunnel."

"Not ice?" Gorov asked.

"No. The obstruction is rising."

"The boxes."

"Yes, sir."

"It's working," Zhukov said.

"Seems to be," the captain agreed.

"Now if the Edgeway people have located the other end of the tunnel—"

"We can get on with the hard part," Gorov finished for him.

Numbers and images blinked, blinked, blinked across the video display terminals.

At last the squawk box rattled, and Lieutenant Timoshenko said, "Aerial's up. Balloon's surfaced, Captain."

Gorov pulled down a microphone, cleared his throat, and said, "Override the automatic system, Lieutenant. Reel out an additional sixty feet of wire."

A moment later Timoshenko said, "Sixty additional feet of wire deployed, Captain."

Emil Zhukov wiped one hand down his saturnine face. "Now the long wait."

Gorov nodded. "Now the long wait."

11:10
DETONATION IN FIFTY MINUTES

The helium balloon broke through at the upper end of the tunnel and bobbled merrily on the swell. Although it was a flat blue-gray color, it looked, at least to Harry, like a bright and cheerful party balloon.

One by one, as Timoshenko reeled out additional wire at the far end, the eight watertight aluminum boxes burst through the surface. They bumped against one another with dull, almost inaudible thumps.

Harry was no longer alone in the dome-ceilinged cavern. Rita, Brian, Franz, Claude, and Roger had joined him. By now George Lin would have set foot on the bottom of the crevasse, and Pete Johnson would have started down the rope from the storm-lashed top of the iceberg.

Picking up the grappling hook that they had jerry-rigged from lengths of copper pipe and twenty feet of heavy-gauge wire, Harry said, "Come on. Let's get that stuff out of the water."

With Franz's and Roger's assistance, he managed to snare the chain and drag the boxes out of the pool. All three men got wet to the knees in the process, and within seconds the storm suits had frozen solid around their calves. Although their boots and clothing were waterproof, even the partial submersion sucked body heat from them. Cold, shuddering, they hurriedly popped open the aluminum cargo boxes and extracted the gear that had been sent up from the *Ilya Pogodin*.

Each box held a self-contained underwater breathing apparatus. But this was not ordinary scuba gear. It had been designed for use in especially deep and/or extremely cold water. Each suit came with a battery pack that was attached to a belt and worn at the waist. When this was plugged into both the skintight pants and the jacket, the lining provided heat in much the same fashion as did any standard electric blanket.

Harry laid out his own equipment on the ice shore, well back from the highest tide line of the constantly surging and ebbing water in the pool. A compressed-air tank came with each suit. The diving mask was large enough to cover most of the face from chin to forehead, eliminating the need for a separate mouthpiece; air was fed directly into the mask, so the diver could breathe through his nose.

Strictly speaking, they would not be breathing air. The tank contained, instead, an oxygen-helium mixture with several special additives prescribed to allow the user to tolerate great depths. On the radio earlier, explaining the equipment, Timoshenko had assured them that the mixture of gases in the tank would allow a deep dive with only "a reasonable degree of danger" to the respiratory and circulatory systems. Harry hadn't found the lieutenant's choice of words particularly reassuring. The thought of fifty-eight massive charges of plastic explosives, however, was sufficient inducement to put his full trust in Russian diving technology.

The suits were different in other, less important ways from standard scuba gear. The pants had feet in them, as if they were the bottoms of a pair of Dr. Denton pajamas; and the sleeves of the jacket ended in gloves. The hood covered all of the head and face that was not protected by the oversize mask, as if leaving one centimeter of skin exposed would result in instant, extremely violent death. The wet suits almost seemed to be snug versions of the loose and bulky pressure suits worn by astronauts in space.

George Lin had entered the cavern while they were unpacking the aluminum boxes. He studied the equipment with unconcealed suspicion. "Harry, there must be something else, some other way. There's got to be—"

"No," Harry said, without his usual diplomacy and patience. "This is it. This or nothing. There's no time for discussion any more, George. Just shut up and suit up."

Lin looked glum.

But he *didn't* look like a killer.

Harry glanced at the others, who were busy unpacking their own boxes of gear. *None* of them looked like a killer, yet one of them had clubbed Brian and, for whatever mad reason, might give them a lot of trouble when they were underwater and moving down through the long tunnel of ice.

Bringing up the rear, Pete Johnson squirmed laboriously out of the crawl space from the crevasse into the cavern, cursing the ice around him. He had been a tighter fit than any of the others. His broad shoulders had probably made it difficult for him to squeeze through the narrowest part of that passageway.

"Let's get dressed," Harry said. His voice had an odd, hollow quality as it resonated through that domed amphitheater of ice. "No time to waste."

They changed from their arctic gear into the scuba suits with an efficient haste born of acute discomfort and desperation. Harry, Franz, and Roger were already paying in pain for their knee-deep immersion in the pool: Their feet had been half numb, not a good sign, but the shock had temporarily restored too *much* feeling, and now their flesh from calves to toes prickled, ached, *burned*. The others had been spared that additional suffering, but they cursed and complained bitterly during their brief nakedness. No wind circulated through the cavern, but the air temperature was perhaps twenty or more degrees below zero. Therefore, they changed lower- and upper-body garments in stages to avoid being entirely unclothed at any one time and vulnerable to the killing cold: Outer boots, felt boots, socks, pants, and long underwear were removed first and were quickly replaced by the skintight, insulation-lined scuba pants; then they changed from coats, vests, sweaters, shirts, and undershirts into lined rubber jackets with snug rubber hoods.

Modesty was potentially as deadly as sloth. When Harry looked up after tucking himself into his scuba pants, he saw Rita's bare breasts as she struggled into her scuba jacket. Her flesh was blue-white and textured with enormous goose pimples.

Then she zipped up her jacket, caught Harry's eye, and winked.

He marveled at that wink. He could guess at the agonizing fear that must be afflicting her. She wasn't just *on* the ice any more. She was now *in* the ice. Entombed. Her terror must already be acute. Before they traveled down the tunnel to the submarine and safety—if, in fact, they were able to make that journey without perishing—she would no doubt relive the death of her parents more than once and recall every hideous detail of the ordeal that she had endured when she was six years old.

Pete was having trouble squeezing into his gear. He said, "Are all these Russians pygmies?"

Everyone laughed.

The joke hadn't been *that* funny. Such easy laughter was an indication of how tense they were. Harry sensed that panic was near the surface in all of them.

11:15
DETONATION IN FORTY-FIVE MINUTES

The overhead speaker brought the bad news that everyone in the control room had been expecting from the torpedo officer: "That bulkhead is sweating again, Captain."

Gorov turned away from the bank of video displays and pulled down a microphone. "Captain to torpedo room. Is it just a thin film, the same as last time?"

"Yes, sir. About the same."

"Keep an eye on it."

Emil Zhukov said, "Now that we know the lay of the ice above us, we could take her up to six hundred feet, up into the bowl of the funnel."

Gorov shook his head. "Right now we have only one thing to worry about—the sweat on that torpedo-room bulkhead. If we ascend to six hundred feet, we might still have that problem, and we'd also have to worry that the iceberg might suddenly enter a new current and be turned out of this one."

If they cautiously ascended a hundred feet or more into the concavity to relieve some of the tremendous pressure on the hull, the *Pogodin* would essentially be tucked into the berg as if it were an unborn baby nestled in the belly of its mother. Then if the berg began to move faster or slower than it was traveling at the moment, they might not realize what was happening until it was too late. They would collide with the deeper ice lying beyond their bow or with that to their stern.

"Steady as she goes," Gorov said.

The notebook had an evil power that Gunvald found horribly compelling. The contents shocked, disgusted, and sickened him, yet he couldn't resist looking at one more page, then one more, then another. He was like a wild animal that had come upon the guts and half-eaten flesh of one of its own kind that had fallen victim to a predator: He poked his nose into the ruins and sniffed eagerly, frightened but curious, ashamed of himself, but utterly and morbidly fascinated by the dreadful fate that could befall one of his own kind.

In a sense, the notebook was a diary of dementia, a week-by-week chronicle of a mind traveling from the borderlands of sanity into the nations of madness—although that was obviously not how its owner thought of it. To that deranged man, it might seem like a research project, a record from public sources of an imagined conspiracy against the United States and against democracy everywhere. Newspaper and magazine clippings had been arranged according to their dates of publication and affixed to the pages of the notebook with cellophane tape. In the margin alongside each clipping, the compiler had written his comments.

The earliest entries seemed to have been snipped from various amateurishly produced political magazines of limited circulation, published in the U.S. by both extreme left- and right-wing groups. This man found fuel for his burning paranoia at both ends of the spectrum. They were wildly overwritten scare stories of the most mindless sort, simple-minded and scandalous: The President was a dedicated hardline communist—yet, in another clipping, he was a

330 · Dean Koontz

dedicated hard-line fascist; the President was a closet homosexual with a taste for underage boys—or perhaps an insatiable satyr for whom ten bimbos a week were smuggled into the White House; the Pope was alternately a despicable right-wing zealot who was secretly supporting Third World dictators *and* a left-wing maniac intent on funding the destruction of democracy and confiscating all the wealth of the world for the benefit of the Jesuits. Here it was reported that the Rockefellers and the Mellons were the descendants of conspiratorially minded families who had been trying to rule the world since the fourteenth century or maybe the twelfth century or maybe even since the dinosaurs had given up the turf. One clipping claimed that in China girls were raised from infancy on government-funded "prostitute farms" and given at the age of ten to sexually demented politicians in the West in return for national-security secrets. Greedy businessmen were said to be polluting the planet, so money-crazed that they didn't give a damn if they killed every baby seal in existence, made patio furniture out of the last of the mighty redwoods, poisoned children, and destroyed the earth in pursuit of the almighty dollar; their evil conspiracies were so complex and so extensive that no one could be sure that even his own mother wasn't in their employ. Space aliens from another galaxy were trying to take over the world, too, with the nefarious, clandestine cooperation of (pick one) the Republican Party, the

Democratic Party, the Libertarian Party, Jews, blacks, born-again Christians, liberals, conservatives, middle-aged white trucking-industry executives. The tenor of the clippings was such that Gunvald wouldn't have been surprised to find one about Elvis faking death in order to secretly control the international banking establishment from an underground mansion in Switzerland.

With the newspaper clipping on page twenty-four, the notebook became uglier and more disturbing. It was a photograph of the late President Dougherty. Above the photograph was a headline: DOUGHTERY ASSASSINATION—TEN YEARS AGO TODAY. In the margin, in cramped but carefully hand-printed red letters, was a psychotic rant: *His brain has rotted away. His mind no longer exists. His tongue can't produce any more lies. He has gone to the worms, and we're spared any more children he might have had. I saw a poster today that said, "I cannot convince a man of my truth simply by silencing him when he tries to speak his own." But that is a lie. Death does convince a man. And I believe it helps to convince his followers. I wish that I had killed him.*

From that point forward, more and more space in the notebook was devoted to the Dougherty family. By page one hundred, a third of the way through the book, they had become his sole obsession. Every clipping in the subsequent two hundred pages dealt with them. He had saved important and trivial stories: a report of a campaign speech that Brian's father had made two years ago, a piece about a surprise birthday party given for the late President's widow, a UPI dispatch concerning Brian's adventures in one of Madrid's bullrings. . . .

On page two hundred ten was a Dougherty family portrait taken at the wedding of Brian's sister and reprinted in *People* magazine. Beneath it was a two-word, handwritten notice in red: *The enemy.*

On page two hundred thirty, the last lingering veils of sanity were cast off, and the screaming face of purest madness was revealed. The compiler had pasted up a page from a magazine, a color photograph of Brian's oldest sister, Emily. A pretty young woman. Button nose. Large green eyes. A splash of freckles. Auburn hair to her shoulders. She was facing sideways and laughing at something that someone had said or done out of camera range. Neat printing spiraled around her face, hundreds of repetitions of three words that filled the rest of the page to every border: *pig, whore, maggot, pig, whore, maggot, pig, whore, maggot. . . .*

The pages that followed were hair-raising.

Gunvald tried calling Harry once more. No response. He could communicate with no one. The storm was his only companion.

What in the name of God was happening on that iceberg?

❄

Brian Dougherty and Roger Breskin were the only members of the group who had extensive diving experience. Because Brian was not an official member of the expedition, merely an observer, Harry didn't think the kid should have to assume the front position in the descent through the tunnel, which might prove to be dangerous in ways that they had not yet imagined. Therefore, Roger Breskin would lead.

They would follow Roger in an orderly procession: Harry second, then Brian, Rita, George, Claude, Franz, and Pete. A lot of thought had gone into that arrangement. Brian would be between Harry and Rita, the only two people that he could fully trust. George Lin was behind Rita and might be a threat to her and Brian. Because of his age and convivial temperament, Claude Jobert seemed the least likely of all suspects other than Pete, so he would be behind Lin, where he would surely notice and attempt to prevent any foul play. If Franz was the guilty party, his freedom to strike out at Brian would be severely limited by the fact that Pete would be keeping a watch on him from behind. And in the unlikely event that Pete Johnson was the would-be murderer, he wouldn't find it easy to get past Franz, Claude, Lin, and Rita to reach Brian.

If they had been descending through the water-filled tunnel in darkness, their order on the line wouldn't have mattered, because in darkness anything could have happened. Fortunately, the aluminum cargo boxes had contained three powerful halogen lamps designed for use underwater at levels of considerable pressure. Roger would carry one at the front of the procession; in the middle, George Lin would have one; and Pete would be in charge of the third. If each member of the group maintained ten feet between himself and the person he was following on the way down, the distance from the first to the third light would be approximately forty yards. They wouldn't be swimming through bright light, but Harry figured the illumination would be sufficient to discourage murder.

Each of the heated wet suits came with a waterproof watch that featured a large, luminescent digital readout. Harry looked at his when he finished suiting up. Eighteen minutes past eleven.

Detonation in forty-two minutes.

He said, "Ready to go?"

Everyone was suited up, masks in place. Even George Lin.

Harry said, "Good luck, my friends." He slipped on his own mask, reached over his left shoulder to activate the air feed on his tank, and took a few deep breaths to be sure that the equipment was working properly. He turned to Roger Breskin and gave him the thumbs-up sign.

Roger picked up his halogen lamp, sloshed through the shallow edge of the pool, hesitated for only a second—and jumped feet-first into the forty-foot-wide mouth of the tunnel.

Harry followed, cutting the water with less of a splash than Roger had made. Although he knew better, he expected the ice-cold embrace of the sea to snatch his breath away and make his heart stutter, and he gasped involuntarily as the water closed around him. But his battery pack and the heated lining of his wet suit functioned extremely well, and he felt no temperature change from the cavern to the tunnel.

The water was murky. Millions of particles of dirt, clouds of tiny diatoms in sufficient quantity to feed a pack of whales, and beads of ice drifted in the diffused, yellowish beam of the waterproof lamp. Behind the halogen glow, Roger was a half-seen shape, perfectly black and mysterious in his rubber suit, like a shadow that had escaped from the person who had cast it, or like Death himself without his customary scythe.

As instructed, Brian plunged into the water without delay, to thwart a possible attempt on his life after Harry and Roger had departed the cavern.

Roger had already begun to pull himself downward on the multicommunications wire that led back to the *Ilya Pogodin.*

Harry brought his left wrist close to his face mask to look at the luminous digital readout on his watch: 11:20.

Detonation in forty minutes.

He followed Roger Breskin down into the unknown.

11:22
DETONATION IN THIRTY-EIGHT MINUTES

"Officer's mess to captain."

In the control room, Nikita Gorov reached for the microphone. "Report."

The words came out of the squawk box so fast that they ran together and were nearly indecipherable. "We've got sweat on the bulkhead here."

"Which bulkhead?" Gorov asked with businesslike calm, though his stomach fluttered with dread.

"Starboard, sir."

"How serious?"

"Not very serious, sir. Not at this point. It's a thin dew, two yards long, a couple of inches wide, just below the ceiling."

"Any indications of buckling?"

"No, sir."

"Keep me informed," he said, without revealing the depth of his concern, and he let go of the microphone.

The technician seated at the surface Fathometer said, "I'm picking up a partial blockage of the hole again."

"Divers?"

The technician studied the graph for a moment. "Yes. That could be the interpretation. Divers. I've got downward movement on all the blips."

The good news affected everyone. The men were no less tense than they had been a minute ago. For the first time in several hours, however, their tension was qualified by guarded optimism.

"Torpedo room to captain."

Gorov surreptitiously blotted his damp hands on his slacks and pulled down the microphone once more. "Go ahead."

The voice was controlled, though an underlying note of distress was apparent. "The sweat on the bulkhead between number four tube and number five tube is getting worse, Captain. I don't like the looks of it."

"Worse to what extent?"

"Water's trickling down to the deck now."

"How much water?" Gorov asked.

The overhead speaker hissed as the torpedo officer assessed the situation. Then: "An ounce or two."

"That's all?"

"Yes, sir."

"Any buckling?"

"Nothing visible."

"The rivets?"

"No distortion of the rivet line."

"Any sounds of metal fatigue?"

"We've been going over it with a stethoscope, sir. No alarming noise, no fatigue signatures, just the usual."

"Then why do you sound so concerned?" Gorov demanded, getting directly to the heart of the issue.

The torpedo officer didn't respond immedi-

338 · *Dean Koontz*

ately, but finally he said, "Well, sir, when you lay your hand against the steel . . . there's a strange vibration."

"Engine vibrations."

From the squawk box, the torpedo room officer said, "No, sir. It's something else. I don't know just what. But something I've never felt before. I think . . ."

"What?"

"Sir?"

"What do you think," Gorov demanded. "Spit it out. What do you think you feel when you put your hand to the steel?"

"Pressure."

Gorov was aware that the control-room crew had already lost its guarded optimism. To the torpedo officer, he said, "Pressure? You can't feel pressure through the steel. I suggest you control your imagination. There's no reason to panic. Just keep a close watch on it."

The torpedo officer evidently had expected more of a reaction. Morosely, he said, "Yes, sir."

Zhukov's lupine face was distorted by fear but also by doubt and anger, a mosaic of emotions that were all dismayingly distinct and readable. A first officer needed to have better control of his expressions if he hoped to become a captain. He spoke so softly that Gorov had to strain to hear: "One pinhole, one hairline crack in the pressure hull, and the boat will be smashed flat."

True enough. And it could all happen in a fraction of a second. It would be over before they even realized that it had begun. At least death would be mercifully swift.

"We'll be all right," Gorov insisted.

He saw the confusion of loyalties in the first officer's eyes, and he wondered if he was wrong. He wondered if he should take the *Pogodin* up a few hundred feet to lessen the crushing pressure on it, and abandon the Edgeway scientists.

He thought of Nikki.

He was a stern enough judge of himself to face the possibility that saving the Edgeway expedition might have become an obsession with him, an act of personal atonement, which was not in the best interest of his crew. If that was the case, he had lost control of himself and was no longer fit to command.

Are we all going to die because of me? he wondered.

11:27
DETONATION IN THIRTY-THREE MINUTES

The descent along the communications wire proved to be far more difficult and exhausting than Harry Carpenter had anticipated. He was not a fraction as experienced in the water as were Brian and

Roger, although he had used scuba gear on several occasions over the years and had thought that he knew what to expect. He had failed to take into account that a diver ordinarily spent the larger part of his time swimming more or less parallel to the ocean floor; their headfirst descent on that seven-hundred-foot line was perpendicular to the seabed, which he found to be tiring. *Inexplicably* tiring, in fact, because there was no physical reason why it should have been markedly more difficult than any other diving he'd ever done. At any angle, he was essentially weightless when he was underwater, and the flippers were as useful as they would have been had he been swimming parallel to the seabed. He suspected that his special weariness was largely psychological, but he could not shake it. In spite of the suit's lead weights, he constantly seemed to be fighting his natural buoyancy. His arms ached. Blood pounded at his temples and behind his eyes. He soon realized that he would have to pause periodically, reverse his position, and get his head up to regain equilibrium; otherwise, although his weariness and growing disorientation were no doubt entirely psychological, he would black out.

In the lead, Roger Breskin appeared to progress effortlessly. He slid his left hand along the communications wire as he descended, held the lamp in his other hand, and relied entirely on his legs to propel him, kicking smoothly. His technique wasn't substantially different from Harry's, but he had the advantage of muscles built through regular, diligent workouts with heavy weights.

As he felt his shoulders crack, as the back of his neck began to ache, and as sharp new currents of pain shot down his arms, Harry wished that he had spent as much time in gyms as Roger had put in over the past twenty years.

He glanced over his shoulder to see if Brian and Rita were all right. The kid was trailing him by about twelve feet, features barely visible in the full-face diving mask. Eruptions of bubbles streamed out of Brian's scuba vent, were briefly tinted gold by the backwash from Roger's lamp, and quickly vanished into the gloom above. In spite of all that he'd endured in the past few hours, he seemed to be having no trouble keeping up.

Behind Brian, Rita was barely visible, only fitfully backlighted by the lamp that George Lin carried in her wake. The yellowish beams were defeated by the murky water; against that eerily luminous but pale haze, she was but a rippling shadow, at times so indistinct and strange that she might have been not human but an unknown denizen of the polar seas. Harry couldn't get a glimpse of her face, but he knew that her psychological suffering, at least, must be great.

❄

Cryophobia: fear of ice.

The frigid water in the tunnel was as dark as if it had been tainted with clouds of squid ink, for it was thick with diatoms and specks of ice and inorganic particulates. Rita wasn't able to see the ice that lay only twenty feet from her in every direction, but she remained acutely aware of it. At times her fear was so overwhelming that her chest swelled and her throat tightened and she was unable to breathe. Each time, however, on the shuddering edge of blind panic, she finally exhaled explosively, inhaled the metallic-tasting mixture of gases from the scuba tank, and staved off hysteria.

Frigophobia: fear of cold. She suffered no chill whatsoever in the Russian wet suit. Indeed, she was warmer than she had been at any time during the past few months, since they had come onto the icecap and established Edgeway Station. Nevertheless, she was unavoidably *aware* of the deadly cold of the water, conscious of being separated from it by only a thin sheath of rubber and electrically heated layers of insulation. The Russian technology was impressive, but if the battery pack at her hip was drained before she reached the submarine far below, her body heat would be quickly leached away. The insistent cold of the sea would insinuate itself deep into her muscles, into her marrow, torturing her body and swiftly numbing her mind. . . .

Down, ever down. Embraced by a coldness that she couldn't feel. Surrounded by ice that she couldn't see. Curved white walls out of sight to the left of her, to the right, above and below, ahead and behind. Surrounding and entrapping her. Tunnel of ice. Prison of ice. Flooded with darkness and bitter cold. Silent but for the susurrant rush of her breathing and the *thud-thud-thudd*ing of her heart. Inescapable. Deeper than a grave.

As she swam down into depths unknown, Rita was sometimes more aware of the light ahead of her than she was at other times, because she was repeatedly flashing back to the winter when she was only six years old.

Happy. Excited. On her way to her first skiing holiday with her mother and father, who are experienced on the slopes and eager to teach her. The car is an Audi. Her mother and father sit up front, and she sits alone in the back. Ascending into increasingly white and fantastic realms. A winding road in the French Alps. An alabaster wonderland all around them, below them, great vistas of evergreen forests shrouded with snow, rocky crags looming high above like the old-men faces of watching gods, bearded with ice. Fat white flakes suddenly begin to spiral out of the iron-gray afternoon sky. She's a child of the Italian Mediterranean, of sun and olive groves and sun-spangled ocean, and she's never before been to the mountains. Now her young heart races with adventure. It's so beautiful: the snow, the steeply rising land, the valleys crowded with trees and purple shadows,

344 · *Dean Koontz*

sprinkled with small villages. And even when Death suddenly comes, it has a terrible beauty, all dressed resplendently in white. Her mother sees the avalanche first, to the right of the roadway and high above, and she cries out in alarm. Rita looks through the side window, sees the wall of white farther up the mountain, sliding down, growing as rapidly as a storm wave sweeping across the ocean toward shore, casting up clouds of snow like sea spray, silent at first, so white and silent and beautiful that she can hardly believe it can hurt them. Her father says, "We can outrun it," and he sounds scared as he jams his foot on the accelerator, and her mother says, "Hurry, for God's sake, hurry," and it comes onward, silent and white and huge and dazzling and bigger by the second . . . silent . . . then a barely audible rumble like distant thunder. . . .

Rita heard strange sounds. Hollow, faraway voices. Shouting or lamenting. Like the voices of the damned faintly wailing for surcease from suffering, issuing from the ether above a séance table.

Then she realized that it was only a single voice. Her own. She was making hard, panicky sounds into her face mask, but since her ears weren't in the mask, she heard her own cries only as they vibrated through the bones of her face. If they sounded like the wails of a damned soul, that was because, at the moment, Hell was a place within her, a dark corner in her own heart.

She squinted past Brian and desperately concentrated on the shadowy shape farther along the line: Harry. He was dimly visible in the murk, kicking down into the black void, so near and yet so far away. Twelve or fifteen feet separated Rita from Brian; count six feet for the kid, and maybe twelve feet between him and Harry: thirty or thirty-five feet altogether, separating her from her husband. It seemed like a mile. As long as she thought about Harry and kept in mind the good times that they would have together when this ordeal ended, she was able to stop screaming into her face mask and continue swimming. Paris. The Hôtel George V. A bottle of fine champagne. His kiss. His touch. They would share it all again if she just didn't let her fears overwhelm her.

Harry glanced back toward Rita. She was still where she should be, following Brian along the communications line.

Looking ahead again, he told himself that he was excessively worried about her. In general, women were supposed to have greater endurance than men. If that was true, it was especially true of *this* woman.

He smiled to himself and said, "Hang in there," as though she could hear him.

Ahead of Harry, when they were perhaps a hundred fifty feet down the dark tunnel, Roger Breskin finally paused for a rest. He performed a somersault as though engaged in a water ballet and turned around on the line until he faced Harry in a more natural position: head up and feet down.

Five yards behind Roger, Harry also paused and was about to do a somersault of his own when Roger's halogen lamp winked out. Two lights still glowed behind Harry, but the beams were diffused by the cloudy water and didn't reach him or Roger. He was enveloped in darkness.

An instant later Breskin collided with him. Harry couldn't hold on to the communications wire. They tumbled down and away into the blackness, at a descending angle toward the tunnel wall, and for an instant Harry didn't understand what was happening. Then he felt a hand clawing at his throat, and he knew that he was in trouble. He flailed at Breskin, putting all his strength into the blows, but the water absorbed the energy of his punches and transformed them into playful pats.

Breskin's hand closed tightly around Harry's throat. Harry tried to wrench his head away, pull back, but he couldn't escape. The weight lifter had an iron grip.

Breskin drove a knee into Harry's stomach, but the water worked against him, slowing and cushioning the blow.

Harder and sooner than he had expected, Harry's back thumped against the tunnel wall, and pain coruscated along his spine. The bigger man pinned him against the ice.

The two remaining halogen lamps—one held by George and one by Pete—were far above and about twenty feet farther toward the center of the tunnel, vaguely luminous ghost lights haunting the cloudy water. Harry was essentially blind. Even at close range, he could not see his assailant.

The hand at his throat slipped higher, pawed at his chin. His face mask was torn off.

With that strategic stroke, Harry was denied his breath and what little vision he'd had, and he was exposed to the killing cold of the water. Helpless, disoriented, he was no longer a threat to Breskin, and the big man let him go.

The cold was like a fistful of nails rammed hard into his face, and his body heat seemed to pour out as though it were a hot liquid streaming through the resultant punctures.

Terrified, on the verge of panic but aware that panic might be the death of him, Harry rolled away into the darkness, grappling behind himself for the precious mask that floated at the end of his air hose.

A second after the lamp went out at the head of the procession, Rita realized what was wrong: Breskin was the would-be killer of Brian Dougherty. And a second after *that,* she knew what she had to do.

Although she couldn't see Harry or Breskin in the gloom below, she was certain that the two men were struggling for their lives. As tough as he was, Harry wouldn't stand much of a chance against an experienced diver. She started to go to his aid, but that was a foolish idea, and she rejected it at once. Emotionally, she was driven toward Harry, but she dared not lose control of her emotions, or they might all die. If Harry was no match for Roger Breskin, then neither was she. The best thing that she could do was trust in Harry to survive, one way or another, and meanwhile fade into the darkness away from the communications wire, wait for her chance, and be prepared to come in behind Breskin when he went after Brian.

She let go of the line and swam out of the amber light from George Lin's lamp, which glowed behind her and silhouetted her for Breskin. Praying that George wouldn't follow her and blow her cover, she soon came up against the wall of the tunnel, the smooth curve of . . . ice.

The rumble swells into a roar, and again her father says, "We'll outrun it," but his words are now more of a prayer than a promise. The great white wall comes down down down down, and her mother screams. . . .

Rita shook off the past and strove to repress her fear of the ice against which she pressed. The wall wasn't going to collapse on her. It was solid, hundreds of feet thick, and until the packages of plastique were detonated at midnight, it was under no pressure great enough to cause it to implode.

Swinging around, putting her back to the wall, she looked out toward the commotion along the communications wire. She resisted the steady downward pull of her weight belt by treading water and pressing one hand tightly against the ice at her side.

The ice wasn't a living thing, not a conscious entity. She *knew* better than that. Yet she felt as though it *wanted* her. She could sense its yearning, its hunger, its conviction that she belonged to it. She would not have been surprised if a mouth had opened in the wall under her hand, savagely biting it off at the wrist or opening wider still and swallowing her whole.

She tasted blood. She was struggling so hard to repress her burgeoning terror that she had bitten into her lower lip. The salty, coppery taste—and the pain—helped clear her mind and focus her on the *real* threat to her survival.

In the center of the tunnel, Roger Breskin soared out of the black depths and into the dim light from George Lin's lamp.

Harry had vanished into the abyss below, which suddenly seemed to bore away not merely thousands of feet but to eternity.

Breskin went straight for Brian.

Clearly, Brian had just begun to understand what

was happening. He would never be able to move fast enough to escape Breskin, even though he was also an experienced diver.

Rita pushed away from the wall and swam in behind the attacker, wishing she had a weapon, hoping that the element of surprise would be all the advantage that she needed.

As Brian saw Roger Breskin soar like a shark from the lightless depths, he recalled a conversation they'd had earlier in the day, just after they'd rescued George from the ledge on the flank of the iceberg. Brian had been hoisted back to the top of the cliff, shaking, weak with relief:

Incredible.

What are you talking about?

Didn't expect to make it.

You didn't trust me?

It wasn't that. I thought the rope would snap or the cliff crack apart or something.

You're going to die. But this wasn't your place. It wasn't the right time.

Brian had thought that Roger was being uncharacteristically philosophical. Now he realized that it had been a blunt threat, a heartfelt promise of violence.

Maybe Breskin hadn't wanted George to be a witness, or maybe he hadn't struck earlier for other, inexplicable, and insane reasons of his own. This time, he had more than one witness, but he seemed not to care.

Even as that conversation replayed in Brian's memory, he tried to turn from Breskin and kick toward the tunnel wall, but they collided and tumbled away together into the darkness. Breskin's powerful legs encircled Brian, clamping like a crab pincer. Then a hand at his throat. At his face mask. *No!*

George Lin thought that Russian divers from the submarine were attacking them.

From the moment the Russians had offered to help, George had known that they had some trick in mind. He'd been trying to figure what it might be, but he hadn't thought of *this*: a murderous act of treachery deep in the tunnel. Why should they go to so much trouble to kill a group of Western scientists who were already destined to be blown to bits or dumped into a deadly cold sea at midnight? This was senseless, pointless lunacy, but on the other hand, he knew that nothing the communists had ever done made sense, not anywhere in the world, not in Russia or in China or anywhere else, not at any time during their reign of terror. Their ideology was nothing but a mad hunger for unrestrained power, politics as a cult religion divorced from morality and reason, and their bloody ram-

pages and bottomless cruelty could never be ana-
lyzed or understood by anyone not of their mad
persuasion.

He preferred to swim straight to the top of the
tunnel, clamber out of the pool, return to the top of
the ice, find a blasting shaft, lie down upon it, and
let the midnight explosion tear him to pieces,
because that would be a cleaner death than any at
the hands of *these* people. But he couldn't move.
His left hand was curled around the communications wire so tightly that the two might have been
soldered together. With his right hand, he gripped
the halogen lamp so hard that his fingers ached.

He waited to die as his sister had died. As
his mother had died. As his grandfather and grandmother had died. The past had surged forward to
overwhelm the present.

He'd been a fool to have believed that he'd
escaped the horror of his childhood. In the end, no
lamb could escape the slaughter.

The air hose trailed along the side of Harry's
head, and the diving mask was attached to the end
of it, floating above him. He pulled the mask down
and clamped it to his face. It was full of water, and
he dared not breathe immediately, even though his
lungs felt as though they were on fire. When he
peeled up one corner of the rubber rim, the influx
of oxygen-helium mixture forced the water out

from behind the Plexiglas faceplate, and when all the water had been purged, he pressed that corner down tight again and sucked in a deep breath, another, another, spluttering and choking and gasping with relief. The slightly odd smell and taste of the gas was more delicious than anything that he had ever eaten or drunk before in his entire life.

His chest was sore, his eyes burned, and his headache was so fierce that his skull seemed to be splitting apart. He wanted only to hang where he was, suspended in the tenebrous sea, recuperating from the assault. But he thought of Rita, and he swam up toward the two remaining lights and a turmoil of shadows.

Brian gripped Breskin's left wrist with both hands and tried to wrench the big man's steely hand from his face, but he wasn't able to resist. The diving mask was torn loose.

The sea was colder than the freezing point of ordinary water, but it still had not turned to ice because of its salt content. When it gushed across his face, the shock was nearly as painful as having a blazing torch shoved against his skin.

Nevertheless, Brian reacted so calmly that he surprised himself. He squeezed his eyelids shut before the water could flash-freeze the surface tissues of his eyeballs, clenched his teeth, and managed not to breathe either through his mouth or nose.

He couldn't hold out long. A minute. A minute and a half. Then he would breathe involuntarily, spasmodically—

Breskin clamped his legs tighter around Brian's midsection, pushed his rubber-sheathed fingers between Brian's compressed lips, and tried to force his mouth open.

Rita swam in behind and above Roger Breskin, into the sour light from George's hand-held lamp. She glided onto Breskin's back and wrapped her long legs around his waist as he had wrapped his legs around Brian.

With reflexes sharpened rather than dulled by maniacal frenzy, Breskin let go of Brian and seized Rita by the ankles.

She felt as though she was riding a wild horse. He twisted and bucked, a powerful beast, but she gripped him with her thighs and grabbed for his mask.

Sensing her intent, insane but not stupid, Breskin released her ankles and seized her wrists just as her hands touched the rim of his faceplate. He bent forward, kicked his flippers, did a somersault. Rolling through the water, he tore her hands from his face, and using the dynamics of the sea to achieve a leverage that she couldn't hope to match, he pitched her away from him. She kicked furiously as she went, hoping to connect with the crazy bastard, but none of her kicks landed.

When she oriented herself again, she saw that Pete and Franz had descended on Breskin. Franz struggled to maintain a wristlock while Pete tried to pin at least one of the madman's arms.

Breskin was a trained diver, however, and they were not. They were slow, clumsy, confused by the physics of the gravity-free realm in which they battled, while Breskin writhed as if he were an eel, supple and quick and fearfully strong, at home in deep water. He broke their hold on him, rammed an elbow into Pete's face, ripped Pete's mask over his head, and shoved him into Franz.

Brian was at the wire, fifteen feet below George Lin. Claude was with him. The Frenchman held Pete's lamp in one hand and was using his free hand to steady Brian while the kid got the water out of his mask.

Kicking away from Pete and Franz as they tumbled in disarray, Breskin streaked toward Brian again.

Rita glimpsed movement out of the corner of her eye, turned her head, and saw Harry shoot up from the darkness below.

Harry knew that Breskin didn't see him coming. Certain that he had temporarily disabled all opposition, the big man spun away from Pete and Franz, kicked with all the power of his muscular legs, and went directly for his preferred prey. He was no doubt sure that he could deal swiftly with a man of Claude's age and then finish Brian before the kid was able to clear his fouled mask and draw a restorative breath.

Rising under Breskin, Harry could have collided with him and hoped to deflect him from Brian. Instead, he kicked to one side, shot past the madman, and grabbed the air hose that connected his face mask to the pressurized tank on his back. Harry flutter-kicked again, soaring up, jerking the hose out of the clamp that held it to the feed valve at the top of the tank. Because he and Breskin were moving in different directions, the hose also uncoupled from the diving mask.

The icy water didn't pour in through Roger's mask coupling when the hose was torn loose. There must be a safety feature, a shutoff valve.

He fumbled for the hose, but he realized that it had been ripped away not merely from the mask but from the tank on his back. It was gone and couldn't be reconnected.

Alarmed, he scissored his legs and went up toward the mouth of the tunnel as fast as he could. His only hope was to reach the surface.

Then he remembered that the pool in the domed

ice cavern was more than a hundred fifty feet above him, too far to reach with the weight belt pulling him down, so he fumbled at his waist, trying to free himself of the burdensome lead. The release wasn't where it ought to be, because the damn belt was made by the Russians, and he had never before used Russian equipment.

Roger stopped kicking so he could concentrate on the search for the belt release. At once he began to sink slowly back into the tunnel. He patted-tugged-wrenched at the belt, but he *still* could not find the release, Jesus, dear Jesus God Almighty, still couldn't find it, and finally he knew that he had wasted too much time, didn't dare waste another second, would have to get to the surface even with the hampering belt. Arms straight down at his sides, trying to be as sleek as an arrow, creating as little resistance to the water as possible, kicking smoothly, rhythmically, he struggled up, up. His chest ached, and his heart was hammering as if it would burst, and he couldn't any longer resist the urge to breathe. He opened his mouth, exhaled explosively, desperately inhaled, but there was nothing to breathe except the meager breath that he had just expelled, which was even thinner the next time he exhaled. His lungs were *ablaze,* and he knew that the darkness around him was no longer that of the tunnel but a darkness *behind* his eyes. He would lose consciousness if he didn't breathe, and if he passed out he would die. So he ripped off his mask and sucked a deep breath of the air in the domed cavern, except he was nowhere *near* the domed cavern, of course—why had he imagined that he'd reached the surface, how could he have been so stupid?—and he inhaled water so bitterly cold that pain shot through his teeth. He closed his mouth, choking violently, but at once he tried to breathe again. There was only more water, water, nothing but water. He clawed at the water with both hands, as if it were a thin curtain that he could tear apart to get to the blessed air just beyond it. Then he realized that he wasn't kicking any longer, was sinking under the influence of the diving weights. He wasn't clawing at the water any more either, just drifting down and down, gasping, and it felt as though he had more lead weights inside his chest than around his waist. . . .

He saw that Death had neither a face of raw bone nor the face of a man. It was a woman. A pale, strong-jawed woman. She was not without some beauty. Her eyes were a lovely, translucent gray. Roger studied her face as it rose out of the water before him, and he realized that she was his mother, from whom he had learned so much, in whose arms he had first heard that the world was a hostile place and that people of exceptional evil secretly ruled ordinary men and women through interlocking conspiracies, with no intention but to crush the free spirit of everyone who defied them. And now, though Roger had made himself strong to resist those conspirators if they ever came for him, although he had applied himself to his studies and had earned two degrees in order to have the knowledge to outwit them, they had crushed him anyway. They had won, just as his mother had told him they would, just as they always won. But losing wasn't so terrible. There was a peace in losing. Gray-haired, gray-eyed death smiling at him, and he wanted to kiss her, and she took him into her motherly embrace.

Harry watched as the corpse, lungs full of water and burdened with lead weights, drifted past them on its journey to the bottom of the sea. Air bubbles gushed from the tank on its back.

11:37
DETONATION IN TWENTY-THREE MINUTES

The tension had sharpened Nikita Gorov's mind and had forced him to confront an unpleasant but undeniable truth. Fools and heroes, he saw now, were separated by a line so thin that it was the next thing to invisible. He had been so intent on being a hero. And for what? For whom? For a dead son? Heroism could not change the past. Nikki was dead and in the grave. Dead! And the crew of the

Ilya Pogodin—the seventy-nine men under his command—were still very much alive. They were his responsibility. It was inexcusable to have risked their lives merely because, in some strange way, he wanted to fulfill an obligation to his dead son. He'd been playing hero, but he'd been only a fool.

Regardless of the danger, regardless of what he *should* have done, the submarine was committed to the rescue mission now. They couldn't abandon it this close to success. Not unless those two sweating bulkheads began to show signs of structural deterioration. He had gotten his men into this, and it was up to him to get them out in a way that would save their hide without humiliating them. Men of their courage didn't deserve to be humbled by his failure, but they surely would be worse than humbled in their own eyes if they turned tail now and ran without good reason. He'd been playing hero, but now he wanted nothing more than to make heroes of *them* in the eyes of the world, and get them home safely.

"Any change?" he asked the young technician reading the surface Fathometer.

"No, sir. The divers are stationary. They haven't descended a foot in the last few minutes."

The captain stared at the ceiling, as if he could see through the double hull and all the way up the long tunnel. What were they doing up there? What had gone wrong?

"Don't they realize there's no time left?" Zhukov said. "When those explosives split the iceberg at midnight, we've got to be out from under. We've *got* to be."

Gorov checked the video displays. He looked at the clock. He pulled on his beard and said, "If they don't start moving down again in five minutes, we'll have to get out of here. One minute later than that, and they can't make it aboard before midnight anyway."

11:38.

Rita swam up to Claude and hugged him. He returned her embrace. Her eyes glistened with tears.

They pressed the faceplates of their diving masks flat against each other. When she spoke, he could hear her as if she were in another room. The Plexiglas conducted their voices well enough.

"Brian didn't fall earlier tonight. He was clubbed, left to die. We didn't know who did it. Until now."

When Rita finished, Claude said, "I wondered what the hell—? I wanted to help subdue him, but Pete shoved this lamp into my hand and pushed me out of the way. I suddenly feel as old as I am."

"You're not even sixty."

"Then I feel *older* than I am."

She said, "We're going to continue the descent. I'll take that lamp back to Pete."

"Is he all right?"

"Yes. Just a bloody nose when the mask was pulled up over his head. He'll make it."

"Something's wrong with George."

"Shock, I think. Harry's explaining to him about Roger."

"You've got tears on your cheeks," Claude said.

"I know."

"What's wrong?"

"Nothing," she said. "Harry's alive."

11:39.

As he followed Claude Jobert down the wire once more, Franz thought about what he would say to Rita if they reached the other side of midnight.

You handled yourself well. You're amazing. You know, I once loved you. Hell, I still do. I never got over you. And I learned a lot from you, whether it was ever apparent or not. Oh, I'm still an asshole, yes, I admit it, but I'm slowly growing up. Old attitudes die hard. I've been acting like a total idiot these past months, quarrelsome with Harry and distant with you. But that's finished. We can never be lovers again. I see what you and Harry have together, and it's unique, more than you and I ever had or ever could have. But I'd like to be friends.

He hoped to God he lived to say all that.

11:40.

Brian swam down along the wire.

He wasn't worried much about the ticking bombs overhead. He was increasingly convinced that he and the others would reach the submarine and survive the explosions. In the throes of the obsession about which Rita had warned him, he was worried instead about the book that he intended to write.

The theme would definitely be heroism. He had come to see that there were two basic forms of it. Heroism that was sought, as when a man climbed a mountain or challenged an angry bull in one of Madrid's rings—because a man had to know his limits, heroism sought was important. It was far less valuable, however, than heroism *unsought*. Harry, Rita, and the others had put their lives on the line in their jobs because they believed that what they were doing would contribute to the betterment of the human condition, not because they wanted to test themselves. Yet, although they would deny it, they were heroes every day of the week. They were heroes in the way that cops and firemen were heroes, in the way that millions of mothers and fathers were quiet heroes for taking on the ominous responsibilities of supporting families and raising children to be good citizens, the way ministers were heroes to dare talk of God in a world that had come to doubt His existence and to mock those who still believed, the way many teachers were heroes when they went into schools racked by violence and nevertheless tried to teach kids what they would need to know to survive in a world that had no mercy for the uneducated. The first brand of heroism—heroism sought—had a distinct quality of selfishness, but heroism unsought was selfless. Brian understood now that it was this unsought heroism, not the tinsel glory of either politics or bullrings, that was the truest courage and the deepest virtue. When he had finished writing the book, when he had worked out all his thoughts on the subject, he would be ready to begin his adult life at last. And he was determined that quiet heroism would be the theme.

11:41.

The technician looked up from the surface-Fathometer graph. "They're moving again."

"Coming down?" Gorov asked.

"Yes, sir."

The squawk box brought them the voice of the petty officer in the forward torpedo room. It contained a new note of urgency.

Taking the neck of the overhead microphone as gingerly as if he were handling a snake, Gorov said, "Go ahead."

"We've got a lot more than a couple ounces of water on the deck now, Captain. Looks like a liter or two. The forward bulkhead is sweating all the way from overhead to deck."

"Distortion of the rivet line?"

"No, sir."

"Hear anything unusual with the stethoscope?"

"No, sir."

"We'll be on our way in ten minutes," Gorov said.

11:42.

In places, the tunnel narrowed just enough for the halogen light to reflect off the ice, and then the fact of their imprisonment could not be as easily put out of mind as when darkness lay to all sides.

Rita was pulled continually between the past and the present, between death and life, courage and cowardice. Minute by minute, she expected her inner turmoil to subside, but it grew worse.

A stand of widely scattered trees spot the steep hillside above the alpine road. It's not a dense forest, but maybe it's enough of a barrier to break the force of the avalanche and dam the roaring flow: tall evergreens with thick trunks, ancient and strong. Then the white tide hits the trees, and they snap as though they're breadsticks. Her mother screams, her father cries out, and Rita can't look away from the onrushing wave of snow, a hundred feet high, growing, disappearing into the winter sky, huge, like the face of God. The juggernaut hits the Audi, tumbles the car, shoves it across the roadway, sweeps under and over it, casting it across the guardrail and into a ravine. An enwrapping white-ness all around. The car turns over, over again, then sleds sideways, down, down, rebounds from a tree, turns into the slide, races down once more in a great river of snow, with another impact, yet another. The windshield implodes, followed by a sudden stillness and a silence deeper than the silence in a deserted church.

Rita wrenched herself from the memory, making meaningless, pathetic sounds of terror.

George Lin was urging her on from behind.

She had stopped swimming.

Cursing herself, she kicked her feet and started down again.

11:43.

At three hundred fifty feet or thereabouts, having covered little more than half the distance to the *Ilya Pogodin*, Harry began to doubt that they could make it all the way down. He was aware of the incredible pressure, primarily because his eardrums kept popping. The roar of his own blood rushing through his veins and arteries was thunderous. He imagined he could hear faraway voices, fairy voices, but the words made no sense, and he figured that he'd *really* be in trouble when he understood what they were saying. He wondered if, like a submarine, he could collapse under extreme pressure and be squashed into a flat mess of blood and bones.

Earlier, on the shortwave radio, Lieutenant Timoshenko had offered several proofs that the descent could be made successfully, and Harry kept repeating a couple of them to himself: In Lake Maggiore, in 1961, Swiss and American divers reached seven hundred and thirty feet in scuba gear. Lake Maggiore. Seven hundred and thirty feet. 1961. Swiss and American divers. In 1990, Russian divers in more modern gear had been as deep as . . . he forgot. But deeper than Lake Maggiore. Swiss, Americans, Russians . . . It could be done. By well-equipped, *professional* divers anyway.

Four hundred feet.

11:44.

Following the wire farther into the shaft, George Lin told himself that the Russians weren't communists any more. At least the communists weren't in charge. Not yet. Maybe one day in the future, they would be back in power; evil never really died. But the men in the submarine were risking their lives, and they had no sinister motives. He tried to convince himself, but it was a hard sell, because he had lived too many years in fear of the red tide.

Canton. Autumn 1949. Three weeks before Chiang Kai-shek was driven from the mainland. George's father had been away, making arrangements to spirit the family and its dwindling assets to the island nation of Taiwan. There were four other people in the house: his grandmother; his grandfather; his mother; his eleven-year-old sister, Yun-ti. At dawn, a contingent of Maoist guerrillas, seeking his father, invaded the house. Nine heavily armed men. His mother managed to hide him inside a fireplace, behind a heavy iron screen. Yun-ti was hidden elsewhere, but the men found her. As George watched from within the fireplace, his grandparents were beaten to their knees and then shot in the head. Their brains splattered the wall. In that same room, his mother and sister were raped by all nine men, repeatedly. Every degradation, every humiliation was perpetrated upon them. George was a child, not even seven years old: small, terrified, powerless. The guerrillas stayed until three o'clock the next morning, waiting for George's father, and when they finally left, they slit Yun-ti's throat. Then his mother's throat. So much blood. His father had come home twelve hours later—and found George still hiding in the fireplace, unable to speak. He remained silent for more than three years after they escaped to Taiwan. And when at last he had broken his silence, he had first spoken the names of his mother and sister. Speaking them, he'd wept inconsolably until a physician came to their house and administered a sedative.

Nevertheless, the men in the submarine below were Russians, not Chinese, and they weren't communists any more. Perhaps they had *never* been true communists. After all, soldiers and sailors sometimes fought for their country even when they believed that the men running it were thugs and fools.

The men below would not be like those who had violated his mother and sister and then killed them. These were different people in a different time. They could be trusted. He *must* trust them.

Nevertheless, he was infinitely more afraid of the *Pogodin*'s crew than of all the high explosives in the world.

11:46.

"Officer's mess to captain."

"I read you."

"That starboard bulkhead is streaming, Captain."

"Buckling?"

"No, sir."

"How much water?"

"Half a liter, sir."

Trouble in both the torpedo room and the officer's mess. They would soon have to get the hell out of there.

"Stethoscope?" Gorov asked.

"Lots of noise past the bulkhead, sir, but no standard stress signatures."

"We'll be on our way in five minutes."

11:47.

With the submarine almost within reach, Harry remembered more reason to be hopeful. According to Lieutenant Timoshenko, British divers at Alverstoke, Hampshire, and French divers at Marseilles had reached fifteen hundred feet with advanced scuba gear in simulated chamber dives.

Of course, that one qualifying phrase prevented the data from being as reassuring as he would have liked: "simulated chamber dives."

This was the real thing.

The tunnel widened out. The ice walls receded until they no longer reflected any of the light.

He had a sense of vastly greater space around him. The water was clearer than it had been above, probably because there were fewer particles of ice in it. Within seconds, he saw colored lights below, first green and then red. Then his hand-held light revealed a great, gray shape hovering in the abyss below him.

Even when he arrived at the sail of the *Ilya Pogodin* and rested against the radar mast, Harry was not sanguine about their chances of surviving the tremendous pressure. He was half convinced that his lungs would explode with the force of grenades and that his blood vessels would pop like balloons. He didn't know much about the effects of great pressure on the body; maybe his lungs wouldn't explode, but the mental image was convincing.

Furthermore, Harry didn't like the looks of the submarine. Waiting for the others to catch up with him, he had nearly a minute to study the boat. All the running lights were aglow: red on the port side, green on the starboard side, white on the sail, a yellow overtaking light . . . Maybe his thought processes were affected by pressure or exhaustion, but the *Pogodin* seemed too gaudy to be substantial. After so much darkness, the boat resembled a damned slot machine or a Christmas tree. It seemed delicate, fragile, a construction of dark cellophane.

11:49.

Rita expected her fear to abate when she reached the bottom of the tunnel and the ice was no longer to every side of her. But the island of ice was still overhead, as high as a seventy-story building and four fifths of a mile long, as enormous as several blocks of Manhattan skyscrapers. She knew that it was buoyant and wouldn't sink on her or crush her into the ocean floor, but she was terrified by the thought of it hanging over her, and she dared not look up.

It's cold in the Audi, because the engine is dead and no heat comes from the vents. Snow and shattered tree limbs have poured into the front seat, through the shattered windshield, covering the dashboard and burying her parents to the waist. They sit silently in the snow, both dead, and as time passes, Rita knows that she can't survive in just her own winter coat until help comes. The dashboard lights are on, as is the dome light, so the interior of the Audi isn't dark; she can see the snow pressing at every window, on all sides of the car; she is an intelligent girl, so she is aware that the snow may be a hundred feet deep, too deep to allow her to dig her way out and escape by herself. Rescuers will be a long time reaching her. She needs her father's heavy coat, and after delaying a dangerously long time, she steels herself for what she will see, and she crawls into the front seat. Icicles of crimson blood hang from her father's ears and nostrils, and her mother's throat is pierced by the jagged end of a tree branch that was driven through the windshield by the avalanche. Their faces are blue-gray. Their open eyes are entirely white, because the frost has sheathed them. Rita takes one look and no more, keeps her head down, and begins to dig the snow away from her father. She is only six years old, an active child and strong for her age, but still so small. She would find it impossible to get the coat off her father's stiffening corpse if his arms were through the sleeves. But during the drive he had shrugged out of the coat. Now his body sits on it, leans back against it, and with a lot of prying and tugging, she works it out from under him. She scrambles with her prize into the backseat where the snow doesn't intrude, curls up, draws the coat tightly around her, and waits for help to come. She even keeps her head under his coat, trapping not merely her body heat but her breath inside the satiny lining, because her breath is warm. After a while she begins to have trouble staying awake, and she drifts out of the cold car into colder places within her own mind. Each time she rises blearily from her dangerous sleep, she is groggier than the time before, but she remembers to listen for the sounds of rescue. After what seems a long time, she hears instead—or thinks she hears—movement in the front seat: the crackle of ice breaking as her dead father and dead mother get tired of sitting there and decide to crawl into the back with her. They want to creep under the comfort of the big heavy coat. Crackle: the sound of bloody icicles falling out of his nostrils. Again, the crackle of ice: Here they come. The terrible crackle of ice: They must be climbing into the rear of the car. The crack-crack-crackle of ice . . . and is that a voice whispering her name, a familiar voice whispering her name? And a cold hand reaching under the coat, envious of her warmth. . . .

Someone touched Rita, and she cried out in horror, but at least the scream drove the Audi and avalanche into the past where they belonged.

Pete was on one side of her, Franz on the other. Evidently, she had stopped moving, and they were holding her by her arms and bringing her down the final few fathoms between them. The submarine was directly ahead. She saw Harry holding on to the radar mast above the sail.

11:50.

Harry shuddered with relief at the sight of Rita between Pete and Franz, and a thrill of hope coursed through him.

When the other six joined him, he half crawled and half swam along the sail, climbed down the short ladder to the bridge, and pulled himself along the line of cleats on the forward superstructure deck. If he floated off the boat, he would not be able to catch up with it easily, for the nine-knot current would not affect him in precisely the same way that it did the three-hundred-foot-long boat.

His relationship to the submarine was much like that of an astronaut to his craft during a spacewalk: There was an illusion of stillness, though they were both moving at considerable speeds.

Cautious, but conscious of the need for haste, he continued to pull himself hand over hand along the cleat line, searching for the air-lock hatch that Timoshenko had described over the radio.

11:51.

A warning siren shrieked.

The green numerals and dimensional diagrams disappeared from the central video display directly above the command pad. Red letters replaced them: EMERGENCY.

Gorov punched a console key labeled DISPLAY. The screen cleared immediately, and the siren shut off. A new message appeared in the usual green letters: MUZZLE DOOR COLLAPSED ON FORWARD TOR-PEDO TUBE NUMBER FIVE. TUBE FILLED WITH WATER TO BREECH DOOR.

"It's happening," Zhukov said.

Number five tube must have torqued when they had collided with the ice floe earlier in the night. Now the muzzle door at the outer hull had given way.

Gorov said quickly, "Only the outer door collapsed. Just the *muzzle* door. Not the breech door. There's no water in the boat. Not yet—and there won't be."

A seaman monitoring one of the safety boards said, "Captain, our visitors have opened the topside hatch to the air lock."

"We're going to make it," Gorov told the control-room crew. "We're damned well going to make it."

11:52.

The air-lock hatch on the forward escape trunk was unlocked by someone at a control panel in the submarine. Harry gazed down into a tiny, brightly lighted, water-filled compartment. As Lieutenant

Timoshenko had warned them, it was large enough to accommodate only four divers at a time—and even at that size, it was twice as large as the escape trunks on many submarines.

One by one, Brian, Claude, Rita, and George went down into the round room and sat on the floor with their backs pressed to the walls.

From outside, Harry closed the hatch, which was faster than waiting for someone inside to use a lanyard to pull it down and then spin the sealing wheel.

He looked at his luminous watch.

11:53.

Gorov anxiously watched the bank of VDTs.

"Escape trunk ready," Zhukov said, repeating the message that he received on his headset, and simultaneously the same information appeared on one of the VDTs.

"Process the divers," Gorov said.

11:54.

In the air lock, Rita held on to wall grips as powerful pumps extracted the water from the chamber in thirty seconds. She didn't remove her mask, but continued to breathe the mixture of gases in her scuba tank, as they had been instructed to do.

A hatch opened in the center of the floor. A

young Russian seaman appeared, smiled almost shyly, and beckoned with one finger.

They moved quickly from the air lock, down a ladder into the escape-chamber control room. The seaman climbed the ladder again behind them, pulled the inner hatch shut, sealed it, and descended quickly to the control panel. With a roar, water flooded into the upper chamber again.

Acutely aware that a huge island of ice, mined with explosives, loomed directly above the boat, Rita went with the others into an adjoining decompression chamber.

11:56.

Harry tried the hatch again, and it swung open.

He waited until Franz and Pete had entered, and then he followed them and dogged down the hatch from inside.

They sat with their backs to the walls.

He didn't even have to look at his watch. An internal crisis clock told him that they were about four minutes from detonation.

The drains dilated, and the pumps drained the escape trunk.

11:57.

A mountain of ice on the verge of violent disintegration loomed over them, and if it went to pieces when they were under it, the boat would most likely be battered to junk. Death would be so swift that many of them might not even have a chance to scream.

Gorov pulled down an overhead microphone, called the maneuvering room, and ordered the boat into immediate full reverse.

The maneuvering room confirmed the order, and a moment later the ship shuddered in response to the abrupt change of engine thrust.

Gorov was thrown against the command-pad railing, and Zhukov almost fell.

From the overhead speaker: "Maneuvering room to captain. Engines full reverse."

"Rudder amidships."

"Rudder amidships."

The iceberg was moving southward at nine knots. The submarine was reversing *northward* at ten . . . twelve . . . now fifteen knots against a nine-knot current, resulting in an effective separation speed of fifteen knots.

Gorov didn't know if that was sufficient speed to save them, but it was the best that they could do at the moment, because to build to greater speed, they needed more time than remained until detonation.

"Ice overhead," the surface-Fathometer operator announced. They were out from under the funnel-shaped concavity in the center of the berg. "Sixty feet. Ice overhead at sixty feet."

11:58.

Harry entered the decompression chamber and sat beside Rita. They held hands and stared at his watch.

11:59.

The center of attention in the control room was the six-figure digital clock aft of the command pad. Nikita Gorov imagined that he could detect a twitch in his crewmen with the passage of each second:

11:59:10.

11:59:11.

"Whichever way it goes," Emil Zhukov said, "I'm glad that I named my son Nikita."

"You may have named him after a fool."

"But an interesting fool."

Gorov smiled.

11:59:30.

11:59:31.

The technician at the surface-Fathometer said, "Clear water. No ice overhead."

"We're out from under," someone said.

"But we're not yet out of the way," Gorov cautioned, aware that they were well within the fallout pattern of blast-hurled ice.

11:59:46.

380 · *Dean Koontz*

11:59:47.

"Clear water. No ice overhead."

11:59:49.

For the second time in ten minutes, a warning siren sounded, and EMERGENCY flashed in red on one of the overhead screens.

Gorov keyed up a display and found that another torpedo tube in the damaged area of the hull had partially succumbed: MUZZLE DOOR COLLAPSED ON FORWARD TORPEDO TUBE NUMBER FOUR. TUBE FILLED WITH WATER TO BREECH DOOR.

Pulling down a microphone, Gorov shouted, "Captain to torpedo room! Abandon your position and seal all watertight doors."

"Oh, dear God," said Emil Zhukov, the atheist.

"The breech doors will hold," Gorov said with conviction, and he prayed that he was right.

11:59:59.

12:00:00.

"Brace yourselves!"

"Clear water."

12:00:03.

"What's wrong?"

"Where is it?"

12:00:07.

The concussion hit them. Transmitted through the shattering iceberg to the water and through the water to the hull, it was a surprisingly mild and distant rumble. Gorov waited for the power of the shock waves to escalate, but it never did.

The sonar operator reported massive fragmentation of the iceberg.

By 12:02, however, when sonar had not located a substantial fragment of ice anywhere near the *Ilya Pogodin*, Gorov knew they were safe. "Take her up."

The control-room crew let out a cheer.

AFTER . . .

[1]
JANUARY 18
DUNDEE, SCOTLAND

Shortly before noon, two and a half days after escaping from their prison of ice, the survivors arrived in Scotland.

Ever since he had escaped on a small boat with his father from mainland China so many years ago, George Lin had not cared much for travel by sea, whether above or below the waves, and he was relieved to be on land once more.

The weather was neither severe nor mild for winter in Dundee. The flat-gray sky was low and threatening. The temperature was twenty degrees Fahrenheit. A cold wind swept in from the North Sea, making the water leap and curl across the entire length of the Firth of Tay.

More than one hundred newsmen from all over the world had flown to Dundee to report on the conclusion of the Edgeway story. With friendly sarcasm, a man from *The New York Times* had dubbed the place "Dandy Dundee" more than twenty-four hours ago, and the name had stuck. Among themselves, reporters apparently had gotten more conversational mileage from the bone-chilling weather than from the news event that they were there to cover.

Even after debarking from the *Pogodin* at 12:30 and standing in the brisk breeze for nearly an hour, George still enjoyed the feel of the wind on his face. It smelled clean and so much better than the canned air of the submarine. And it was neither so cold nor so fierce that he needed to fear frostbite, which was a vast improvement over the weather with which he had lived for the past few months.

Pacing energetically back and forth at the edge of the wharf, followed by a covey of reporters, he said, "This boat—isn't she a beautiful sight?"

Anchored in a deepwater berth behind him, the submarine was flying an enormous Russian flag and, for courtesy, a Scottish flag of somewhat smaller dimensions. Sixty-eight crewmen were in two facing lines on the main deck, all in dress blues and navy pea coats, standing at attention for a ceremonial inspection. Nikita Gorov, Emil Zhukov, and the other officers looked splendid in their uniforms and gray winter parade coats with brass buttons. A number of dignitaries were also on the bridge and on the railed gangplank that connected the submarine to the dock: a representative of Her Majesty's government, the Russian ambassador to Britain, two of the ambassador's aides, the mayor of Dundee, two representatives of the United Nations, and a handful of functionaries from the Russian trade embassy in Glasgow.

One of the photographers asked George to pose

beside a weathered concrete piling with the *Ilya Pogodin* as a backdrop. Smiling broadly, he obliged.

A reporter asked him what it felt like to be a hero on the front pages of newspapers worldwide.

"I'm no hero," George said at once. He turned to point at the officers and crew of the boat behind him. "*They* are the heroes here."

[2]
JANUARY 20
EDGEWAY STATION

During the night, the wind velocity began to fall for the first time in five days. By morning, ice spicules stopped ticking against the roof and walls of the communications shack, and soft snowflakes filled the air again. The violent storms in the extreme North Atlantic had begun to break up.

Shortly after two o'clock that afternoon, Gunvald Larsson finally established contact with the United States military base at Thule, Greenland. The American radio operator immediately reported that the Edgeway Project had been suspended for the remainder of the winter. "We've been asked to bring you off the icecap. If we get the good weather they're predicting, we should be able to come for you the day after tomorrow. Will that be enough time to close down your buildings and machinery?"

"Yes, plenty of time," Gunvald said, "but for

God's sake, never mind about that! What's happened to the others? Are they alive?"

The American was embarrassed. "Oh, I'm sorry.
Of course, you couldn't know, isolated as you've
been." He read two of the newspaper stories and
then added what else he knew.

After five days of continuous tension, Gunvald
decided that a celebration was in order. He lit his
pipe and broke out the vodka.

[3]
JANUARY 25
E-MAIL MESSAGE TRANSMITTED FROM
MONTEGO BAY, JAMAICA,
TO PARIS, FRANCE

Claude, Franz, and I got here January 23. Within
an hour of arrival, both the taxi driver who brought
us from the airport and the hotel clerk referred to
us as "an unlikely group." Man, they don't know
the half of it.

Can't get enough sun. Even I'm acquiring a tan.

I think I've met the woman of my dreams. Her
name is Majean. Franz got picked up in the bar by
a modern woman who doesn't believe in standard
genderroles, and he's trying to learn to let her open
doors for herself if she wants. He's piss-poor at it,
and sometimes they *fight* over a door, but he's
learning. Meanwhile, Claude seems to be con-

stantly in the company of a twenty-eight-year-old blonde who thinks he's indescribably cute and swoons at his French accent.

We're talking about maybe changing careers and opening a bar in some tropical resort. Maybe you and Rita want to think about going into business with us. We could sit around all day, swilling down rum drinks with funny little paper umbrellas in them. It sure beats frostbite, high explosives, and underwater life-or-death battles with psychopaths. The most serious problem we face here is humidity.

As ever, Pete.

[4]
JANUARY 26
PARIS, FRANCE

In their suite at the Hôtel George V, a bottle of Dom Perignon stood in an ice bucket beside the bed.

They were in each other's arms, as close as two people could get without actually melting together and becoming a single entity, generating enough heat to keep an entire Arctic outpost warm for a long winter, when they were startled by a clatter beside the bed. They had been rescued by the *Pogodin* more than a week ago, but their nerves were still wound too tight. He sat up, and she fell off him, and they both turned toward the sound, but they were alone in the room.

"Ice," she said.

"Ice?"

"Yes, ice. Shifting in the champagne bucket."

He glanced at the bucket on its silver-plated stand, and the ice shifted again.

"Ice," she repeated.

He looked at her. She smiled. He grinned. She giggled as if she were a schoolgirl, and he roared with laughter.

A NOTE TO THE READER

I receive over ten thousand letters a year from readers, and a significant number urge me to reissue more of my early books that have been out of print for some time. Many do more than urge. They make ominous references to voodoo curses and hit contracts placed with guys named Slash. They suggest that it would be a good idea to reissue those books before my face gets rearranged—although I might welcome some rearrangement, especially if it involved more hair. They threaten to kidnap me and force me to watch reruns of *The Partridge Family* twenty-four hours a day until I go stark, raving mad.

I'm charmed that readers care so much about my books that they want to read everything. I have already allowed a number of out-of-print books to come back into circulation, including *Shadowfires*, *The Servants of Twilight*, and *The Voice of the Night*, which were originally all published under pen names.

Icebound was originally published as *Prison of Ice*, under the name "David Axton," in a much rougher form. I have revised it and updated the technological and cultural references while trying not to get carried away and alter the entire storyline and feel of it.

This book was meant to be something of a homage to Alistair MacLean, that master of the adventure-suspense novel, whose books include *The Guns of Navarone*, *Where Eagles Dare*, and *Ice Station Zebra*. As a reader, I loved those books, and I wrote the original version of *Icebound* to see if I could pull one off.

In adventure-suspense of this type, the elements that count above all others are tension, pace, and plot—preferably a plot with a series of surprises and escalating physical challenges for the characters. The characters themselves generally have to be straightforward, and certainly less complex than those who appear in most of my books.

As always, I try to get the technical and background details correct—though when writing about submarines, for instance, it isn't my intent to layer on the technological detail as heavily and brilliantly as Tom Clancy. In the MacLean-style adventure, a degree of authenticity must be sacrificed to *speed*.

I hope you liked *Icebound,* though I sort of hope you like the new books more. After all, this is the only book of its type I've written, and if readers wanted another, I'd have nothing to offer to protect myself from being subjected to those reruns of *The Partridge Family*.

—DEAN KOONTZ, May 1994

LARGE PRINT EDITIONS

Look for these at your local bookstore

American Heart Association, *American Heart Association Cookbook, 5th Edition* (abridged)
Lauren Bacall, *Now* (paper)
Barbara Taylor Bradford, *Angel* (paper)
Barbara Taylor Bradford, *Remember*
Marlon Brando with Robert Lindsey, *Brando: Songs My Mother Taught Me* (paper)
Leo Buscaglia, Ph.D., *Born for Love*
Joe Claro, editor, *The Random House Large Print Book of Jokes and Anecdotes* (paper)
Michael Crichton, *Disclosure* (paper)
Michael Crichton, *Rising Sun*
E. L. Doctorow, *The Waterworks* (paper)
Dominick Dunne, *A Season in Purgatory*
Fannie Flagg, *Daisy Fay and the Miracle Man* (paper)
Fannie Flagg, *Fried Green Tomatoes at the Whistle Stop Cafe* (paper)
Robert Fulghum, *It Was on Fire When I Lay Down on It* (hardcover and paper)
Robert Fulghum, *Maybe (Maybe Not): Second Thoughts from a Secret Life*
Robert Fulghum, *Uh-Oh*
Martha Grimes, *The End of the Pier*
Martha Grimes, *The Horse You Came In On* (paper)
Lewis Grizzard, *If I Ever Get Back to Georgia, I'm Gonna Nail My Feet to the Ground*
David Halberstam, *The Fifties* (2 volumes, paper)
Katharine Hepburn, *Me* (hardcover and paper)

(continued)

P. D. James, *The Children of Men*
Naomi Judd, *Love Can Build a Bridge* (paper)
Dean Koontz, *Dark Rivers of the Heart* (paper)
Judith Krantz, *Dazzle*
Judith Krantz, *Lovers* (paper)
John le Carré, *The Night Manager* (paper)
John le Carré, *The Secret Pilgrim*
Robert Ludlum, *The Bourne Ultimatum*
Cormac McCarthy, *The Crossing* (paper)
Audrey Meadows with Joe Daley, *Love, Alice* (paper)
James A. Michener, *Mexico* (paper)
James A. Michener, *The Novel*
James A. Michener, *Recessional* (paper)
James A. Michener, *The World Is My Home* (paper)
Sherwin B. Nuland, *How We Die* (paper)
Richard North Patterson, *Degree of Guilt*
Louis Phillips, editor, *The Random House Large Print Treasury of Best-Loved Poems*
Maria Riva, *Marlene Dietrich* (2 volumes, paper)
Margaret Truman, *Murder at the National Cathedral*
Margaret Truman, *Murder at the Pentagon*
Margaret Truman, *Murder on the Potomac* (paper)
Anne Tyler, *Saint Maybe*
John Updike, *Rabbit at Rest*
Phyllis A. Whitney, *Daughter of the Stars* (paper)
Phyllis A. Whitney, *Star Flight* (paper)
Lois Wyse, *Grandchildren Are So Much Fun I Should Have Had Them First*

———————

The New York Times Large Print Crossword Puzzles (paper)

Will Weng, editor, Volumes 1–3
Eugene T. Maleska, editor, Volumes 4–7
Eugene T. Maleska, editor, Omnibus Volume 1